J. J. Connington and The Murder Room

››› This title is part of The Murder Room, our series dedicated to making available out-of-print or hard-to-find titles by classic crime writers.

Crime fiction has always held up a mirror to society. The Victorians were fascinated by sensational murder and the emerging science of detection; now we are obsessed with the forensic detail of violent death. And no other genre has so captivated and enthralled readers.

Vast troves of classic crime writing have for a long time been unavailable to all but the most dedicated frequenters of second-hand bookshops. The advent of digital publishing means that we are now able to bring you the backlists of a huge range of titles by classic and contemporary crime writers, some of which have been out of print for decades.

From the genteel amateur private eyes of the Golden Age and the femmes fatales of pulp fiction, to the morally ambiguous hard-boiled detectives of mid twentieth-century America and their descendants who walk our twenty-first century streets, The Murder Room has it all. ›››

The Murder Room
Where Criminal Minds Meet

themurderroom.com

J. J. Connington (1880–1947)

Alfred Walter Stewart, who wrote under the pen name J. J. Connington, was born in Glasgow, the youngest of three sons of Reverend Dr Stewart. He graduated from Glasgow University and pursued an academic career as a chemistry professor, working for the Admiralty during the First World War. Known for his ingenious and carefully worked-out puzzles and in-depth character development, he was admired by a host of his better-known contemporaries, including Dorothy L. Sayers and John Dickson Carr, who both paid tribute to his influence on their work. He married Jessie Lily Courts in 1916 and they had one daughter.

By J. J. Connington

Sir Clinton Driffield Mysteries

Murder in the Maze
Tragedy at Ravensthorpe
The Case with Nine Solutions
Mystery at Lynden Sands
Nemesis at Raynham Parva
The Boathouse Riddle
The Sweepstake Murders
The Castleford Conundrum
The Ha-Ha Case
In Whose Dim Shadow
A Minor Operation
Murder Will Speak
Truth Comes Limping
The Twenty-One Clues
No Past is Dead
Jack-in-the-Box
Common Sense is All You Need

Supt Ross Mysteries

The Eye in the Museum
The Two Tickets Puzzle

Novels

Death at Swaythling Court
The Dangerfield Talisman
Tom Tiddler's Island
The Counsellor
The Four Defences

The Case with Nine Solutions

J. J. Connington

An Orion book

This edition published by
The Orion Publishing Group Ltd
Orion House
5 Upper St Martin's Lane
London WC2H 9EA

An Hachette UK company
A CIP catalogue record for this book is available from the British Library

ISBN 978 1 4719 0597 1

www.orionbooks.co.uk

CONTENTS

Introduction
by
Curtis Evans

During the Golden Age of the detective novel, in the 1920s and 1930s, J. J. Connington stood with fellow crime writers R. Austin Freeman, Cecil John Charles Street and Freeman Wills Crofts as the foremost practitioner in British mystery fiction of the science of pure detection. I use the word 'science' advisedly, for the man behind J. J. Connington, Alfred Walter Stewart, was an esteemed Scottish-born scientist. A 'small, unassuming, moustached polymath', Stewart was 'a strikingly effective lecturer with an excellent sense of humour, fertile imagination and fantastically retentive memory', qualities that also served him well in his fiction. He held the Chair of Chemistry at Queens University, Belfast for twenty-five years, from 1919 until his retirement in 1944.

During roughly this period, the busy Professor Stewart found time to author a remarkable apocalyptic science fiction tale, *Nordenholt's Million* (1923), a mainstream novel, *Almighty Gold* (1924), a collection of essays, *Alias J. J. Connington* (1947), and, between 1926 and 1947, twenty-four mysteries (all but one tales of detection), many of them sterling examples of the Golden Age puzzle-oriented detective novel at its considerable best. 'For those who ask first of all in a detective story for exact and mathematical accuracy in the construction of the plot', avowed a contemporary *London Daily Mail* reviewer, 'there is no author to equal the distinguished scientist who writes under the name of J. J. Connington.'[1]

Alfred Stewart's background as a man of science is reflected in his fiction, not only in the impressive puzzle plot mechanics he devised for his mysteries but in his choices of themes and depictions of characters. Along with Stanley Nordenholt of *Nordenholt's Million*, a novel about a plutocrat's pitiless efforts to preserve a ruthlessly remolded remnant of human life after a global environmental calamity, Stewart's most notable character is Chief Constable Sir Clinton Driffield, the detective in seventeen of the twenty-four Connington crime novels. Driffield is one of crime fiction's most highhanded investigators, occasionally taking on the functions of judge and jury as well as chief of police.

Absent from Stewart's fiction is the hail-fellow-well-met quality found in John Street's works or the religious ethos suffusing those of Freeman Wills Crofts, not to mention the effervescent novel-of-manners style of the British Golden Age Crime Queens Dorothy L. Sayers, Margery Allingham and Ngaio Marsh. Instead we see an often disdainful cynicism about the human animal and a marked admiration for detached supermen with superior intellects. For this reason, reading a Connington novel can be a challenging experience for modern readers inculcated in gentler social beliefs. Yet Alfred Stewart produced a classic apocalyptic science fiction tale in *Nordenholt's Million* (justly dubbed 'exciting and terrifying reading' by the *Spectator*) as well as superb detective novels boasting well-wrought puzzles, bracing characterization and an occasional leavening of dry humour. Not long after Stewart's death in 1947, the Connington novels fell entirely out of print. The recent embrace of Stewart's fiction by Orion's Murder Room imprint is a welcome event indeed, correcting as it does over sixty years of underserved neglect of an accomplished genre writer.

Born in Glasgow on 5 September 1880, Alfred Stewart had significant exposure to religion in his earlier life. His father was William Stewart, longtime Professor of Divinity and Biblical Criticism at Glasgow University, and he married Lily Coats, a daughter of the Reverend Jervis Coats and member of one of Scotland's preeminent Baptist families. Religious sensibility is entirely absent from the Connington corpus, however. A confirmed secularist, Stewart once referred to one of his wife's brothers, the Reverend William Holms Coats (1881–1954), principal of the Scottish Baptist College, as his 'mental and spiritual antithesis', bemusedly adding: 'It's quite an education to see what one would look like if one were turned into one's mirror-image.'

Stewart's J. J. Connington pseudonym was derived from a nineteenth-century Oxford Professor of Latin and translator of Horace, indicating that Stewart's literary interests lay not in pietistic writing but rather in the pre-Christian classics ('I prefer the *Odyssey* to *Paradise Lost*,' the author once avowed). Possessing an inquisitive and expansive mind, Stewart was in fact an uncommonly well-read individual, freely ranging over a variety of literary genres. His deep immersion in French literature and supernatural horror fiction, for example, is documented in his lively correspondence with the noted horologist Rupert Thomas Gould.[2]

It thus is not surprising that in the 1920s the intellectually restless Stewart, having achieved a distinguished middle age as a highly regarded man of science, decided to apply his creative energy to a new endeavour, the writing of fiction. After several years he settled, like other gifted men and women of his generation, on the wildly popular mystery genre. Stewart was modest about his accomplishments in this particular field of light fiction, telling Rupert Gould later in life that 'I write these things [what Stewart called tec yarns] because they amuse me in parts when I am putting them together and because they are the only writings of mine that the public will look at. Also, in a minor degree, because I like to think some people get pleasure out of them.' No doubt Stewart's single most impressive literary accomplishment is *Nordenholt's Million*, yet in their time the two dozen J. J. Connington mysteries did indeed give readers in Great Britain, the United States and other countries much diversionary reading pleasure. Today these works constitute an estimable addition to British crime fiction.

After his 'prentice pastiche mystery, *Death at Swaythling Court* (1926), a rural English country-house tale set in the highly traditional village of Fernhurst Parva, Stewart published another, superior country-house affair, *The Dangerfield Talisman* (1926), a novel about the baffling theft of a precious family heirloom, an ancient, jewel-encrusted armlet. This clever, murderless tale, which likely is the one that the author told Rupert Gould he wrote in under six weeks, was praised in *The Bookman* as 'continuously exciting and interesting' and in the *New York*

Times Book Review as 'ingeniously fitted together and, what is more, written with a deal of real literary charm'. Despite its virtues, however, *The Dangerfield Talisman* is not fully characteristic of mature Connington detective fiction. The author needed a memorable series sleuth, more representative of his own forceful personality.

It was the next year, 1927, that saw J. J. Connington make his break to the front of the murdermongerer's pack with a third country-house mystery, *Murder in the Maze*, wherein debuted as the author's great series detective the assertive and acerbic Sir Clinton Driffield, along with Sir Clinton's neighbour and 'Watson', the more genial (if much less astute) Squire Wendover. In this much-praised novel, Stewart's detective duo confronts some truly diabolical doings, including slayings by means of curare-tipped darts in the double-centered hedge maze at a country estate, Whistlefield. No less a fan of the genre than T. S. Eliot praised *Murder in the Maze* for its construction ('we are provided early in the story with all the clues which guide the detective') and its liveliness ('The very idea of murder in a box-hedge labyrinth does the author great credit, and he makes full use of its possibilities'). The delighted Eliot concluded that *Murder in the Maze* was 'a really first-rate detective story'. For his part, the critic H. C. Harwood declared in *The Outlook* that with the publication of *Murder in the Maze* Connington demanded and deserved 'comparison with the masters'. 'Buy, borrow, or – anyhow – get hold of it', he amusingly advised. Two decades later, in his 1946 critical essay 'The Grandest Game in the World', the great locked-room detective novelist John Dickson Carr echoed Eliot's assessment of the novel's virtuoso setting, writing: 'These 1920s [. . .] thronged with sheer brains. What would be one of the best possible settings for violent death? J. J. Connington found the answer, with *Murder in the Maze*.' Certainly in retrospect *Murder in the Maze* stands as one of the finest English country-house mysteries of the 1920s, cleverly yet fairly clued, imaginatively detailed and often grimly suspenseful. As the great American true-crime writer Edmund Lester Pearson noted in his review of *Murder in the Maze* in *The Outlook*, this Connington novel had everything that one could desire in a detective story: 'A shrubbery maze, a hot day, and somebody potting at you with an air gun loaded with darts covered with a deadly South-American arrow-poison – *there* is a situation to wheedle two dollars out of anybody's pocket.'[3]

Staying with what had worked so well for him to date, Stewart the same year produced yet another country-house mystery, *Tragedy at Ravensthorpe*, an ingenious tale of murders and thefts at the ancestral home of the Chacewaters, old family friends of Sir Clinton Driffield. There is much clever matter in *Ravensthorpe*. Especially fascinating is the author's inspired integration of faerie folklore into his plot. Stewart, who had a lifelong – though skeptical – interest in paranormal phenomena, probably was inspired in this instance by the recent hubbub over the Cottingly Faeries photographs that in the early 1920s had famously duped, among other individuals, Arthur Conan Doyle.[4] As with *Murder in the Maze*, critics raved about this new Connington mystery. In the *Spectator*, for example, a reviewer hailed *Tragedy at Ravensthorpe* in the strongest terms, declaring of the novel: 'This is more than a good detective tale. Alike in plot, characterization, and literary style, it is a work of art.'

In 1928 there appeared two additional Sir Clinton Driffield detective novels, *Mystery at Lynden Sands* and *The Case with Nine Solutions*. Once again there was great praise for the latest Conningtons. H. C. Harwood, the critic who had so much admired *Murder in the Maze*, opined of *Mystery at Lynden Sands* that it 'may just fail of being the detective story of the century', while in the United States author and book reviewer Frederic F. Van de Water expressed nearly as high an opinion of *The Case with Nine Solutions*. 'This book is a thoroughbred of a distinguished lineage that runs back to "The Gold Bug" of [Edgar Allan] Poe,' he avowed. 'It represents the highest type of detective fiction.' In both of these Connington novels, Stewart moved away from his customary country-house milieu, setting *Lynden Sands* at a fashionable beach resort and *Nine Solutions* at a scientific research institute. *Nine Solutions* is of particular interest today, I think, for its relatively frank sexual subject matter and its modern urban setting among science professionals, which rather resembles the locales found in P. D. James' classic detective novels *A Mind to Murder* (1963) and *Shroud for a Nightingale* (1971).

By the end of the 1920s, J. J. Connington's critical reputation had achieved enviable heights indeed. At this time Stewart became one of the charter members of the Detection

Club, an assemblage of the finest writers of British detective fiction that included, among other distinguished individuals, Agatha Christie, Dorothy L. Sayers and G. K. Chesterton. Certainly Victor Gollancz, the British publisher of the J. J. Connington mysteries, did not stint praise for the author, informing readers that 'J. J. Connington is now established as, in the opinion of many, the greatest living master of the story of pure detection. He is one of those who, discarding all the superfluities, has made of deductive fiction a genuine minor art, with its own laws and its own conventions.'

Such warm praise for J. J. Connington makes it all the more surprising that at this juncture the esteemed author tinkered with his successful formula by dispensing with his original series detective. In the fifth Clinton Driffield detective novel, *Nemesis at Raynham Parva* (1929), Alfred Walter Stewart, rather like Arthur Conan Doyle before him, seemed with a dramatic dénouement to have devised his popular series detective's permanent exit from the fictional stage (read it and see for yourself). The next two Connington detective novels, *The Eye in the Museum* (1929) and *The Two Tickets Puzzle* (1930), have a different series detective, Superintendent Ross, a rather dull dog of a policeman. While both these mysteries are competently done – the railway material in *The Two Tickets Puzzle* is particularly effective and should have appeal today – the presence of Sir Clinton Driffield (no superfluity he!) is missed.

Probably Stewart detected that the public minded the absence of the brilliant and biting Sir Clinton, for the Chief Constable – accompanied, naturally, by his friend Squire

Wendover – triumphantly returned in 1931 in *The Boathouse Riddle*, another well-constructed criminous country-house affair. Later in the year came *The Sweepstake Murders*, which boasts the perennially popular tontine multiple-murder plot, in this case a rapid succession of puzzling suspicious deaths afflicting the members of a sweepstake syndicate that has just won nearly £250,000.[5] Adding piquancy to this plot is the fact that Wendover is one of the imperiled syndicate members. Altogether the novel is, as the late Jacques Barzun and his colleague Wendell Hertig Taylor put it in *A Catalogue of Crime* (1971, 1989), their magisterial survey of detective fiction, 'one of Connington's best conceptions'.

Stewart's productivity as a fiction writer slowed in the 1930s, so that, barring the year 1938, at most only one new Connington appeared annually. However, in 1932 Stewart produced one of the best Connington mysteries, *The Castleford Conundrum*. A classic country-house detective novel, Castleford introduces to readers Stewart's most delightfully unpleasant set of greedy relations and one of his most deserving murderees, Winifred Castleford. Stewart also fashions a wonderfully rich puzzle plot, full of meaty material clues for the reader's delectation. *Castleford* presented critics with no conundrum over its quality. 'In *The Castleford Conundrum* Mr Connington goes to work like an accomplished chess player. The moves in the games his detectives are called on to play are a delight to watch,' raved the reviewer for the *Sunday Times*, adding that 'the clues would have rejoiced Mr. Holmes' heart.' For its part, the *Spectator* concurred in the *Sunday Times*' assessment of the novel's masterfully constructed plot: 'Few detective stories show such sound reasoning as that by which the Chief Constable brings the crime home to the culprit.' Additionally, E. C. Bentley, much admired himself as the author of the landmark detective novel *Trent's Last Case*, took time to praise Connington's purely literary virtues, noting: 'Mr Connington has never written better, or drawn characters more full of life.'

With *Tom Tiddler's Island* in 1933 Stewart produced a different sort of Connington, a criminal-gang mystery in the rather more breathless style of such hugely popular English thriller writers as Sapper, Sax Rohmer, John Buchan and Edgar Wallace (in violation of the strict detective fiction rules of Ronald Knox, there is even a secret passage in the novel). Detailing the startling discoveries made by a newlywed couple honeymooning on a remote Scottish island, *Tom Tiddler's Island* is an atmospheric and entertaining tale, though it is not as mentally stimulating for armchair sleuths as Stewart's true detective novels. The title, incidentally, refers to an ancient British children's game, 'Tom Tiddler's Ground', in which one child tries to hold a height against other children.

After his fictional Scottish excursion into thrillerdom, Stewart returned the next year to his English country-house roots with *The Ha-Ha Case* (1934), his last masterwork in this classic mystery setting (for elucidation of non-British readers, a ha-ha is a sunken wall, placed so as to delineate property boundaries while not obstructing views). Although

The Ha-Ha Case is not set in Scotland, Stewart drew inspiration for the novel from a notorious Scottish true crime, the 1893 Ardlamont murder case. From the facts of the Ardlamont affair Stewart drew several of the key characters in *The Ha-Ha Case*, as well as the circumstances of the novel's murder (a shooting 'accident' while hunting), though he added complications that take the tale in a new direction.[6]

In newspaper reviews both Dorothy L. Sayers and 'Francis Iles' (crime novelist Anthony Berkeley Cox) highly praised this latest mystery by 'The Clever Mr Connington', as he was now dubbed on book jackets by his new English publisher, Hodder & Stoughton. Sayers particularly noted the effective characterisation in *The Ha-Ha Case*: 'There is no need to say that Mr Connington has given us a sound and interesting plot, very carefully and ingeniously worked out. In addition, there are the three portraits of the three brothers, cleverly and rather subtly characterised, of the [governess], and of Inspector Hinton, whose admirable qualities are counteracted by that besetting sin of the man who has made his own way: a jealousy of delegating responsibility.' The reviewer for the *Times Literary Supplement* detected signs that the sardonic Sir Clinton Driffield had begun mellowing with age: 'Those who have never really liked Sir Clinton's perhaps excessively soldierly manner will be surprised to find that he makes his discovery not only by the pure light of intelligence, but partly as a reward for amiability and tact, qualities in which the Inspector [Hinton] was strikingly deficient.' This is true enough, although the classic Sir Clinton emerges a number of times in the novel, as in his subtly sarcastic recurrent backhanded praise of Inspector Hinton: 'He writes a first class report.'

Clinton Driffield returned the next year in the detective novel *In Whose Dim Shadow* (1935), a tale set in a recently erected English suburb, the denizens of which seem to have committed an impressive number of indiscretions, including sexual ones. The intriguing title of the British edition of the novel is drawn from a poem by the British historian Thomas Babington Macaulay: 'Those trees in whose dim shadow/The ghastly priest doth reign/The priest who slew the slayer/And shall himself be slain.' Stewart's puzzle plot in *In Whose Dim Shadow* is well clued and compelling, the kicker of a closing paragraph is a classic of its kind and, additionally, the author paints some excellent character portraits. I fully concur with the *Sunday Times*' assessment of the tale: 'Quiet domestic murder, full of the neatest detective points [. . .] These are not the detective's stock figures, but fully realised human beings.'[7]

Uncharacteristically for Stewart, nearly twenty months elapsed between the publication of *In Whose Dim Shadow* and his next book, *A Minor Operation* (1937). The reason for the author's delay in production was the onset in 1935–36 of the afflictions of cataracts and heart disease (Stewart ultimately succumbed to heart disease in 1947). Despite these grave health complications, Stewart in late 1936 was able to complete *A Minor Operation*, a first-rate Clinton Driffield story of murder and a most baffling disappearance.

A *Times Literary Supplement* reviewer found that *A Minor Operation* treated the reader 'to exactly the right mixture of mystification and clue' and that, in addition to its impressive construction, the novel boasted 'character-drawing above the average' for a detective novel.

Alfred Stewart's final eight mysteries, which appeared between 1938 and 1947, the year of the author's death, are, on the whole, a somewhat weaker group of tales than the sixteen that appeared between 1926 and 1937, yet they are not without interest. In 1938 Stewart for the last time managed to publish two detective novels, *Truth Comes Limping* and *For Murder Will Speak* (also published as *Murder Will Speak*). The latter tale is much the superior of the two, having an interesting suburban setting and a bevy of female characters found to have motives when a contemptible philandering businessman meets with foul play. Sexual neurosis plays a major role in *For Murder Will Speak*, the ever-thorough Stewart obviously having made a study of the subject when writing the novel. The somewhat squeamish reviewer for *Scribner's Magazine* considered the subject matter of *For Murder Will Speak* 'rather unsavoury at times', yet this individual conceded that the novel nevertheless made 'first-class reading for those who enjoy a good puzzle intricately worked out'. 'Judge Lynch' in the *Saturday Review* apparently had no such moral reservations about the latest Clinton Driffield murder case, avowing simply of the novel: 'They don't come any better'.

Over the next couple of years Stewart again sent Sir

Clinton Driffield temporarily packing, replacing him with a new series detective, a brash radio personality named Mark Brand, in *The Counsellor* (1939) and *The Four Defences* (1940). The better of these two novels is *The Four Defences*, which Stewart based on another notorious British true-crime case, the Alfred Rouse blazing-car murder. (Rouse is believed to have fabricated his death by murdering an unknown man, placing the dead man's body in his car and setting the car on fire, in the hope that the murdered man's body would be taken for his.) Though admittedly a thinly characterised academic exercise in ratiocination, Stewart's *Four Defences* surely is also one of the most complexly plotted Golden Age detective novels and should delight devotees of classical detection. Taking the Rouse blazing-car affair as his theme, Stewart composes from it a stunning set of diabolically ingenious criminal variations. 'This is in the cold-blooded category which [. . .] excites a crossword puzzle kind of interest,' the reviewer for the *Times Literary Supplement* acutely noted of the novel. 'Nothing in the Rouse case would prepare you for these complications upon complications [. . .] What they prove is that Mr Connington has the power of penetrating into the puzzle-corner of the brain. He leaves it dazedly wondering whether in the records of actual crime there can be any dark deed to equal this in its planned convolutions.'

Sir Clinton Driffield returned to action in the remaining four detective novels in the Connington oeuvre, *The Twenty-One Clues* (1941), *No Past is Dead* (1942), *Jack-in-the-Box* (1944) and *Commonsense is All You Need* (1947), all of which were written as Stewart's heart disease steadily worsened and reflect to some extent his diminishing physical and mental energy. Although *The Twenty-One Clues* was inspired by the notorious Hall-Mills double murder case – probably the most publicised murder case in the United States in the 1920s – and the American critic and novelist Anthony Boucher commended *Jack-in-the-Box*, I believe the best of these later mysteries is *No Past Is Dead*, which Stewart partly based on a bizarre French true-crime affair, the 1891 Achet-Lepine murder case.[8] Besides providing an interesting background for the tale, the ailing author managed some virtuoso plot twists, of the sort most associated today with that ingenious Golden Age Queen of Crime, Agatha Christie.

What Stewart with characteristic bluntness referred to as 'my complete crack-up' forced his retirement from Queen's University in 1944. 'I am afraid,' Stewart wrote a friend, the chemist and forensic scientist F. Gerald Tryhorn, in August 1946, eleven months before his death, 'that I shall never be much use again. Very stupidly, I tried for a session to combine a full course of lecturing with angina pectoris; and ended up by establishing that the two are immiscible.' He added that since retiring in 1944, he had been physically 'limited to my house, since even a fifty-yard crawl brings on the usual cramps'. Stewart completed his essay collection and a final novel before he died at his study desk in his Belfast home on 1 July 1947, at the age of sixty-six. When death came to the author he was busy at work, writing.

More than six decades after Alfred Walter Stewart's death, his J. J. Connington fiction is again available to a wider audience of classic-mystery fans, rather than strictly limited to a select company of rare-book collectors with deep pockets. This is fitting for an individual who was one of the finest writers of British genre fiction between the two world wars. 'Heaven forfend that you should imagine I take myself for anything out of the common in the tec yarn stuff,' Stewart once self-deprecatingly declared in a letter to Rupert Gould. Yet, as contemporary critics recognised, as a writer of detective and science fiction Stewart indeed was something out of the common. Now more modern readers can find this out for themselves. They have much good sleuthing in store.

1. For more on Street, Crofts and particularly Stewart, see Curtis Evans, *Masters of the 'Humdrum' Mystery: Cecil John Charles Street, Freeman Wills Crofts, Alfred Walter Stewart and the British Detective Novel, 1920–1961* (Jefferson, NC: McFarland, 2012). On the academic career of Alfred Walter Stewart, see his entry in *Oxford Dictionary of National Biography* (London and New York: Oxford University Press, 2004), vol. 52, 627–628.
2. The Gould–Stewart correspondence is discussed in considerable detail in *Masters of the 'Humdrum' Mystery*. For more on the life of the fascinating Rupert Thomas Gould, see Jonathan Betts, *Time Restored: The Harrison Timekeepers and R. T. Gould, the Man Who Knew (Almost) Everything* (London and New York: Oxford University Press, 2006) and *Longitude,* the 2000 British film adaptation of Dava Sobel's book *Longitude: The True Story of a Lone Genius Who Solved the Greatest Scientific Problem of His Time* (London: Harper Collins, 1995), which details Gould's restoration of the marine chronometers built by in the eighteenth century by the clockmaker John Harrison.
3. Potential purchasers of *Murder in the Maze* should keep in mind that $2 in 1927 is worth over $26 today.

4. In a 1920 article in *The Strand Magazine,* Arthur Conan Doyle endorsed as real prank photographs of purported fairies taken by two English girls in the garden of a house in the village of Cottingley. In the aftermath of the Great War Doyle had become a fervent believer in Spiritualism and other paranormal phenomena. Especially embarrassing to Doyle's admirers today, he also published *The Coming of the Faeries* (1922), wherein he argued that these mystical creatures genuinely existed. 'When the spirits came in, the common sense oozed out,' Stewart once wrote bluntly to his friend Rupert Gould of the creator of Sherlock Holmes. Like Gould, however, Stewart had an intense interest in the subject of the Loch Ness Monster, believing that he, his wife and daughter had sighted a large marine creature of some sort in Loch Ness in 1935. A year earlier Gould had authored *The Loch Ness Monster and Others*, and it was this book that led Stewart, after he made his 'Nessie' sighting, to initiate correspondence with Gould.
5. A tontine is a financial arrangement wherein shareowners in a common fund receive annuities that increase in value with the death of each participant, with the entire amount of the fund going to the last survivor. The impetus that the tontine provided to the deadly creative imaginations of Golden Age mystery writers should be sufficiently obvious.
6. At Ardlamont, a large country estate in Argyll, Cecil Hambrough died from a gunshot wound while hunting. Cecil's tutor, Alfred John Monson, and another man, both of whom were out hunting with Cecil, claimed that Cecil had accidentally shot himself, but Monson was arrested and tried for Cecil's murder. The verdict delivered was 'not proven', but Monson was then – and is today – considered almost certain to have been guilty of the murder. On the Ardlamont case, see William Roughead, *Classic Crimes* (1951; repr., New York: New York Review Books Classics, 2000), 378–464.
7. For the genesis of the title, see Macaulay's 'The Battle of the Lake Regillus', from his narrative poem collection *Lays of Ancient Rome.* In this poem Macaulay alludes to the ancient cult of Diana Nemorensis, which elevated its priests through trial by

combat. Study of the practices of the Diana Nemorensis cult influenced Sir James George Frazer's cultural interpretation of religion in his most renowned work, *The Golden Bough: A Study in Magic and Religion*. As with *Tom Tiddler's Island* and *The Ha-Ha Case* the title *In Whose Dim Shadow* proved too esoteric for Connington's American publishers, Little, Brown and Co., who altered it to the more prosaic *The Tau Cross Mystery*.

8. Stewart analysed the Achet-Lepine case in detail in 'The Mystery of Chantelle', one of the best essays in his 1947 collection *Alias J. J. Connington*.

CHAPTER I

THE DYING MAN

Dr. Ringwood pushed his chair back from the dinner-table. A glance at the clock on the mantelpiece told him that on this evening he had been even later than usual in getting home for dinner. The expression in his eyes showed that he had gone short of sleep for some time past ; and when he rose to his feet, every movement betrayed his over-tired condition.

" Bring my coffee to the study, please, Shenstone," he ordered. " And you might take the telephone in there as well."

He crossed the hall wearily, switched on the study lights, and stood for a moment on the threshold as if undecided what to do. A bright fire burned on the hearth ; the heavy pile of the carpet was soft to his feet ; and the big saddlebag armchairs spoke to him of pure physical comfort and relaxation after the strain of the day. He moved over to a table, hesitated again, and then picked up a copy of the *B.M.J.* in its postal wrapper. Taking a cigar from a box on the table, he clipped it mechanically and sat down in one of the chairs by the fire.

Shenstone drew a small table to Dr. Ringwood's elbow and placed the coffee on it ; then, retiring for a moment, he returned with the telephone, which he plugged to a connection in the room.

" Bring it over here, Shenstone. I want to be sure that the bell will wake me if I happen to doze."

Shenstone did as he was ordered and was about to leave the room when Dr. Ringwood spoke again.

" Fog clearing off, by any chance ? "

Shenstone shook his head.

" No, sir. Worse now than when you came in. Very thick indeed, sir. One can't see even the nearest street lamp."

Dr. Ringwood nodded gloomily.

" It's to be hoped no one wants me to go out this evening. Difficult enough to find one's way about a strange town in the daytime with a fog like this over everything. But in the daytime there are always people about who can give you some help. Nobody bar policemen will be out to-night, I should think."

Shenstone's face showed his sympathy.

" Very difficult for you, sir. If there's a night call, perhaps you'd knock me up, sir, and I could go out with you and help you to find your way. I'd be quite glad to do it, sir, if I could be of any service. When Dr. Carew went into the nursing home he specially impressed on me that I was to give you every assistance I could."

A tired smile crossed Dr. Ringwood's face.

" Doubtful if you can see any further through pea-soup than I can myself, Shenstone. Half the time, as I was coming back for dinner, I couldn't see even the pavement ; so I'm afraid your local knowledge wouldn't give you much of a pull. Thanks all the same. I've got a map of the town and I'll try to find my way by it."

He paused, and then, as Shenstone turned to go, he added :

" Put a decanter—Scotch—and some soda on the

table over yonder. Then I shan't need to worry you again to-night."

"Very good, sir."

As Shenstone left the room, Dr. Ringwood tore open the wrapper of the *B.M.J.*, threw the paper into the fire, and unfolded the journal. He scanned the contents while sipping his coffee ; but in a few minutes the bulky magazine slipped down on to his knees and he resigned himself completely to the comfort of his surroundings.

"Thank the Lord I didn't need to become a G.P." he reflected. "Specialism's a tough enough row to hoe, but general practice is a dog's life, if this is a sample of it."

He picked up the *B.M.J.* again ; but as he did so his sharp ear caught the sound of the front door bell. An expression of annoyance crossed his features and deepened as he heard Shenstone admit some visitor. In a few seconds the door of the study opened and Shenstone announced.

"Dr. Trevor Markfield, sir."

Dr. Ringwood's face cleared as a clean-shaven man of about thirty entered the room ; and he rose from his chair to greet the newcomer.

"Come in, Trevor. Try that pew beside the fire. I've been meaning to ring you up ever since I came last week, but I haven't had a moment. This 'flu epidemic has kept me on the run."

Trevor Markfield nodded sympathetically as he moved towards the fire and extended his hands to the blaze.

"I'd have looked you up before, but it was only this morning I heard from someone that you were doing *locum* for old Carew. It's a bit out of your line, isn't it ?"

" Carew's an old friend of ours ; and when he went down with appendicitis he asked me in a hurry to look after his practice and I could hardly refuse. It's been an experience, of sorts. I haven't had two hours continuous sleep in the last five days, and I feel as if the next patient runs the risk of a free operation. I'm fit to bite him in the gizzard without anæsthetics."

Markfield's stern features relaxed slightly.

" As bad as all that ? " he asked.

" Oh, I don't mind real cases. But last night I was called out at two in the morning, when I'd just got back from a relapsed 'flu case. A small boy. 'Dreadfully ill, doctor. Please come at once.' When I got there, it was simply an acute case of over-stuffing. ' It was his birthday, doctor, and of course we had to let him do as he liked on that day.' By the time I'd got there, he'd dree'd his weird—quite empty and nothing whatever the matter with him. No apologies for dragging me out of bed, of course. A doctor isn't supposed to have a bed at all. I expect the next thing will be a fatal case of ingrowing toe-nails. It's a damned nuisance to have one's time frittered away on that sort of thing when one's at one's wits end to do what one can for people at the last gasp with something really dangerous."

" Still got the notion that human life's valuable ? The war knocked that on the head," Markfield commented, rubbing his hands together to warm them: " Human life's the cheapest thing there is. It's a blessing I went over to the scientific side, instead of going in for physicking. I'd never have acquired a good sympathetic bedside manner."

Dr. Ringwood made a gesture towards the decanter on the table.

" Have a spot ? " he invited. " It's a miserable night."

Markfield accepted the offer at once, poured out half a tumblerful of whisky, splashed in a very little soda, and drank off his glass with evident satisfaction. Putting down the tumbler, he moved across and sat down by the fire.

" It's an infernal night," he confirmed. " If I didn't know this end of the town like the palm of my hand, I'd have lost my way coming here. It's the thickest fog I've seen for long enough."

" I'm in a worse box, for I don't know the town," Dr. Ringwood pointed out. " And we're not near the peak of this 'flu epidemic yet, by a long way. You're lucky to be on the scientific side. Croft-Thornton Research Institute, isn't it ? "

" Yes, I came here three years ago, in 1925. Silverdale beat me for the head post in the chemical department ; they gave me the second place."

" Silverdale ? " Dr. Ringwood mused. " The fellow who works on alkaloids ? Turned out a new condensate lately as side-line ? I seem to know the name."

" That's him. He doesn't worry me much. I dine at his house now and again ; but beyond that we don't see much of each other outside the Institute."

" I've a notion I ran across him once at a smoker in the old days. He played the banjo rather well. Clean-shaven, rather neatly turned out ? He'll be about thirty-five or so. By the way, he's married now, isn't he ? "

A faint expression of contempt crossed Markfield's face.

" Oh, yes, he's married. A French girl. I came across her in some amateur theatricals after they arrived here. Rather amusing at first, but a bit too exacting if one took her on as a permanency, I should think. I used to dance with her a lot at first, but the pace got a bit too hot for my taste. A man must have some evenings to himself, you know ; and what she wanted was a permanent dancing-partner. She's taken on a cub at the Institute—young Hassendean—for the business."

" Doesn't Silverdale do anything in that line himself? "

" Not a damn. Hates dancing except occasionally. They're a weird couple. Nothing whatever in common, that I can see ; and they've apparently agreed that each takes a separate road. You never see 'em together. She's always around with this Hassendean brat—a proper young squib ; and Silverdale's turned to fresh woods in the shape of Avice Deepcar, one of the girls at the Institute."

" Serious ? " Dr. Ringwood inquired indifferently.

" I expect he'd be glad of a divorce, if that's what you mean. But I doubt if he'll get it, in spite of all the scandal about Yvonne. If I can read the signs, she's just keeping the Hassendean cub on her string for her own amusement, though she certainly advertises her conquest all over the shop. He's not much to boast about : one of these young pseudo-romantic live-your-own-lifer's with about as much real backbone as a filleted sole."

" A bit rough on Silverdale," commented Dr. Ringwood apathetically.

Trevor Markfield's short laugh betrayed his scorn.

" A man's an ass to get tied up to a woman. Silverdale got caught by one side of her—oh, she's very attractive on that side, undoubtedly. But it didn't last, apparently, for either of them—and there you are ! Outside their own line, women are no use to a man. They want too much of one's time if one marries them, and they're the very devil, generally. I've no sympathy with Silverdale's troubles."

Dr. Ringwood, obviously bored, was seeking for a fresh subject.

" Comfortable place, the Institute ? " he inquired.

Markfield nodded with obvious approval.

" First-rate. They're prepared to spend money like water on equipment. I've just come in from the new Research Station they've put up for agricultural experiments. It's a few miles out of town. I've got a room or two in it for some work I'm doing in that line."

Before Dr. Ringwood could reply, the telephone bell trilled and with a stifled malediction he stepped over to the instrument.

" Dr. Ringwood speaking."

As the message came through, his face darkened.

" Very well. I'll be round to see her shortly. The address is 26 Lauderdale Avenue, you say ? . . . I'll come as soon as I can."

He put down the telephone and turned to his guest.

" I've got to go out, Trevor."

Markfield looked up.

" You said 26 Lauderdale Avenue, didn't you ? " he asked. " Talk of the Devil ! That's Silverdale's house. Nothing wrong with Yvonne, is there ? Sprained her ankle, or what not, by any chance ? "

" No. One of the maids turned sick, it seems ; and the other maid's a bit worried because all the family are out to-night and she doesn't know what to do with her invalid. I'll have to go. But how I'll find my way in a fog like this, is beyond me. Where is the place ? "

" About a couple of miles away."

" That'll take a bit of finding," Dr. Ringwood

grumbled, as he thought of the fog and his own sketchy knowledge of the local geography.

Markfield seemed to reflect for a moment or two before answering.

" Tell you what," he said at last, " I've got my car at the door—I'm just down from the Research Station. If you like, I'll pilot you to Silverdale's. I'll manage it better than you possibly could, on a night like this. You can drive behind me and keep your eye on my tail-light. You could get home again all right, I expect ; it's easier, since you've only got to find your way to a main street and stick to it."

Dr. Ringwood made no attempt to dissemble his relief at this solution of his difficulties.

" That's decent of you, Trevor. Just let me have a look at the map before we start. I'll take it with me, and I expect I'll manage to get home again somehow or other."

He glanced ruefully round the comfortable room and then went to the window to examine the night.

" Thicker than ever," he reported. " You'll need to crawl through that fog."

In a few minutes, Dr. Ringwood had put on his boots, warned Shenstone to attend to the telephone in his absence, and got his car out of the garage. Meanwhile Markfield had started his own engine and was awaiting the doctor at the gate.

" Hoot like blazes the moment you lose sight of me," he recommended. " If I hear your horn I'll stop and hoot back. That should keep us in touch if the worst comes to the worst."

He climbed into his driving-seat and started slowly down the road. Dr. Ringwood fell in behind. The fog was denser than ever, and the headlights of the cars merely illuminated its wreaths without piercing them. As soon as his car had started, Dr. Ringwood felt that he had lost touch with all the world except the tail-light ahead of him, and a few square feet of roadway immediately under his eyes. The kerb of the pavement had vanished ; no house-window showed through the mist. From time to time the pale beacon of a street-lamp shone high in the air without shedding any illumination upon the ground.

Once the guiding tail-lamp almost disappeared from view. After that, he crept up closer to the leading car, shifted his foot from the accelerator to the brake, and drove on the hand-throttle. His eyes began to smart with the nip of the fog and his throat was rasped as he drew his breath. Even in the saloon the air had a lung-catching tang, and he could see shadows in it, thrown by the nimbus of the headlights in the fog.

Almost from the start he had lost his bearings and now he pinned his whole attention on Markfield's tail-lamp. Once or twice he caught sight of tram-lines beside his wheels and knew that they were in a main thoroughfare ; but this gave him only the vaguest information of their position. The sound-deadening quality of the vapour about him completed the sense of isolation. Except for the faint beat of his own engine, he seemed to be in a silent world.

Suddenly Markfield's horn surprised him, and he had to jam on his brakes to avoid colliding with the car in front of him. A shadowy figure, hardly to be recognised as human, moved past him to the rear and vanished in the fog-wreaths. Then once more he had to concentrate his attention on the dim lamp ahead.

At last Markfield's car slid softly alongside a pavement and came slowly to rest. Dr. Ringwood pulled up and waited until his guide got down from his seat and came back to him.

" We're just at the turn into Lauderdale Avenue."

Dr. Ringwood made no attempt to conceal his admiration.

" That's a pretty good bit of navigation," he said. " I didn't notice you hesitate once in the whole trip."

" I've a fairly good head for locality," Markfield returned carelessly. " Now all you have to do is to turn to the left about ten yards further on. The numbering starts from this end of the road, and the even numbers are on the left-hand side. The houses are villas with big gardens, so you've only got to keep count of the gates as you pass them. Stick by the pavement and you'll see the motor-entrances easily enough."

" Thanks. I doubt if I'd have got here without you, Trevor. Now what about the road home ? "

" Come straight back along here. Cross three roads—counting this as No. 1. Then turn to the right and keep straight on till you cross tram-lines. That'll be Park Road. Keep along it to the left till you've crossed two more sets of tram-lines and then turn to the right. That'll be Aldingham Street, at the Blue Boar pub. You'll find your way from there simply enough, I think. That's the easiest way home. I brought you by a shorter route, but you'd never find it on a night like this. See you again soon. 'Night ! "

Without waiting for more, Markfield strode off to his car and soon Dr. Ringwood saw the red star, his only point of contact with the real world, slip away from him and vanish in the fog. When it had gone, he let his clutch in and began to grope his way laboriously along the pavement-edge and into Lauderdale Avenue.

The fog was as thick as ever, and he had some

difficulty in detecting even the breaks at the edge of the pavement which indicated the positions of house-gates. The walls of the gardens were concealed behind the climbing curtain of vapour. He counted seven entrances and was well on the way to the next when suddenly the roar of a horn made him lift his eyes to the spaces ahead; two golden discs shone almost upon him and only a wild wrench at the wheel saved him from a collision as the strange car swept past on the wrong side.

"Damn their eyes!" he grumbled to himself. "People like that should be hanged. No one has a right to go barging along at twenty miles an hour on a night like this, hustling everyone out of their way. And on the wrong side of the road, too."

In his swerve he had lost touch with the pavement and he now crept back to the left, steering in gently for fear of rubbing his tyres on the kerb. Then he began counting the gates once more.

"Eight . . . Nine . . . Ten . . . Eleven . . . Twelve. It's the next one."

He passed the next gate and drew up just beyond it. Then reflecting that it was hardly safe to leave a car on the street in a night like this, he got down from his seat and went across the pavement to open the gate of the short drive leading up to the house. The entrance was clear, however, and he was about to return to his car when a thought struck him and he lit a match to examine the pillar of the gate.

"No number, of course!" he commented in annoyance. "Ivy Lodge. This must be the place, anyhow."

Returning to his car, he backed it past the gate and then drove in and up the carriage-way. Just in time, as he came near the front door, the lights of a standing car warned him and he pulled up short to avoid a collision. Shutting off his engine, he got out and approached the house, passing a lighted window as he did so. The standing car was empty, and he climbed the steps to the front door, from which a light was shining. After some searching he discovered the press-button and rang the bell. The fog seemed thicker than ever ; and as he stood on the steps and gazed out into it, he could see no lights except those of the empty motor and his own headlamps. The house seemed completely isolated from the world.

Growing impatient, as no one came to open the door, he rang again ; and then, after a shorter interval, he held his finger down on the button until it seemed impossible that anyone in the house could fail to hear the sound of the bell. But still no one appeared. The lighted rooms and the waiting car convinced him that there must be someone on the premises ; and once more he set the bell in action.

As its notes died away again, he bent towards the door and strained his ears to catch any sound of movement within the building. At first he heard nothing ; but all at once something attracted his attention : a noise like a muffled cough. Dr. Ringwood hesitated for only a moment or two.

" Something damned queer about this house, it seems to me," he commented inwardly. " Technically it's burglary, I suppose ; but if the door's unlocked, I think I'd better go in and look round."

The door opened as he turned the handle, and he stepped softly into the hall. Everything seemed normal in the house. He could hear the ticking of a grandfather's clock further back on the stairs ; but the noise which had first attracted his attention was not repeated.

Gently closing the door to shut out the fog, he stood for a moment listening intently.

"Anybody here?" he demanded in a carrying voice.

There was no answer; but after a short time he heard again the sound which had puzzled him, evidently coming from the lighted room on the ground floor. Half a dozen swift steps took him to the door which he flung open.

"Good God! What's wrong with you?" he ejaculated, as his glance caught the only occupant of the smoke-room into which he had come.

On a chesterfield, a fair-haired young man was lying helpless. From the red stain on the lips, Dr. Ringwood guessed at a hæmorrhage of the lungs; and the quantity of blood on the boy's shirt-front and the dark pool on the carpet pointed to the severity of the attack. The youth's eyes caught the newcomer, and he beckoned feebly to the doctor. Ringwood crossed to the chesterfield and bent down. It hardly needed an expert to see that assistance had come too late. The sufferer made an effort, and the doctor stooped to catch the words.

"... Caught me ... pistol ... shot ... thought it was ... all right ... never guessed ..."

Dr. Ringwood bent closer.

"Who was it?" he demanded.

But that broken and gasped-out message had been the victim's last effort. With the final word, a cough shook him; blood poured from his mouth; and he fell back among the cushions in the terminal convulsion.

Dr. Ringwood saw the jaw drop and realised that he could be of no further service. Suddenly his weariness, accentuated by the strain of the drive through the fog, descended upon him once more. He straightened himself with something of an effort and gazed down at the body, feeling himself curiously detached from this suddenly-emergent mystery, as though it were no direct concern of his. Then, in his own despite, his cool medical brain began to work as though by some volition independent of his own. He drew out his note-book and jotted down the few disjointed words which he had caught, lest he should forget them later on.

Still held by the rigour of his training, he stooped once more and made a close examination of the body, discovering in the course of it two tiny tears in the dress shirt which evidently marked the entries of the bullets which had pierced the lungs. Then, his inspection completed, he left the body undisturbed, noted the time on his wrist-watch, and made a further jotting in his pocket-book.

As he did so, a fresh idea crossed his mind. Had there been more murders ? What about the maids in the house ? The one who had rung him up must have been somewhere on the premises, dead or alive. Possibly the murderer himself was still lurking in the villa.

Too tired to think of risk, Dr. Ringwood set himself to explore the house ; but to his amazement he discovered that it was empty. Nowhere did he see the slightest sign of anything which suggested a divergence from normal routine. The cloak-room showed that two men lived on the premises, since he noted hats of two different sizes on the pegs ; and there appeared to be three bedrooms in use, apart from the servants' rooms on the upper floor.

The next step was obviously to ring up the police, he reflected. The sooner this affair was off his shoulders, the better. But at this point there flashed across his mind the picture of a methodical and possibly slow detective who might even be suspicious of Ringwood himself and wish to detain him till the whole affair was cleared up. That would be a nuisance. Then a way out of the difficulty opened up before him. He remembered paying a visit on the previous night to a butler down with 'flu. When he had seen the patient, the man's master had come and made inquiries about the case; and Ringwood had been able to reassure him as to the man's condition.

"What was that chap's name?" Ringwood questioned his memory. "Sir Clinton Something-or-other. He's Chief Constable or some such big bug. When in doubt, go to headquarters. He'll remember me, I expect; he didn't look as if much slipped past him. And that'll save me from a lot of bother at the hands of underlings. What the devil was his name? Sir Clinton . . . Driffield, that's it. I'll ring him up."

He glanced round the hall in which he was standing but saw no telephone.

"It's probably in the smoke-room where the body is," he suggested to himself.

But though he searched all the likely places in the house he was unable to find any instrument.

"They haven't a 'phone, evidently," he was driven to admit. "But in that case, I can't be in Silverdale's house at all. This must be the wrong shop."

Then he remembered the moment when the other car had swept down upon him out of the fog.

"That probably explains it," he said aloud. "When I had to swerve out of his way, I must have missed one of the entrance gates before I got back in touch with the pavement again. If that's so, then obviously I'm in the wrong house. But whose house is it?"

He re-entered the smoke-room and looked round in

search of some clue. A writing-desk stood over against one of the walls, and he crossed to it and took up a sheet of paper from a note-paper case. The heading was what he wanted : " Ivy Lodge, 28 Lauderdale Avenue, Westerhaven."

" That's what happened," he reflected, with a faint satisfaction at having cleared the point up so simply. " I'm next door to Silverdale's place, evidently, I can 'phone from there."

It occurred to him that he had better be on the safe side and make sure of his information by adding the name of the householder when he rang up the Chief Constable. A fresh search among the pigeon-holes of the desk produced a letter in its original envelope addressed to " Edward Hassendean, Esq." Dr. Ringwood put it down again and racked his memory for an association with the name. He had paid only the most perfunctory attention to Markfield's talk, earlier in the evening, and it was some seconds before his mind could track down the elusive data.

" Hassendean ! That was the name of the cub who was hanging round the skirts of Silverdale's wife, I believe."

He glanced at the body on the chesterfield.

" It might be that youngster. The police will soon find out from the contents of his pockets, I expect. Besides, the rest of the family will be home soon. They must be out for the evening, and the maids too. That accounts for the house being empty."

He pulled out his pocket-book and scanned the note he had made of the boy's disjointed utterance.

" Caught me . . . thought it was . . . all right . . . never guessed . . . "

A flash of illumination seemed to pass across Dr.

Ringwood's mind as he re-read the words. In it he saw a frivolous wife, a dissolute boy, and a husband exasperated by the sudden discovery of an intrigue ; a sordid little tragedy of three characters. That seemed to be a plain enough explanation of the miserable affair. Markfield's suspicions had clearly been fairly near the truth ; if anything, they had fallen short of the real state of affairs. Something had precipitated the explosion ; and Dr. Ringwood idly speculated for a moment or two upon what could have led to the husband's enlightenment.

Then he awoke to a fresh aspect of the affair. The Hassendean family would be coming home again shortly, or else the maids would put in an appearance. The sooner the police were on the premises, the better. In the meanwhile, it seemed advisable to prevent any disturbance of things, if possible.

Dr. Ringwood left the smoke-room, locked the door after him, and removed the key, which he slipped into his pocket. Then, making sure that the front door could be opened from the outside when he returned, he went down the steps and out into the fog once more.

CHAPTER II

THE HOUSE NEXT DOOR

The box edging of the drive gave Dr. Ringwood sufficient guidance through the darkness down to the gate ; and by following the garden wall thereafter, he had little difficulty in making his way to the entrance of No. 26. By the light of a match he read the name *Heatherfield* on the gate-pillar, but here also there was no distinguishing number. This time, however, there could be no mistake and he groped his way cautiously up the drive until the light over the front door shone faintly through the fog.

As he went, a fresh complication in the situation presented itself to his mind. What would be the effect if he blurted out the news of the tragedy at Ivy Lodge ? If the maid at Silverdale's happened to be of a nervous type, she might take fright when she heard of the murder and might refuse to be left alone in the house with only a sick companion. That would be very awkward. Dr. Ringwood decided that his best course would be to say nothing about the affair next door, and merely make some simple excuse for going to the telephone. If he could shut himself up while he telephoned, she would learn nothing ; if not, then he would need to invent some pretext for getting her out of the way while he communicated with the police.

He climbed the steps and pressed the bell-button. This time he was not kept waiting, for almost immediately the door opened and a middle-aged woman, apparently a cook, peered nervously out at his figure framed in the fog. Seeing a stranger before her, she kept the door almost closed.

" Is that Dr. Ringwood ? " she asked.

Then, as he nodded assent, she broke into a torrent of tremulous explanation :

" I thought you were never coming, doctor. It's such a responsibility being left with Ina upstairs ill and no one else in the house. First of all, she was headachy ; then she was sick ; and her skin's hot and she looks all flushed. I think she's real ill, doctor."

" We'll see about it," Dr. Ringwood assured her. " But first of all, I have to ring up about another patient. You've a 'phone, of course ? It won't take me a minute ; and it's important."

The maid seemed put out that he did not go straight to his patient ; but she led the way to the cloakroom where the telephone was fixed. Dr. Ringwood paused before going to the instrument. He bethought himself of a pretext to get this nervous creature out of earshot.

" Let's see," he said. " I may need some boiling water—a small jug of it. Can you go and put on a kettle now, so that it'll be ready if I want it ? "

The maid went off towards the kitchen, whereupon he closed the door behind him and rang up. To his relief, Sir Clinton Driffield was at home ; and in less than a couple of minutes Dr. Ringwood was able to tell his story.

" This is Dr. Ringwood speaking, Sir Clinton. You may remember me ; I'm attending your butler."

" Nothing wrong in the case, I hope ? " the Chief Constable demanded.

" No, it's not that. I was called here—Heatherfield,

26 Lauderdale Avenue, this evening. I'm Dr. Carew's *locum* and a stranger in Westerhaven ; and in this fog I went to the wrong house—the one next door to here : Ivy Lodge, 28 Lauderdale Avenue. Mr. Hassendean's house. The place was lit up and a car was at the door ; but I got no answer when I rang the bell. Something roused my suspicions and I went inside. The house was empty : no maids or anyone on the premises. In a smoke-room on the ground floor I found a youngster of about twenty-two or so, dying. He'd been shot twice in the lung and he died on my hands almost as I went in."

He paused ; but as Sir Clinton made no comment, Dr. Ringwood continued :

" The house hadn't a telephone. I came in here, after locking the smoke-room door. I've a patient to see in this house. How long will it take your people to get to Ivy Lodge and take charge ? "

" I'll be over myself in twenty minutes," Sir Clinton replied. " Probably the local police will be there about the same time. I'll ring them up now."

" Very well. I'll see to my patient here ; and then I'll go back to Ivy Lodge to wait for you. Someone ought to be on the premises in case the maids or the family come home again."

" Right. I'll be with you shortly. Good-bye."

Dr. Ringwood, glancing at his watch, saw that it was twenty minutes past ten.

" They ought to be here about a quarter to eleven, if they can find their way in that fog," he reflected.

Leaving the cloakroom, he made his way to the nearest sitting-room and rang the bell for the maid.

" The water will be boiling in a minute or two, doctor," she announced, coming from the back premises. " Will you need it before you go up to see Ina, or shall I bring it up to you ? "

" I may not need it at all. Show me the way, please."

She led him up to the patient's room and waited while he made his examination.

" What is it, doctor ? " she demanded when he came out again.

" She's got scarlatina, I'm afraid. Rather a bad attack. She ought to be taken to hospital now, but on a night like this I doubt if the hospital van could get here easily. Have you had scarlet yourself, by any chance ? "

" Yes, doctor. I had it when I was a child."

Dr. Ringwood nodded, as though contented by the information.

" Then you don't run much risk of taking it from her. That simplifies things. I'd rather not shift her to-night, just in case the van lost its way. But if you can look after her for a few hours, it will be all right."

The maid did not seem altogether overjoyed at this suggestion. Dr. Ringwood sought for some way out of the difficulty.

" There's nobody at home to-night, is there ? "

" No, sir. Mr. Silverdale hasn't been home since lunch-time, and Mrs. Silverdale went out immediately after dinner."

" When will she be back ? "

" Not till late, sir, I expect. Young Mr. Hassendean came to dinner, and they went off in his car. I expect they've gone to the Alhambra to dance, sir."

Dr. Ringwood repressed his involuntary movement at the name Hassendean.

" When in doubt, play the medicine-man card," he

concluded swiftly in his mind, without betraying anything outwardly. It seemed possible that he might get some evidence out of the maid before she became confused by any police visit. He assumed an air of doubt as he turned again to the woman.

" Did Mrs. Silverdale come much in contact with the housemaid during the day ? "

" No, sir. Hardly at all."

" H'm ! When did Mrs. Silverdale have dinner ? "

" At half-past seven, sir."

" Was this Mr. Hassendean here long before dinner ? "

" No, sir. He came in a few minutes before the half-hour."

" Where were they before dinner ? "

" In the drawing-room, sir."

" The maid had been in that room during the day, I suppose ? "

" Only just doing some dusting, sir. She had been complaining of a sore throat and being out of sorts, and she didn't do anything she could avoid bothering with."

Dr. Ringwood shook his head as though he were not very easy in his mind.

" Then Mrs. Silverdale and Mr. Hassendean went in to dinner ? Did the housemaid wait at dinner ? "

" No, sir. By that time she was feeling very bad, so I sent her to bed and looked after the dinner myself."

" She hadn't touched the dishes, or anything of that sort ? "

" No, sir."

" And immediately after dinner, Mrs. Silverdale and Mr. Hassendean went out ? "

The maid hesitated for a moment.

" Yes, sir. At least——"

Dr. Ringwood made his face grave.

" Tell me exactly what happened. One never can tell with these scarlet cases."

" Well, sir, I was just going to bring in coffee when Mr. Hassendean said : ' Let's have our coffee in the drawing-room, Yvonne. This room's a bit cold." Or something like that. I remember he didn't want the coffee in the dining-room, at any rate. So I went to get it ; and when I came back with it they were sitting beside the fire in the drawing-room. I was going to take the tray over to them, when Mr. Hassendean said : ' Put it down on the table over there.' So I put it down and went away to clear the dining-room table."

" And the housemaid had dusted the drawing-room this morning," Dr. Ringwood said thoughtfully. " Mr. Hassendean wasn't long in the drawing-room after dinner, was he ? "

" No, sir. They didn't take very long over their coffee."

Dr. Ringwood looked judicial and seemed to consider some abstruse point before speaking again.

" Mrs. Silverdale didn't look ill during the day, did she ? "

" No, sir. But now you mention it, I did think she seemed rather strange just before she went out."

" Indeed ? I was afraid of something of the sort. What do you mean, exactly ? " Dr. Ringwood demanded, concealing his interest as well as he could.

" Well, sir, it's hard to say exactly. She came out of the drawing-room and went upstairs to get her cloak ; and as she came down again, I passed her in the hall, taking some dishes to the kitchen. She seemed dazed-like, now you mention it."

" Dazed ? "

" Funny sort of look in her eyes, sir. I can't describe it well. Seemed as if she wasn't taking notice of me as I passed."

Dr. Ringwood's face showed an increase in gravity.

" I'm afraid Mrs. Silverdale may have got infected too. What about Mr. Hassendean ? "

The maid considered for a moment before answering.

" I didn't notice anything strange about Mr. Hassendean, sir. Unless, perhaps, he *did* seem a bit nervous—high-strung like, I thought. But I'd never have paid attention to it if you hadn't asked me the question."

Dr. Ringwood made a gesture of approval, inwardly thanking his stars for the lay public's ignorance of diseases.

" And then they went off together ? "

" Yes, sir. Mr. Hassendean took the cloak from Mrs. Silverdale and put it over her shoulders. Then he took her arm and they went out to his car. It was waiting in front of the door."

" H'm ! I suppose the housemaid hadn't touched the cloak to-day ? "

" Oh, no, sir. She'd been in Mrs. Silverdale's room, of course ; but she wouldn't have any reason to go near the cloak."

Dr. Ringwood feigned a difficulty in recollection.

" Hassendean ! I surely know him. Isn't he about my height, fair, with a small moustache ? "

" Yes, sir. That's him."

Dr. Ringwood had confirmed his guess. It was young Hassendean's body that lay next door.

" Let's see," he said. " I may have to come back here in an hour or so. I'd like to have another look at my patient upstairs. Will Mrs. Silverdale be back by that time, do you think ? "

" That would be about half-past eleven, sir ? No, I don't think she'd be back as soon as that. She's usually out until after midnight, most nights."

" Well, you might sit up and wait for me, please. Go to bed if I'm not here by twelve. But—— No, if you can manage it, I think you ought to keep awake till Mrs. Silverdale comes home. That patient shouldn't be left with no one to look after her. I'm just afraid she may get a little light-headed in the night. It's hard lines on you ; but you must do your best for her."

" Very well, sir, if you say so."

" Perhaps Mr. Silverdale will turn up. Is he usually late ? "

" One never can tell with him, sir. Some days he comes home to dinner and works late in his study. Other times he's out of the house from breakfast-time and doesn't get back till all hours. He might be here in five minutes now, or he mightn't come home till two in the morning."

Dr. Ringwood felt that he had extracted all the information he could reasonable expect to get. He gave the maid some directions as to what she should do in possible emergencies ; then, glancing at his watch, he took his departure.

As he went down the steps of the house, he found no signs of the fog lifting ; and he had to exercise as much care as ever in making his way through it. He was not unsatisfied with the results of his interrogation. Young Hassendean had met Silverdale's wife by appointment, evidently. They had dined together ; and then they had gone away in the fog. Clearly enough, from what the maid said, both of them were in a somewhat abnormal state when they left the house. " Dazed-like," " a bit nervous—high strung." He recalled the expressions with a faint annoyance at the vagueness of the descriptions.

It seemed quite likely that, instead of going to a dance-hall, they had simply driven round to Ivy Lodge, which young Hassendean must have known to be empty at that time. And there, something had happened. The girl had gone away or been taken away, and the youngster had been left to die. But where had Yvonne Silverdale gone ?

Dr. Ringwood opened the door of Ivy Lodge and took the key of the smoke-room from his pocket. The house was silent as when he left it. Evidently no one had come home.

CHAPTER III

SIR CLINTON AT IVY LODGE

Dr. Ringwood left the smoke-room door open to ensure that he would hear anyone who entered the house. He made a second cursory inspection of young Hassendean's body ; but as he took care not to alter the position of anything, he discovered no more than he had done when he inspected it originally. There seemed to be nothing further for him to do until the police came upon the scene ; so he picked out a comfortable chair and let himself relax whilst he had the chance.

The patient next door worried him a little. Perhaps he ought to have got the girl off to hospital at once, fog or no fog. It would be awkward if she turned delirious in the night. And from that, his mind drifted to other cases which were giving him anxiety. With this 'flu epidemic, Carew's practice had been anything but the nice, quiet, jog-trot business he had imagined it to be when he promised to come as *locum.*

By some incongruous linking, his thoughts came back to the events through which he had just passed. Death was all in the day's work for a medical man, but he had hardly bargained for murder. At least, he had hitherto assumed that this was a case of murder, but possibly it was suicide. He recalled that he had not seen any pistol ; and he felt a momentary inclination to search the room for the weapon ; but his fatigue was greater than his interest, and he abandoned the project. After all, it was an affair for the police, when they came to take charge; it was no business of his.

Nevertheless, he could not shake off the subject of the tragedy; and, despite himself, he began to speculate on the possibilities of the situation. Suppose that, after dinner, young Hassendean and Mrs. Silverdale had simply driven round to Ivy Lodge. That would account for the empty car at the door. Then they must have come into the house. He had found the door unlocked, so that anyone could enter. That seemed rather a peculiar point. Surely, if they had come here for the only purpose which seemed covered by the case, they would have taken the obvious precaution of closing the front door against intruders. But if they had done that, how could Silverdale have got in? He could hardly have had a latch-key for his neighbours' house.

It occurred to Dr. Ringwood that possibly Silverdale might have gained admittance through some unlatched window. He might have seen something through the smoke-room window and got into the house like a burglar. But all the curtains were tightly drawn. No one could see in from the outside, even if they had wished to do so. Obviously, then, it could not have been a chance discovery of his wife's guilt that had roused Silverdale to the pitch of murder. He must have had his suspicions and deliberately tracked down the guilty couple.

Almost against his will, Dr. Ringwood's mind persisted in an attempt to reconstruct the happenings of the night. Suppose Silverdale got in—no matter how—then evidently he must have surprised the two; and the end of that business had been the shooting of young Hassendean. But that left Yvonne Silverdale and her husband still unaccounted for. Had she fled into the night before Silverdale could shoot her in her turn. Or had her husband forced her to go with him—whither? And if this were the truth of the matter, why had Silverdale not locked the door? There seemed to be many things needing explanation before one could feel that the case was clear. Well, that was the business of the police.

His train of thought was suddenly interrupted by the sound of feet at the front door, and he pulled himself together with a start and rose from his chair. He was just moving towards the door when it opened and Sir Clinton Driffield, accompanied by another man, entered the room.

" Good evening, Dr. Ringwood," the Chief Constable greeted him. " I think we've managed to get here at the time I promised, though it was a difficult business with all this fog about."

He turned to introduce his companion.

" This is Inspector Flamborough, doctor. He's in charge of the case. I'm merely here as an onlooker. I've given him the facts, so far as I know them from you; but I expect that he may wish further information if you have any."

At Sir Clinton's words, the mouth under Inspector Flamborough's tooth-brush moustache curved in a smile, half-friendly and half-inscrutable. Simultaneously, he seemed to be establishing good relations with the doctor and appreciating some obscure joke in the Chief Constable's remarks.

" It's very lucky you're a medical man, sir. Death's all in the day's work with you and me; neither of us is likely to be put off our balance by it. Most witnesses in cases of this sort get so confused by the shock that it's difficult to squeeze any clear story out of them. A doctor's different."

Dr. Ringwood was not particularly susceptible to flattery, but he recognised that the Inspector probably was voicing his real sentiments. All three of them were experts in death, and among them there was no need to waste time in polite lamentations. None of them had ever set eyes on the victim before that night, and there was no object in becoming sentimental over him.

" Sit down, doctor," Sir Clinton broke in, after a glance at the medical man's face. " You look as if you were about tired out. This 'flu epidemic must be taking it out of you."

Dr. Ringwood did not wait to be asked twice. Sir Clinton followed his example, but the Inspector, pulling a notebook from his pocket, prepared to open his investigation.

" Let's see, now, doctor," he began pleasantly. " I'd like to start from the beginning. You might tell us just how you happened to come into the business ; and if you can give us some definite times, it'll be a great help."

Dr. Ringwood nodded, but seemed to hesitate for a moment before replying :

" I think I could give you it clearest if I were sure of one thing first. I believe that's the body of young Hassendean who lived in this house, but I haven't examined it closely—didn't wish to disturb it in any way before you turned up. If it is young Hassendean's body, then I can fit some other things into my evidence. Perhaps you'll have a look for yourselves and see if you can identify him."

The Inspector exchanged a glance with his superior

" Just as you please, sir," he answered.

He crossed the room, knelt beside the chesterfield, and began to search the pockets in the body's clothes. The first two yielded nothing in the way of identification, but from one of the pockets of the evening waistcoat the Inspector fished out a small card.

" Season ticket for the Alhambra," he reported, after glancing over it. " You're right, doctor. The signature's here : Ronald Hassendean."

" I was pretty sure of it," Dr. Ringwood answered. " But I like to be certain."

The Inspector rose to his feet and came back to the hearthrug.

" Now, perhaps, sir, you'll tell us the story in your own way. Only let's have it clear. I mean, tell us what you saw yourself and let's know when you're bringing anything else in."

Dr. Ringwood had a clear mind and could put his facts together in proper order. In spite of his physical weariness, he was able to take each incident of the evening in its proper turn and make it fit neatly into its place in his narrative. When he had finished, he had brought the story up to the point when the police arrived. As he closed his tale, the Inspector shut his notebook with a nod of approval.

" There's a lot of useful information there, doctor. We're lucky in having your help. Some of what you've told us would have cost a lot of bother to fish out of different people."

Sir Clinton rose to his feet with a gesture which invited the doctor to remain in his chair.

" Of course, doctor," he pointed out, " a good deal of your story is like What the Soldier Said—it isn't first-hand evidence. We'll have to get it for ourselves, again, from the people who gave it to you : Dr. Markfield and this maid next door. That's only routine ; and doesn't imply that we disbelieve it in the slightest, naturally."

Dr. Ringwood agreed with a faint smile.

" I prefer getting a patient's symptoms at first-hand myself," he said. " Things do get distorted a bit in the re-telling. And some of what I gave you is quite possibly just gossip. I thought you ought to hear it ; but most certainly I don't guarantee its accuracy."

The Inspector beamed his approval of the doctor's views.

" And now, sir," he said, glancing at Sir Clinton, " I think I'd better go over the ground here and see if there's anything worth picking up."

He suited the action to the word, and began a systematic search of the room, commenting aloud from time to time for his companions' benefit.

" There's no pistol here, unless it's hidden away somewhere," he reported after a while. " The murderer must have taken it away with him."

Sir Clinton's face took on a quizzical expression.

" Just one suggestion, Inspector. Let's keep the facts and the inferences in separate boxes, if you please. What we really *do* know is that you haven't found any pistol up to the present."

Flamborough's grin showed that the Chief Constable's shot had gone home without wounding his feelings.

" Very good, sir. ' Pistol *or pistols*, not found.' I'll note that down."

He went down on hands and knees to examine the carpet.

" Here's something fresh, sir," he announced. " The carpet's so dark that I didn't notice it before. The pattern concealed it, too. But here it is, all right."

He drew his fore-finger over the fabric at a spot near the door, and then held it for their inspection, stained with an ominous red.

" A blood-spot, and a fair-sized one, too ! There may be more of them about."

" Yes," said Sir Clinton mildly. " I noticed some on the hall-carpet as I came in. There's a trail of them from the front door into this room. Perhaps you didn't see them ; they're not conspicuous."

The Inspector looked a trifle crestfallen.

" I know you've a sharp eye, sir. I didn't spot them myself."

" Suppose we finish up this room before going elsewhere. All the windows are fast, are they ? " the Chief Constable asked.

Flamborough examined them and reported that all the catches were on. Then he gazed up and down the room inquisitively.

" Looking for bullet-holes ? " Sir Clinton questioned. " Quite right. But you won't find any."

" I like to be certain about things, sir."

" So do I, Inspector. So does Dr. Ringwood, if you remember. Well, you can be certain of one thing. If two shots had been fired in here this evening, and if all the windows had been left closed as they are now, then I'd have smelt the tang of the powder in the air when we came in. I didn't. Ergo, no shots were fired in this room. Whence it follows that it's no use hunting for bullet-holes. Does that chain of reasoning satisfy you, Inspector ? "

Flamborough made a gesture of vexation.

" That's true enough," he confessed. " I ought to have thought of it."

" I think we've got the main points, now, so far as

this room itself goes," Sir Clinton observed, without paying any heed to the Inspector's annoyance. "Would you mind examining the body, doctor, just to confirm your view that he was shot in the lung?"

Dr. Ringwood assented and, crossing over, he subjected young Hassendean's body to a careful scrutiny. A few minutes sufficed to prove that the only wounds were those in the chest; and when the doctor had satisfied himself that his earlier diagnosis was correct, he turned to the Chief Constable.

"There's no certainty without a P.M., of course, but from the way the bullets have gone in, it's pretty obvious that the shots took effect on the left lung. There's very little external bleeding, apparently; and that rather looks as if one of the intercostal arteries may be involved. He must have bled a lot internally, I suspect. Probably the P.M. will confirm that."

Sir Clinton accepted the verdict without demur.

"And what do you make out of things, Inspector?" he demanded, turning to Flamborough.

"Well, sir, with these small-calibre pistols, it's difficult to give more than a guess. So far as I can see, it looks as if the pistol had been quite close-up when it was fired. I think I can see something that looks like scorching or discoloration on his dress shirt round about the wound, though the blood makes it hard to be sure. That's really as far as I'd like to go until I've had a better chance of examining the thing."

Sir Clinton turned back to the doctor.

"I suppose a wound in the lung may produce death at almost any length of time after the shot's actually fired. I mean that a man may live for quite a long while even with a wound like this and might be able to move about to some extent after being shot?"

Dr. Ringwood had no hesitation in agreeing with this.

" He might have lived for an hour or two—even for days. Or else, of course, he might have collapsed almost at once. You never can tell what will happen in lung wounds."

Sir Clinton seemed to give this a certain consideration. Then he moved towards the door.

" We'll take up the blood-trail now. You'd better switch off the light and lock the door, Inspector. We don't want anyone blundering in here and getting a fright by any mischance."

They went out into the hall, where Sir Clinton drew the attention of the Inspector to the traces of blood which he had noticed on the carpet.

" Now we'd better have a look at that car outside," he suggested.

As they descended the steps from the front door, the Inspector took a flash-lamp from his pocket and switched it on. Its rays merely served to light up the fog ; and it was not until they came almost to the side of the car that they could see much. The Inspector bent across, rubbed his finger over the driving-seat, and then examined his hand in the light of the lamp.

" Some more blood there, sir," he reported.

He cleaned away the marks on his finger-tip and proceeded to explore the other seats in the same manner. The results were negative. Apart from one or two spots on the running-board at the driving-seat door, the car seemed otherwise clean. Inspector Flamborough straightened himself up and turned to Sir Clinton.

" It seems that he must have driven the car back himself, sir. If someone else had done the driving, the blood would have been on some of the other seats instead of this one."

Sir Clinton acquiesced with a gesture.

" I suppose that's possible, doctor ? A wound in the lung wouldn't incapacitate him completely ? "

Dr. Ringwood shook his head.

" It would depend entirely on the sort of wound it was. I see nothing against it, *prima facie*. Driving a car isn't really much strain on the body muscles."

Sir Clinton ran his eye over the lines of the car in the light of the side-lamps.

" It's an Austin, so he'd be able to get the engine going with the self-starter, probably, even on a night like this. He wouldn't need to crank up the car. There would be no exertion on his part."

The Inspector had been examining the ground.

" It's frozen fairly hard," he reported. " There's no hope of tracing the car's track on a night like this, even if one could have done that through all the marks of the town traffic. That's a blank end."

" You may as well take the number, Inspector. It's just possible that some constable may have noticed it, though the chances are about a thousand to one against that, on a night of this sort."

Flamborough went round to the rear number-plate and jotted down the figures in his pocket-book, repeating them aloud as he did so :

" GX. 6061."

He came round the car again and subjected the whole interior to a minute scrutiny under the light of his flashlamp.

" Here's a girl's handkerchief lying on the floor," he said, as he peered down at the place beside the driver. Then, holding it in the light from the side-lamp, he turned it over and reported.

" It's got ' Y.S.' embroidered in one corner. That

would be for Yvonne Silverdale, I suppose. It doesn't take us much further. Except that it proves this was the car she went off in with young Hassendean, and I expect we could have got better proof of that elsewhere."

" Nothing else you can find ? " Sir Clinton inquired.

" No, sir."

Before the Chief Constable could say anything further, two figures loomed up through the fog and a startled exclamation in a female voice reached the group around the car. Sir Clinton caught Dr. Ringwood's arm and whispered hurriedly in his ear :

" The maids coming back to the house. Spin them a yarn that young Hassendean's met with an accident and been brought home. Tell them who you are. We don't want to have them in hysterics."

Dr. Ringwood moved towards the dim figures in the fog.

" I'm Dr. Ringwood," he explained. " I suppose you're the maids, aren't you ? You must go in very quietly. Young Mr. Hassendean's had a bad accident and mustn't be disturbed. He's in the room to the right as you go in at the door, so don't make a fuss in the house. You'd better get off to bed."

There was a sound of rapid whispering and then one of the maids enquired :

" Was it a motor accident, sir ? "

Dr. Ringwood, anxious not to commit himself to details, made a gesture to the window behind him.

" Don't make a row, please. Mr. Hassendean mustn't be disturbed in any way. Get off to bed as soon as you can, and keep quiet. By the way, when do you expect the rest of the family home ? "

" They've gone out to play bridge, sir," answered

the maid who had spoken before. " Usually they get home about half-past eleven."

" Good. I shall have to wait for them."

The bolder of the two maids had advanced as he was speaking, and now she stared suspiciously at him in the dim light from the car lamps.

" Excuse me, sir," she ventured. " How do I know that it's all right ? "

" You mean I might be a burglar, I suppose ? " Dr. Ringwood answered patiently. " Well, here's Inspector Flamborough. He's surely protection enough for you."

The maid examined Flamborough with relief.

" Oh, that's all right, sir. I saw Inspector Flamborough once at the police sports. That's him, right enough. I'm sorry to have been a bit suspicious, sir——"

" Quite right," Dr. Ringwood reassured her. " Now, just get off to bed, will you. We've got the patient to think about."

" Is it a bad accident, sir ? "

" Very serious, perhaps. Talking won't mend it, anyhow."

Dr. Ringwood's temper was becoming slightly frayed by the maid's persistence. However, she took the hint and retired with her companion into the house. Inspector Flamborough made a gesture which arrested them at the door.

" By the way, when did young Mr. Hassendean leave the house to-night ? " he demanded.

" I couldn't say, sir. We left ourselves at seven o'clock. Mr. Hassendean and Miss Hassendean were just going out then—they were dining out. And Mr. Ronald was dressing, I think. He was going out to dinner, too."

Flamborough dismissed them, and they vanished into the hall. Sir Clinton gave them a reasonable time to get out of the way before making any further move. The Inspector occupied himself with writing a note in his pocket-book.

" I think we may as well go into the house again," the Chief Constable suggested. " Just fasten that front door after us, Inspector, if you please. We may as well have some warning when the family turns up."

He led the way up the steps, entered the hall, and, after opening one or two doors at random, selected the drawing-room of the house, in which a banked-up fire was burning.

" We may as well wait here. It's to be hoped they won't be long, now. Sit down, doctor."

Then, noticing the expression on Dr. Ringwood's face, he continued :

" I'm sorry to detain you, doctor ; but now we've got you, I think we'll have to keep you until the Hassendeans come in. One never knows what may turn up. They may have something to tell us which might need medical checking and you've been too much of a gift from the gods to part with so long as there's a chance of our utilising you."

Dr. Ringwood tried to make his acquiescence a cheerful one, though he was thinking regretfully of his bed.

" It's all in the day's work," he said. " I'm only a bit worried about that case of scarlet next door. I'll have to look in there before I go."

" So shall we," Sir Clinton explained. " Once we've got all the evidence from the family, we'll need to ring up and get the body taken off to the mortuary. You say we can telephone from the house next door ? "

" Yes. I had to go there to ring you up myself. The Hassendeans have no 'phone."

" We'll go round with you then. . . . H'm ! There's the door-bell, Inspector. You'd better attend to it. Bring them in here, please."

Flamborough hurried out of the room ; they heard some muffled talk broken by ejaculations of surprise and horror ; and then the Inspector ushered Mr. and Miss Hassendean into the drawing-room. Dr. Ringwood was unfavourably impressed at the first glance. Mr. Hassendean was a red-faced, white-haired man of about seventy, with a feebly blustering manner. His sister, some five years younger, aped the air and dress of women twenty years her junior.

" What this ? What's this, eh ? " Mr. Hassendean demanded as he came into the room. " God bless my soul ! My nephew shot ? What does it mean, eh ? "

" That's what we should like to know, sir," Inspector Flamborough's quiet voice cut into the frothing torrent of the old man's eloquence. " We're depending on you to throw some light on the affair."

" On me ? " Mr. Hassendean's voice seemed to strain itself in the vain attempt to express his feelings at the Inspector's suggestion. " I'm not a policeman, my good fellow ; I'm a retired drysalter. God bless me ! Do I look like Sherlock Holmes ? "

He paused, apparently unable to find words for a moment.

" Now, look here, my good man," he went on, " I come home and I find you occupying my house, and you tell me that my young nephew has been shot. He's a good-for-nothing cub, I admit ; but that's beside the point. I want to know who's to blame for it. That's a simple enough question, surely. And instead of answering it, you have the nerve to ask me to do your work for you ! What do we pay police rates for, tell me that ! And who are these men in my drawing-room ? How did they come here ? "

" This is Sir Clinton Driffield ; this is Dr. Ringwood," the Inspector answered smoothly, taking no notice of Mr. Hassendean's other remarks.

" Ah ! I've heard of you, Sir Clinton," Mr. Hassendean acknowledged, less ungraciously. " Well, what about it ? "

" We've met under rather unfortunate conditions, Mr. Hassendean," Sir Clinton admitted soothingly, " but they're none of our choosing, you know. I quite understand your feelings ; it must be a bad shock to come home to an affair like this. But I hope you'll see your way to give us any information you have—anything that will assist us to get on the track of the person who shot your nephew. We really depend on you to help us at once, for every hour lost may make it more difficult to lay our hands on the criminal. Without knowing it, you may have the key to the thing in your hands."

More by his manner than by his words, the Chief Constable had succeeded in pacifying the old man.

" Well, if it's put like that, I don't mind," he conceded, with a slight lessening in the asperity of his tone. " Ask your questions and I'll see what I can do for you."

Dr. Ringwood, watching the change in the situation, reflected sardonically to himself that a title had its uses when one came to deal with a snob.

" That old bounder was rude to the Inspector on

principle ; but when Sir Clinton Driffield asks precisely the same question, he's quite amenable," he thought to himself. " What a type ! "

The Chief Constable, when he began his interrogatory, was careful not to betray that he already had some information.

" Perhaps we'd better begin at the beginning, Mr. Hassendean," he suggested, with the air of one consulting a valued collaborator. " Could you throw any light on your nephew's arrangements for this evening ? Did he mean to stay in the house, or had he any outside engagement that you knew about ? "

" He told me he was going out to dinner with that hussy next door."

Sir Clinton's smile further disarmed old Hassendean.

" I'm afraid you'll need to be more definite. There are so many hussies nowadays."

"You're right there, sir ! You're right there. I agree with you. I'm speaking of the French one next door, her name's Silverdale. My nephew was always hanging round her skirts, sir. I warned him against her, often enough."

" I always *knew* something would happen ! " Miss Hassendean declared with the air of a justified Cassandra. " And now it *has* happened."

Sir Clinton returned to the main track.

" Have you any idea if he meant to spend the evening next door ? "

Miss Hassendean interrupted before her brother could reply.

" He mentioned to me that he was going with her to the Alhambra to dance. I remember that, because he actually asked me where I was going myself to-night, which was unusual interest on his part."

"Scattering his money, of course!" her brother rapped out angrily.

"He had money to scatter, then?" Sir Clinton asked casually. "He must have been lucky for his age."

For some reason, this reflection seemed to stir a grievance in the old man's mind.

"Yes, he had about £500 a year of his own. A very comfortable income for a single young man. And I had to sit, sir, as his trustee; pay over the money quarterly to him; and see it wasted in buying jewellery and what-not for that wench next door. I'm not a rich man, sir; and I give you my word I could have spent it better myself. But I'd no control over him, none whatever. I had to stand by and see all that good money flung into the gutter."

Dr. Ringwood turned aside to hide his smile at this revelation of the drysalter's soul.

"By the way, who gets that money now?" Sir Clinton inquired.

"I do, sir. And I hope I'll put it to better use."

Sir Clinton nodded in response to this sentiment, and seemed to ponder before he asked his next question.

"I suppose you can't think of anyone who might have had a grudge against him?"

The old man's glance showed some suspicion at the question; but his sister seemed to have less compunction, for she answered instead.

"I warned Ronald again and again that he was playing with fire. Mr. Silverdale never took any open offence, but . . ."

She left her sentence unfinished. Sir Clinton seemed less impressed than she had expected. He made no comment on her statement.

"Then I take it, Mr. Hassendean, that you can

throw no light on the affair, beyond what you have told us ? "

The old man seemed to think that he had given quite enough information, for he merely answered with a non-committal gesture.

" I must thank you for your assistance," Sir Clinton pursued. " You understand, of course, that there are one or two formalities which need to be gone through. The body will have to be removed for a *post mortem* examination, I'm afraid ; and Inspector Flamborough will need to go through your nephew's papers to see if anything in them throws light on this affair. He can do that now, if you have no objections."

Old Hassendean seemed rather taken back by this.

" Is that necessary ? "

" I'm afraid so."

The old man's face bore all the marks of uneasiness at this decision.

" I'd rather avoid it if possible," he grumbled. " It's not for use in Court, is it ? I shouldn't like that, not by any means. To tell you the truth, sir," he continued in a burst of frankness, " we didn't get on well, he and I ; and it's quite on the cards that he may have said—written, I mean—a lot of things about me that I shouldn't care to have printed in the newspapers. He was a miserable young creature, and I never concealed my opinion about him. Under his father's will, he had to live in my house till he was twenty-five, and a pretty life he led me, sir. I suspect that he may have slandered me in that diary he used to keep."

" You'd better make a note about that diary, Inspector," Sir Clinton suggested in a tone which seemed to indicate that Flamborough must be discreet. " You needn't trouble yourself too much about it,

Mr. Hassendean. Nothing in it will come out in public unless it bears directly on this case ; I can assure you of that."

The drysalter recognised that this was final ; but he could hardly be described as giving in with a good grace.

" Have it your own way," he grunted crossly.

Sir Clinton ignored this recrudescence of temper.

" I'll leave the Inspector to see to things," he explained. " I'll go with Dr. Ringwood, Inspector, and do the telephoning. You'd better stay here, of course, until someone relieves you. You'll find plenty to do, I expect."

He bade good-night to his involuntary host and hostess and, followed by the doctor, left the house.

CHAPTER IV

THE CRIME AT HEATHERFIELD

"That's a fine old turkey-cock," Dr. Ringwood commented, as he and Sir Clinton groped their way down the drive towards the gate of Ivy Lodge.

The Chief Constable smiled covertly at the aptness of the description.

"He certainly did gobble a bit at the start," he admitted. "But that type generally stops gobbling if you treat it properly. I shouldn't care to live with him long, though. A streak of the domestic tyrant in him somewhere, I'm afraid."

Dr. Ringwood laughed curtly.

"It must have been a pretty household," he affirmed. "You didn't get much valuable information out of him, in spite of all his self-importance and fuss."

"A character-sketch or two. Things like that are always useful when one drops like a bolt from the blue into some little circle, as we have to do in cases of this sort. I suppose it's the same in your own line when you see a patient for the first time: he may be merely a hypochondriac or he may be out of sorts. You've nothing to go on in the way of past experience of him. We're in a worse state, if anything, because you can't have a chat with a dead man and find out what sort of person he was. It's simply a case of collecting other people's impressions of him in a hurry and *discarding* about half that you hear, on the ground of prejudice."

" At least you'll get his own impressions this time, if it's true that he kept a diary," the doctor pointed out.

" It depends on the diary," Sir Clinton amended. " But I confess to some hopes."

As they drew near the door of Heatherfield, Dr. Ringwood's thoughts reverted to the state of things in the house. Glancing up at the front, his eye was caught by a lighted window which had been dark on his previous visit.

" That looks like a bedroom up there with the light on," he pointed out to his companion. " It wasn't lit up last time I was here. Perhaps Silverdale or his wife has come home."

A shapeless shadow swept momentarily across the curtains of the lighted room as they watched.

" That's a relief to my mind," the doctor confessed. " I didn't quite like leaving that maid alone with my patient. One never can tell what may happen in a fever case."

As they were ascending the steps, a further thought struck him.

" Do you want to be advertised here—your name, I mean ? "

" I think not, at present, so long as I can telephone without being overheard."

" Very well. I'll fix it," Dr. Ringwood agreed, as he put his finger on the bell-push.

Much to his surprise, his ring brought no one to the door.

" That woman must be deaf, surely," he said, as he pressed the button a second time. " She came quick enough the last time I was here. I hope nothing's gone wrong."

Sir Clinton waited until the prolonged peal of the

bell ended when the doctor took his finger away, then he bent down to the slit of the letter-box and listened intently.

" I could swear I heard someone moving about, just then," he said, as he rose to his full height again. " There mûst be someone on the premises to account for the shadow we saw at the window. This looks a bit rum, doctor. Ring again, will you ? "

Dr. Ringwood obeyed. They could hear the trilling of a heavy gong somewhere in the back of the house.

" That ought to wake anyone up, surely," he said with a nervous tinge in his voice. " This is my second experience of the sort this evening. I don't much care about it."

They waited for a minute, but no one came to the door.

" It's not strictly legal," Sir Clinton said at last, " but we've got to get inside somehow. I think we'll make your patient an excuse, if the worst comes to the worst. Just wait here a moment and I'll see what can be done."

He went down the steps and disappeared in the fog. Dr. Ringwood waited for a minute or two, and then steps sounded in the hall behind the door. Sir Clinton opened it and motioned him to come in.

" The place seems to be empty," he said hurriedly. " Stay here and see that no one passes you. I want to go round the ground floor first of all."

He moved from door to door in the hall, switching on the lights and swiftly inspecting each room as he came to it.

" Nothing here," he reported, and then made his way into the kitchen premises.

Dr. Ringwood heard his steps retreating ; then, after a short interval, there came the sound of a door closing and the shooting of a bolt. It was not long before Sir Clinton reappeared.

" Somebody's been on the premises," he said curtly. " That must have been the sound I heard. The back door was open."

Dr. Ringwood felt himself at a loss amid the complexities of his adventures.

" I hope that confounded maid hasn't got the wind up and cleared out," he exclaimed, his responsibility for his patient coming foremost in the confusion of the situation.

" No use thinking of chasing anyone through this fog," Sir Clinton confessed, betraying in his turn his own professional bias. " Whoever it was has got clean away. Let's go upstairs and have a look round, doctor."

Leading the way, he snapped down the switch at the foot of the stair-case ; but to Dr. Ringwood's surprise, no light appeared above. Sir Clinton pulled a flash-lamp from his pocket and hurried towards the next flat ; as he rounded the turn of the stair, he gave a muffled exclamation. At the same moment, a high-pitched voice higher up in the house broke into a torrent of aimless talk.

" That girl's a bit delirious," Dr. Ringwood diagnosed, as he heard the sound ; and he quickened his ascent. But as he reached a little landing and could see ahead of him, he was brought up sharply by the sight which met his eyes. Sir Clinton was bending with his flash-lamp over a huddled mass which lay on the floor at the head of the flight, and a glance showed the doctor that it was the body of the maid who had admitted him to the house on his earlier visit.

" Come here, doctor, and see if anything can be done for her," Sir Clinton's voice broke in on his surprise.

He leaped up the intervening steps and stooped in his turn over the body, while Sir Clinton made way for him and kept the flash-lamp playing on the face. Down the well of the stairs came the voice of the delirious patient, sunk now to a querulous drone.

The briefest examination showed that the victim was beyond help.

" We might try artificial respiration, but it would really be simply time lost. She's been strangled pretty efficiently."

Sir Clinton's face had grown dark as he bent over the body, but his voice betrayed nothing of his feelings.

" Then you'd better go up and look after that girl upstairs, doctor. She's evidently in a bad way. I'll attend to things here."

Dr. Ringwood mechanically switched on the light of the next flight in the stairs and then experienced a sort of subconscious surprise to find it in action.

" I thought the fuse had gone," he explained involuntarily, as he hurried up the stairs.

Left to himself, Sir Clinton turned his flash-lamp upwards on to the functionless electric light bracket above the landing and saw, as he had expected, that the bulb had been removed from the socket. A very short search revealed the lamp itself lying on the carpet. The Chief Constable picked it up gingerly and examined it minutely with his pocket-light ; but his scrutiny merely proved that the glass was unmarked by any recent finger-prints. He put it carefully aside, entered the lighted bedroom, and secured a fresh bulb from one of the lamp-sockets there.

With this he returned to the landing and glanced

round in search of something on which to stand, so that he could put the new bulb in the empty socket. The only available piece of furniture was a small table untidily covered with a cloth, which stood in one corner of the landing. Sir Clinton stepped across to it and inspected it minutely.

" Somebody's been standing on that," he noted. " But the traces are just about nil. The cloth's thick enough to have saved the table-top from any marks of his boot-nails."

Leaving the table untouched, he re-entered the room he had already visited and secured another small table, by means of which he was able to climb up and fix the new bulb in the empty socket over the landing. It refused to light, however, and he had to go to the foot of the stairs and reverse the switch before the current came on.

Shutting off his flash-lamp, Sir Clinton returned to the landing and bent once more over the body. The cause of death was perfectly apparent : a cord with a rough wooden handle at each end had been slipped round the woman's throat and had been used as a tourniquet on her neck. The deep biting of the cord into the flesh indicated with sufficient plainness the brutality of the killer. Sir Clinton did not prolong his examination, and when he had finished, he drew out his pocket-handkerchief and covered the distorted face of the body. As he did so, Dr. Ringwood descended the stairs behind him.

" I'll need to telephone for the hospital van," he said. " It's out of the question to leave that girl here in the state she's in."

Sir Clinton nodded his agreement. Then a thought seemed to strike him.

" Quite off her rocker, I suppose ? " he demanded. " Or did she understand you when you spoke to her ? "

" Delirious. She didn't even seem to recognise me," Dr. Ringwood explained shortly.

Then the reason for the Chief Constable's questions seemed to occur to him.

" You mean she might be able to give evidence ? It's out of the question. She's got a very bad attack. She won't remember anything, even if she's seen something or heard sounds. You'd get nothing out of her."

Sir Clinton showed no particular disappointment.

" I hardly expected much."

Dr. Ringwood continued his way down stairs and made his way to the telephone. When he had sent his message, he walked up again to the first floor. A light was on in one of the rooms, and he pushed open the door and entered, to find Sir Clinton kneeling on the floor in front of an antique chest of drawers.

A glance round the room showed the doctor that it belonged to Mrs. Silverdale. Through the half-open door of a wardrobe he caught sight of some dresses ; the dressing-table was littered with feminine knick-knacks, among which was a powder-puff which the owner had not replaced in its box ; a dressing-jacket hung on a chair close to the single bed. The whole room betrayed its constant use by some woman who was prepared to spend time on her toilette.

" Found anything further ? " Dr. Ringwood inquired as Sir Clinton glanced up from his task.

" Nothing except this."

The Chief Constable indicated the lowest drawer in front of him.

" Somebody's broken the lock and gone inside in a hurry. The drawer's been shoved home anyhow and left projecting a bit. It caught my eye when I came in."

He pulled the drawer open as he spoke, and Dr. Ringwood moved across and looked down into it over the Chief Constable's shoulder. A number of jewel-boxes lay in one corner, and Sir Clinton turned his attention to these in the first place. He opened them, one after another, and found the contents of most of them in place. One or two rings, and a couple of small articles seemed to be missing.

" Quite likely these are things she's wearing to-night," he explained, replacing the leather cases in the drawer as he spoke. " We'll try again."

The next thing which came to his hand was a packet of photographs of various people. Among them was one of young Hassendean, but it seemed to have no special value for Mrs. Silverdale, since it had been carelessly thrust in among the rest of the packet.

" Nothing particularly helpful there, it seems," was Sir Clinton's opinion.

He turned next to several old dance-programmes which had been preserved with some care. Lifting them in turn and holding them so that the doctor could see them, the Chief Constable glanced at the scribbled names of the various partners.

" One gentleman seems to have been modest, any-how," he pointed out. " No initials, even—just an asterisk on the line."

He flipped the programmes over rapidly.

" Mr. Asterisk seems to be a favourite, doctor. He occurs pretty often at each dance."

" Her dancing-partner, probably," Dr. Ringwood

surmised. " Young Hassendean, most likely, I should think."

Sir Clinton put down the programmes and searched again in the drawer. His hand fell on a battered note-book.

" Part of a diary she seems to have kept while she was in a convent. . . . H'm ! Just a school-girl's production," he turned over a few pages, reading as he went, " and not altogether a nice school-girl," he concluded, after he had paused at one entry. " There's nothing to be got out of that just now. I suppose it may be useful later on, in certain circumstances."

He laid the little book down again and turned once more to the drawer.

" That seems to be the lot. One thing's pretty clear. The person who broke that lock wasn't a common burglar, for he'd have pouched the trinkets. The bother is that we ought to find out what this search was for ; and since the thing has probably been removed, it leaves one with a fairly wide field for guessing. Let's have another look round."

Suddenly he bent forward and picked up a tiny object from the bottom of the drawer. As he lifted it, Dr. Ringwood could see that it was a scrap of paper ; and when it was turned over he recognised it as a fragment torn from the corner of an envelope with part of the stamp still adhering to it.

" H'm ! Suggestive rather than conclusive," was Sir Clinton's verdict. " My first guess would be that this has been torn off a roughly-opened letter. So there must have been letters in this drawer at one time or another. But whether our murderous friend was after a packet of letters or not, one can't say definitely."

He stood up and moved under the electric light in order to examine the fragment closely.

" It's got the local post-mark on it. I can see the VEN. The date's 1925, but the month part has been torn."

He showed the scrap to Dr. Ringwood and then placed it carefully in his note-case.

" I hate jumping to conclusions, doctor ; but it certainly does look as if someone had broken in here to get hold of letters. And they must have been pretty important letters if it was worth while to go the length of casual murder to secure them."

Dr. Ringwood nodded.

" He must have been a pretty hard case to murder a defenceless woman."

Sir Clinton's face showed a faint trace of a smile.

" There are *two* sexes, doctor."

" What do you mean ? . . . Oh, of course. I said ' *he* must,' and you think it might have been a woman ? "

" I don't think so ; but I hate to prejudge the case, you know. All that one can really say is that *someone* came here and killed that unfortunate woman. The rest's simply conjecture and may be right or wrong. It's easy enough to make up a story to fit the facts."

Dr. Ringwood walked across to the nearest chair and sat down.

" My brain's too fagged to produce anything of the sort, I'm afraid," he admitted, " but I'd like to hear anything that would explain the damned business."

Sir Clinton closed the drawer gently and turned round to face the doctor.

" Oh, it's easy enough," he said, " whether it's the true solution or not's quite another question. You came here about twenty past ten, were let in by the maid, saw your patient, listened to what the maid had to tell you—lucky for us you took that precaution or we'd have missed all that evidence, since she can't tell us now—and left this house at twenty-five to eleven. We came back again, just an hour later. The business was done in between those times, obviously."

"Not much theory there," the doctor pointed out.

"I'm simply trying it over in my mind," Sir Clinton explained, "and it's just as well to have the time-limits clear to start with. Now we go on. Some time after you had got clear away from here, the murderer comes along. Let's call that person X, just to avoid all prejudice about age or sex. Now X has thought out this murder beforehand, but not very long beforehand."

"How do you make that out?" Dr. Ringwood demanded.

"Because the two bits of wood which form the handles of the tourniquet are simply pieces cut off a tree, and freshly cut, by the look of the ends. X must have had possession of these before coming into the house—hence premeditation. But if it had been a case of long premeditation, X would have had something better in the way of handles. I certainly wouldn't have risked landing on a convenient branch at the last moment if I'd been doing the job myself; and X, I may say, strikes me as a remarkably cool, competent person, as you'll see."

"Go on," the doctor said, making no attempt to conceal his interest.

"Our friend X probably had the cord in his or her pocket and had constructed the rough tourniquet while coming along the road. Our friend X was wearing gloves, I may say."

" How do you know that ? " Ringwood asked.

" You'll see later. Now X went up to the front door and rang the bell. The maid came along, recognised X. . . ."

" How do you know that ? " Ringwood repeated.

" I don't know it. I'm just giving you the hypothesis you asked for. I don't say it's correct. To continue : this person X inquired if Silverdale (or Mrs. Silverdale, perhaps) was at home. Naturally the maid said no. Most likely she told X that her companion had scarlatina. Then X decided to leave a note, and was invited into the house to write it. It was a long note, apparently ; and the maid was told to go to the kitchen and wait till X had finished. So off she went."

" Well ? "

" X had no intention of putting pen to paper, of course. As soon as the maid was out of the way, X slipped upstairs and switched on the light in this room."

" I'd forgotten it was the light in this window that we saw from the outside," Dr. Ringwood interrupted. " Go on."

" Then, very quietly, by shifting the table on the landing under the electric light, X removed the bulb that lighted the stair. One can reach it by standing on that table. Then X shifted the table back to its place. There were no finger-prints on the bulb—ergo, X must have been wearing gloves, as I told you."

" You seem to have got a lot of details," the doctor admitted. " But why all this manœuvring ? "

" You'll see immediately. I think I said already that whoever did the business was a very cool and competent person. When all was ready, X attracted the maid's attention in some way. She came to the foot of the stairs, suspecting nothing, but probably wondering what X was doing, wandering about the house. It's quite likely that X made the sick girl upstairs the pretext for calling and wandering out of bounds. Anyhow, the maid came to the foot of the stairs and moved the switch of the landing light. Nothing happened, of course, since the bulb had been removed. She tried the switch backwards and forwards once or twice most likely, and then she would conclude that the lamp was broken or the fuse gone. Probably she saw the reflection of the light from the room-door. In any case, she came quite unsuspiciously up the stair."

Sir Clinton paused, as though to allow the doctor to raise objections ; but none came, so he continued :

" Meanwhile X had taken up a position opposite the door of the room, at the foot of the second flight of stairs. If you remember, a person crouching there in semi-darkness would be concealed from anyone mounting the first flight. The tourniquet was ready, of course."

Dr. Ringwood shuddered slightly. Apparently he found Sir Clinton's picture a vivid one, in spite of the casual tone in which it had been drawn.

" The girl came up, quite unsuspicious," Sir Clinton continued. " She knew X ; it wasn't a question of a street-loafer or anything of that sort. An attack would be the last thing to cross her mind. And then, in an instant, the attack fell. Probably she turned to go into the lighted room, thinking that X was there ; and then the noose would be round her neck, a knee would be in her back and . . ."

With a grim movement, Sir Clinton completed his narrative of the murder more effectively than words could have done.

" That left X a clear field. The girl upstairs was

light-headed and couldn't serve as a witness. X daren't go near her for fear of catching scarlatina—and that would have been a fatal business, for naturally we shall keep our eye on all fresh scarlet cases for the next week or so. It's on the cards that her scarlatina has saved her life."

Dr. Ringwood's face showed his appreciation of this point.

" And then ? " he pressed Sir Clinton.

" The rest's obvious. X came in here, hunting for something which we haven't identified. Whatever it was, it was in this drawer and X knew where it was. Nothing else has been disturbed except slightly—possibly in a hunt for the key of the drawer in case it had been left lying around loose. Not finding the key, X broke open the drawer and then we evidently arrived. That must have been a nasty moment up here. I don't envy friend X's sensations when we rang the front door bell. But a cool head pulls one through difficulties of that sort. While we were standing unsuspiciously on the front door steps, X slipped down stairs, out of the back door, and into the safety of the fog-screen."

The Chief Constable rose to his feet as he concluded.

" Then that's what happened, you think ? " Doctor Ringwood asked.

" That's what *may* have happened," Sir Clinton replied cautiously. " Some parts of it certainly are correct, since there's sound evidence to support them. The rest's no more than guess-work. Now I must go to the 'phone."

As the Chief Constable left the room, the sick girl upstairs whimpered faintly, and Dr. Ringwood got out of his chair with a yawn which he could not suppress.

He paused on the threshold and looked out across the body to the spot at the turn of the stair. Sir Clinton's word-picture of the murderer crouching there in ambush with his tourniquet had been a little too vivid for the doctor's imagination.

CHAPTER V

THE BUNGALOW TRAGEDY

In the course of his career, Sir Clinton Driffield had found it important to devote some attention to his outward appearance ; but his object in doing so had been different from that of most men, for he aimed at making himself as inconspicious as possible. To look well-dressed, but not too smart ; to seem intelligent without betraying his special acuteness ; to be able to meet people without arousing any speculations about himself in their minds ; above all, to eliminate the slightest suggestion of officialism from his manner : these had been the objects of no little study on his part. In the days when he had held junior posts, this protective mimicry of the average man had served his purposes excellently, and he still cultivated it even though its main purpose had gone.

Seated at his office desk, with its wire baskets holding packets of neatly-docketed papers, he would have passed as a junior director in some big business firm. Only a certain tiredness about his eyes hinted at the sleepless night he had spent at Heatherfield and Ivy Lodge, and when he began to open his letters, even this symptom seemed to fade out.

As he picked up the envelopes before him, his eye was caught by the brown cover of a telegram, and he opened it first. He glanced over the wording and his eyebrows lifted slightly. Then, putting down the document, he picked up his desk-telephone and spoke to one of his subordinates.

" Has Inspector Flamborough come in ? "

" Yes, sir. He's here just now."

" Send him along to me, please."

Replacing the telephone on its bracket, Sir Clinton picked up the telegram once more and seemed to reconsider its wording. He looked up as someone knocked on the door and entered the room.

" Morning, Inspector. You're looking a bit tired. I suppose you've fixed up all last night's business ? "

" Yes, sir. Both bodies are in the mortuary ; the doctor's been warned about the P.M.'s ; the coroner's been informed about the inquests. And I've got young Hassendean's papers all collected. I haven't had time to do more than glance through them yet, sir."

Sir Clinton gave a nod of approval and flipped the telegram across his desk.

" Sit down and have a look at that, Inspector. You can add it to your collection."

Flamborough secured the slip of paper and glanced over it as he pulled a chair towards the desk.

" '*Chief Constable, Westerhaven. Try hassendean bungalow lizardbridge road justice.*' H'm ! Handed in at the G.P.O. at 8.5 a.m. this morning. Seems to err a bit on the side of conciseness. He could have had three more words for his bob, and they wouldn't have come amiss. Who sent it, sir ? "

" A member of the Order of the Helpful Hand, perhaps. I found it on my desk when I came in a few minutes ago. Now you know as much about it as I do, Inspector."

" One of these amateur sleuths, you think, sir ? " asked the Inspector, and the sub-acid tinge in his tone betrayed his opinion of uninvited assistants. " I had about my fill of that lot when we were handling that Laxfield affair last year."

He paused for a moment, and then continued :

" He's been pretty sharp with his help. It's handed in at 8.5 a.m. and the only thing published about the affair is a stop-press note shoved into the *Herald.* I bought a copy as I came along the road. Candidly, sir, it looks to me like a leg-pull."

He glanced over the telegram disparagingly.

" What does he mean by ' Lizardbridge road justice ' ? There's no J.P. living on the Lizardbridge Road ; and even if there were, the thing doesn't make sense to me."

" I think ' justice ' is the signature, Inspector—what one might term his *nom-de-kid,* if one leaned towards slang, which of course you never do."

The Inspector grinned. His unofficial language differed considerably from his official vocabulary, and Sir Clinton knew it.

" Justice ? I like that ! " Flamborough ejaculated contemptuously, as he put the telegram down on the desk.

" It looks rather as though he wanted somebody's blood," Sir Clinton answered carelessly. " But all the same, Inspector, we can't afford to put it into the waste-paper basket. We're very short of anything you could call a real clue in both these cases last night, remember. It won't do to neglect this, even if it does turn out to be a mare's nest."

Inspector Flamborough shrugged his shoulders almost imperceptibly, as though to indicate that the decision was none of his.

" I'll send a man down to the G.P.O. to make

inquiries at once, sir, if you think it necessary. At that time in the morning there can't have been many wires handed in and we ought to be able to get some description of the sender."

" Possibly," was as far as Sir Clinton seemed inclined to go. " Send off your man, Inspector. And while he's away, please find out something about this Hassendean Bungalow, as our friend calls it. It's bound to be known to the Post Office people, and you'd better get on the local P.O. which sends out letters to it. The man who delivers the post there will be able to tell you something about it. Get the 'phone to work at once. If it's a hoax, we may as well know that at the earliest moment."

" Very well, sir," said the Inspector, recognising that it was useless to convert Sir Clinton to his own view.

He picked up the telegram, put it in his pocket, and left the room.

When the Inspector had gone, Sir Clinton ran rapidly through his letters, and then turned to the documents in the wire baskets. He had the knack of working his mind by compartments when he chose, and it was not until Flamborough returned with his report that the Chief Constable gave any further thought to the Hassendean case. He knew that the Inspector could be trusted to get the last tittle of useful information when he had been ordered to do so.

" The Hassendeans *have* a bungalow on the Lizardbridge Road, sir," Flamborough confessed when he came back once more. " I got the local postman to the 'phone and he gave me as much as one could expect. Old Hassendean built the thing as a spec., hoping to get a good price for it. Ran it up just after the war. But it cost too much, and he's been left with it on his hands.

It's just off the road, on the hill about half-way between here and the new place they've been building lately, that farm affair."

" Oh, there ? " Sir Clinton answered. " I think I know the place. I've driven past it often : a brown-tiled roof and a lot of wood on the front of the house."

" That's it, sir. The postman described it to me."

" Anything more about it ? "

" It's empty most of the year, sir. The Hassendeans use it as a kind of summer place—shift up there in the late spring, usually, the postman said. It overlooks the sea and stands high, you remember. Plenty of fresh air. But it's shut up just now, sir. They came back to town over two months ago—middle of September or thereabouts."

Sir Clinton seemed to wake up suddenly.

" That fails to stir you, Inspector ? Strange ! Now it interests me devilishly, I can assure you. We'll run up there now in my car."

The Inspector was obviously disconcerted by this sudden desire for travel.

" It's hardly worth your while to go all that way, sir," he protested. " I can easily go out myself if you think it necessary."

Sir Clinton signed a couple of documents before replying. Then he rose from his chair.

" I don't mind saying, Inspector, that two murders within three hours is too high an average for my taste when they happen in my district. It's a case of all hands to the pumps, now, until we manage to get on the track. I'm not taking the thing out of your hands. It's simply going on the basis that two heads are better than one. We've got to get to the bottom of the business as quick as we can."

" I quite understand, sir," Flamborough acknowledged without pique. " There's no grudge in the matter. I'm only afraid that this business is a practical joke and you'll be wasting your time."

Sir Clinton dissented from the last statement with a movement of his hand.

" By the way," he added, " we ought to take a doctor with us. If there's anything in the thing at all, I've a feeling that Mr. Justice hasn't disturbed us for a trifle. Let's see. Dr. Steel will have his hands full with things just now ; we'll need to get someone else. That Ringwood man has his wits about him, from what I saw of him. Ring him up, Inspector, and ask him if he can spare the time. Tell him what it's about, and if he's the sportsman I take him for, he'll come if he can manage it. Tell him we'll call for him in ten minutes and bring him home again as quick as we can. And get them to bring my car round now."

Twenty minutes later, as they passed up an avenue, Sir Clinton turned to Dr. Ringwood :

" Recognise it, doctor ? "

Dr. Ringwood shook his head.

" Never seen it before to my knowledge."

" You were here last night, though. Look, there's Ivy Lodge."

" So I see by the name on the gate-post. But remember it's the first time I've seen the house itself. The fog hid everything last night."

Sir Clinton swung the car to the left at the end of the avenue.

" We shan't be long now. It's a straight road out from here to the place we're bound for."

As they reached the outskirts of Westerhaven, Sir Clinton increased his speed, and in a very short time

Dr. Ringwood found himself approaching a long low bungalow which faced the sea-view at a little distance from the road. It had been built in the shelter of a plantation, the trees of which dominated it on one side ; and the garden was dotted with clumps of quick-growing shrubs which helped to give it the appearance of maturity.

Inspector Flamborough stepped down from the back seat of the car as Sir Clinton drew up.

" The gate's not locked," he reported, as he went up to it. " Just wait a moment, sir, while I have a look at the surface of the drive."

He walked a short distance towards the house, with his eyes on the ground ; then he returned and swung the leaves of the gate open for the car to pass.

" You can drive in, sir," he reported. " The ground was hard last night, you remember ; and there isn't a sign of anything in the way of footmarks or wheel-prints to be seen there."

As the car passed him, he swung himself aboard again ; and Sir Clinton drove up to near the house.

" We'll get down here, I think, and walk the rest," he proposed, switching off his engine. " Let's see. Curtains all drawn. . . . Hullo ! One of the small panes of glass on that front window has been smashed, just at the lever catch. You owe an apology to Mr. Justice, Inspector, I think. He's not brought us here to an absolute mare's nest, at any rate. There's been house-breaking going on."

Followed by the others, he walked over to the damaged window and examined it carefully.

" No foot-prints or anything of that sort to be seen," he pointed out, glancing at the window-sill. " The window's been shut, apparently, after the housebreaker got in—if he did get in at all. That would be an obvious precaution, in case the open window caught someone's eye."

He transferred his attention to the casement itself. It was a steel-framed one, some four feet high by twenty inches wide, which formed part of a set of three which together made up the complete window. Steel bars divided it into eight small panes.

"The Burglar's Delight!" Sir Clinton described it scornfully. "You knock in one pane, just like this; then you put your hand through; turn the lever-fastener; swing the casement back on its hinges—and walk inside. There isn't even the trouble of hoisting a sash as you have to do with the old-fashioned window. Two seconds would see you inside the house, with only this affair to tackle."

He glanced doubtfully at the lever handle behind the broken glass.

"There might be finger-prints on that," he said. "I don't want to touch it. Just go round to the front door, Inspector, and see if it's open by any chance. If not, we'll smash the glass at the other end of this window and use the second casement to get in by, so as not to confuse things."

When the Inspector had reported the front door locked, the Chief Constable carried out his proposal; the untouched casement swung open, and they prepared to enter the room, which hitherto had been concealed from them by the drawn curtains. Sir Clinton led the way, and as he pushed the curtain out of his road, his companions heard a bitten-off exclamation.

"Not much of a mare's nest, Inspector," he continued in a cooler tone. "Get inside."

The Inspector, followed by Dr. Ringwood, climbed through the open casement and stared in astonishment at the sight before them. The place they had entered was evidently one of the sitting-rooms of the bungalow, and the dust-sheets which covered the furniture indicated that the building had been shut up for the winter. In a big arm-chair, facing them as they entered, sat the body of a girl in evening dress with a cloak around her shoulders. A slight trail of blood had oozed from a wound in her head and marked her shoulder on the right side. On the floor at her feet lay an automatic pistol. One or two small chairs seemed to have been displaced roughly in the room, as though some struggle had taken place ; but the attitude of the girl in the chair was perfectly natural. It seemed as though she had sat down merely to rest and death had come upon her without any warning, for her face had no tinge of fear in its expression.

" I wasn't far out in putting my money on Mr. Justice, Inspector," Sir Clinton said thoughtfully, as he gazed at the dead girl. " It might have been days before we came across this affair without his help."

He glanced round the room for a moment, biting his lip as though perplexed by some problem.

" We'd better have a general look round before touching the details," he suggested, at last ; and he led the way out of the room into the hall of the bungalow. " We'll try the rooms as we come to them."

Suiting the action to the word, he opened the first door that came to hand. It proved to be that of a dismantled bedroom. The dressing-table was bare and everything had been removed from the bed expect a wire mattress. The second door led into what was obviously the dining-room of the bungalow ; and here again the appearance of the room showed that the house had been shut up for the season. A third trial revealed a lavatory.

" H'm ! Clean towels hanging on the rail ? " Sir Clinton pointed out. " That's unusual in an empty house, isn't it ? "

Without waiting for a minuter examination, he turned to the next door.

" Some sort of store-room, apparently. These mattresses belong to the beds, obviously."

Along one side of the little room were curtained shelves. Sir Clinton slid back the curtains and revealed the stacked house-napery, towels, and sheets.

" Somebody seems to have been helping themselves here," he indicated, drawing his companions' attention to one or two places where the orderly piling of the materials had been disturbed by careless withdrawals. " We'll try again."

The next room provided a complete contrast to the rest of the house. It was a bedroom with all its fittings in place. The bed, fully made up, had obviously not been slept in. The dressing-table was covered with the usual trifles which a girl uses in her toilette. Vases, which obviously did not belong to the normal equipment of the room, had been collected here and filled with a profusion of expensive flowers. Most surprising of all, an electric stove, turned on at half power, kept the room warm.

" She's been living here ! " the Inspector exclaimed in a tone which revealed his astonishment.

Sir Clinton made a gesture of dissent. He crossed the room, and threw open the door of a cupboard wardrobe, revealing empty hooks and shelves.

" She'd hardly be living here with nothing but an

evening frock in the way of clothes, would she ? " he asked. " You can look round if you like, Inspector ; but I'm prepared to bet that she never set foot in this room. You won't find much."

He stepped over to the dressing-table and examined one by one the knick-knacks placed upon it.

" These things are all split-new, Inspector. Look at this face-powder box—not been opened, the band's still intact on it. And the lip-stick's unused. You can see that at a glance."

Flamborough had to admit the truth of his superior's statements.

" H'm ! " he reflected. " Of course it's Mrs. Silverdale, I suppose, sir ? "

" I should think so, but we can make sure about it very soon. In the meantime, let's finish going round the premises."

The rest of the survey revealed very little. The remainder of the house was obviously dismantled for the winter. Only once did Sir Clinton halt for any time, and that was in the pantry. Here he examined the cups suspended from hooks on the wall and pointed out to Flamborough the faint film of accumulated dust on each of them.

" None of that crockery has been used for weeks, Inspector. One can't live in a house without eating and drinking, you know."

" A port of call, then ? " the Inspector persisted. " She and young Hassendean could drop in here without rousing any suspicion."

" Perhaps," Sir Clinton conceded abstractedly. " Now we'll get Dr. Ringwood to give his assistance."

He led the way back to the room through which they had entered the house.

" She was dead before that shot was fired, of course," he said as they crossed the threshold. " But beyond that there ought to be something to be seen."

" What makes you so sure that the shot didn't kill her, sir ? " the Inspector demanded.

" Because there wasn't half enough blood scattered about the place. She was dead when the shot was fired —must have been dead for some minutes, I suspect. There was no heart-action to lift the blood in her body, so consequently it sank under gravity and left her skull nearly empty of it. Then when the shot was fired, only the merest trickle came from the wound. I think that's right, isn't it, doctor ? "

" It's quite on the cards," Dr. Ringwood agreed. " Certainly there wasn't the normal amount of bleeding that one might have expected."

" Then the really important point is : how did she come to die. This is where we rely on you, doctor. Go ahead, please, and see what you make of it."

Dr. Ringwood went over to the arm-chair and began his examination of the dead girl. His glance travelled first to the open eyes, which seemed curiously dark ; and a very brief inspection of their abnormal appearance suggested one possible verdict.

" It looks as if she'd had a dose of one of these mydriatic drugs—atropine, or something of that sort. The eye-pupils are markedly dilated," he pronounced.

Sir Clinton refrained from glancing at the Inspector.

" I suppose you couldn't make a guess at the time of death ? " he inquired.

Dr. Ringwood tested the stiffness of the limbs, but from his face they gathered that it was almost a purely formal experiment.

" I'm not going to bluff about the thing. You know

yourselves that *rigor mortis* is only the roughest test; and when there's an unknown poison to complicate matters, I simply couldn't give you a figure that would be worth the breath spent on it. She's been dead for some hours—and you could have guessed that for yourselves."

"Congratulations, doctor! There are so few people in this world who have the honesty to say: 'I don't know,' when they're questioned on their own speciality. Now you might have a look at the wound, if you don't mind."

While Dr. Ringwood was carrying out this part of his examination, Inspector Flamborough occupied himself in a search of the room. An ejaculation from him brought Sir Clinton to his side, and the Inspector pointed to a dark patch on the floor which had hitherto been concealed by one of the displaced chairs.

"There's quite a big pool of blood here, sir," he said tilting the chair so that the Chief Constable could see it better. "What do you make of that?"

Sir Clinton looked at him quizzically.

"Think you've caught me tripping, Inspector? Not in this, I'm afraid. That's not the girl's blood at all. Unless I'm far out, it's young Hassendean's. Now, while you're about it, will you have a good look for empty cartridge-cases on the floor. There ought to be three of them."

The Inspector set to work, industriously grovelling on the floor as he searched under the heavier articles of furniture in the room.

"Well, doctor, what do you make of it?" Sir Clinton asked, when he saw that Ringwood had completed his examination.

"It's plain enough on the surface," the doctor

answered, as he turned away from the body. " She must have been shot at quite close quarters, just above the ear. Her hair is singed with the flame of the powder. The bullet went clean through the head and then into the padded ear-piece of the chair. I expect it's stuck there. You can see for yourself that the shot didn't produce any twitch in the body ; the position she's sitting in shows that well enough. I'm quite prepared to bet that she was dead before the shot was fired."

" The P.M. will clear that up for us definitely, if the poison can be detected," Sir Clinton answered. " But these vegetable poisons are sometimes the very devil to spot, if they're at all out-of-the-way ones."

He turned back to the Inspector, who was now on his feet again, dusting the knees of his trousers.

" I've found three cartridge-cases sure enough, sir," he reported. " Two of them are under that couch over there ; the third's in the corner near the window. I didn't pick them up. We'll need to make a plan of this room, I expect ; and it's safest to leave things as they are, so as to be sure of the exact spots."

Sir Clinton signified his approval.

" On the face of things, judging by the way an automatic ejects its cartridge, one might say that the single case near the window came from the shot that killed the girl. The other two, which landed somewhere near each other, might represent the two shots that made the wounds in young Hassendean's lung. But that's mere speculation. Let's have a look at the pistol, Inspector."

Flamborough put his hand into his waistcoat pocket, stooped down, picked up the pistol gingerly, and drew a rough outline of its position on the floor with a piece of chalk.

" Try it for finger-prints, sir ? " he inquired. " I've got an insufflator in the car."

Receiving permission, he hurried off to procure his powder-sprayer, and in a few minutes he had treated the pistol with the revealing medium. As he did so, his face showed deepening disappointment.

" Nothing worth troubling about here, sir. Whoever it was handled this pistol last must have been wearing gloves. There's nothing to be seen but a few smears of no use to us at all."

Sir Clinton seemed in no wise depressed by the news.

" Then just open it up, Inspector, and have a look at the magazine."

" It's three shots short of being full, sir, counting the cartridge that must be in the barrel now," Flamborough explained, after he had slid the magazine from the butt.

" Then you've found all the empty cases corresponding to the number of shots fired from *this* pistol, at anyrate. We can leave someone else to hunt for extras when the plan's being made. I don't expect they'll discover any. Now we'll—H'm ! What's this ? "

He stepped swiftly across the room and lifted something which had rolled under a little book-case standing on four feet. As he picked it up, his companions saw that it was an amber cigarette holder. Flamborough's face betrayed some mortification.

" I could have sworn I looked under there," he declared.

" So you did, Inspector ; but it happened to be close up to one of the feet of the bookcase, and probably it was hidden from you in the position you were when you lay on the floor. It just happened to be in the right line from where I was standing a moment ago. Now let's have a look at it."

He held it out, handling it by the tip with the greatest precaution to avoid leaving his finger-prints upon the tube. At first sight, it seemed simply a cigarette-holder such as could be bought in any tobacconist's shop ; but as he rotated it between his finger and thumb, the other side of the barrel came into view and revealed a fly embedded in the material.

" One hears a lot about flies in amber," Sir Clinton said, " but this is the first time I've seen one."

Dr. Ringwood bent over and examined the imprisoned insect.

" That ought to be easy enough to identify," he commented. " I never saw a fly in amber before ; and that one, with its wings half-spread, must be fairly well known to most of the owner's friends."

" It may have nothing to do with the case, though," Inspector Flamborough put in. " It's quite on the cards that it was dropped there at the time the house was open for the summer. Some visitor may have lost it, for all one can tell. Or it may belong to either of the Hassendeans."

Sir Clinton twisted the little object into a vertical position and peered into the cavity which had received the cigarettes' ends.

" It's not a left-over from summer, Inspector. The tube's got quite a lot of tarry liquid in it. That would have gone viscid if the thing had been lying there for a couple of months. No, it's been used quite recently—within the last day or two, certainly."

He moved towards the window.

" Just bring that machine of yours, Inspector, and blow some powder over it, please."

Flamborough obeyed ; but the application of the powder revealed nothing except a few shapeless blotches on the stem of the holder.

" Nothing ! " Ringwood exclaimed, with more than a tinge of disappointment in his tone.

" Nothing," Sir Clinton admitted.

He handed the holder to Flamborough, who stowed it away safely.

" We've still to overhaul the body," the Chief Constable suggested. " You'd better do that, Inspector."

" Not much help in these modern dresses," said Flamborough, eyeing the girl's evening frock with a disparaging glance. " But she ought to have a bag with her, surely. . . . Here it is ! "

He plunged his hand between the body and the chair and withdrew a little bag, which he proceeded to open.

" The usual powder-box," he began, enumerating the articles as they came to hand, " Small mirror, silver-mounted, no initials on it. Small comb. Lipstick—been used once or twice. No money. No handkerchief."

" You found Mrs. Silverdale's handkerchief in the car last night," Sir Clinton reminded him.

" Then I suppose this must be her body, right enough, sir. Well, that seems to be all that's here."

" What about these rings she's wearing," the Chief Constable suggested. " See if you can get them off. There may be some inscriptions on the inside ; some women go in for that kind of thing."

Fortunately the hands of the body were relaxed, and it was possible to remove the circlets from the fingers. Flamborough rose with three rings in his possession, which he examined with care.

" You're on the mark there, sir, right enough. Here's

her wedding-ring. It's engraved ' 7–11–23 '—that'll be the date of her marriage, I suppose. Then on each side of the date are initials. ' Y. S.'—that's for Yvonne Silverdale, obviously ; and ' F. S.'—these'll be her husband's initials. Then there's a diamond ring that she was using for a keeper. Let's see. It's got the same pairs of initials on each side of the date '4–10–23.' That'll be her engagement-ring, I expect. H'm ! They don't seem to have given themselves much time for second thoughts if the engagement lasted only a month and three days."

He passed the two rings to Sir Clinton and picked the last one from his palm for examination.

" This is off the little finger. It's a plain gold signet with Y and S intertwined on it. Evidently it's Mrs. Silverdale right enough, sir. The inscription's inside . . . H'm ! there's a variation here. The date's ' 15–11–25 ' here ; but there's only a single letter at each end : a Y at one side and a B at the other. That's a bit of a puzzle," he concluded, glancing at his superior to see if he could detect anything in his face.

" I agree with you, Inspector," was all that he elicited for his pains. " Now take off the bracelet, and that string of pearls round her neck. Anything of note on the bracelet ? "

" Nothing whatever, sir," the Inspector reported after a glance at it.

" Well, you'd better put these in a safe place when we get back to town. Now does that finish us here ? "

He glanced round the room and his eye was caught by the second window which looked out from the side of the bungalow. The curtains were still undrawn, and he noticed a minute gap through which the outer daylight could pass freely. A thought seemed to strike him as he ran his eyes over the fabric.

" We'll just go outside for a minute," he announced, and led the way through the hall and out of the front door. " Let's see, that window's round here, isn't it. Keep back for a moment."

He halted outside the window and scrutinised the ground with care for a few seconds.

" See that, Inspector ? " he inquired. " There aren't any foot-prints that one could make anything out of ; but someone has put his foot on the box edging of the path just in front of the window. It's quite obviously crushed . . . and freshly crushed, too, by the look of it."

Stepping softly on to the flower-bed which lay under the window-sill, he bent down until his eye was level with the chink between the curtains and peered through into the room.

" That's interesting," he said, as he turned again to face his companions. " One gets quite a good view of the room from here ; and it looks as if somebody had taken advantage of it last night. Nobody would attempt to look into a shut-up house in the dark, so presumably the lights were on when he took the trouble to put his eye to the crack."

The Inspector made no pretence of concealing his delight.

" If we could only get hold of him. Perhaps he saw the murder actually done, sir."

Sir Clinton seemed disinclined to rejoice too fervently.

" It's all pure hypothesis," he pointed out, rather frigidly.

Flamborough's rectitude forced him into a semi-apology for past doubts.

" You were quite right about Mr. Justice, sir. He's

been a trump-card ; and if we can only get hold of him and find out what he saw here last night, the rest ought to be as easy as kiss-your-hand."

Sir Clinton could not restrain a smile.

" You're devilish previous, Inspector, in spite of all I can do. This Peeping Tom may be Mr. Justice, or again he may not. There isn't any evidence either way."

He stepped back on to the path again.

" Now, Inspector, we'll have to leave you here in charge. It seems to be your usual rôle in these days. I'll send a couple of men up to relieve you—the fellow who makes our scale-models, too. You can set him to work. And I'll make arrangements for the removal of Mrs. Silverdale's body."

" Very good, sir. I'll stay here till relieved."

" Then Dr. Ringwood and I had better get away at once."

They walked round the bungalow to the car. As he drove away, Sir Clinton turned to the doctor.

" We must thank you again, doctor, for coming out here."

" Oh, that's all right," Ringwood assured him. " I got Ryder to look after my patients—at least the worst ones—this morning. Very decent of him. He made no bones about it when he heard it was you who wanted me. It hasn't been a pleasant job, certainly ; but at least it's been a change from the infernal grind of Carew's practice."

Sir Clinton drove for a few minutes in silence, then he put a question to the doctor.

" I suppose it's not out of the question that young Hassendean might have driven from the bungalow to Ivy Lodge with those wounds in his lungs ? "

" I see nothing against it, unless the P.M. shows

something that makes it impossible. People with lung-wounds—even fatal ones—have managed to get about quite spryly for a time. Of course, it's quite on the cards that his moving about may have produced fresh lesions in the tissues. What surprises me more is how he managed to find his way home through that fog last night."

"That wouldn't be so difficult," Sir Clinton rejoined. "This road runs right from the bungalow to the end of Lauderdale Avenue. He'd only to keep his car straight and recognise the turn when he came to it. It wasn't a case of having to dodge through a network of streets."

A thought seemed to occur to him.

"By the way, doctor, did you notice any peculiar coincidence in dates that we've come across?"

"Dates? No, can't say I did. What do you mean?"

"Well," the Chief Constable pointed out deliberately, "the date on that scrap from the torn envelope we found in the drawer was 1925, and the figures on that mysterious signet-ring were 5–11–25. It just happened to strike me."

His manner suggested that he had no desire to furnish any further information. Dr. Ringwood changed the subject.

"By the way, you didn't examine the lever handle of the window for finger-prints," he said, with a note of interrogation in his voice.

"The Inspector will do that. He's very thorough. In any case, I don't expect to find much on the lever."

For a few moments Sir Clinton concentrated his attention on his driving, as they were now within the outskirts of Westerhaven. When he spoke again, his remark struck the doctor as obscure.

" I wish that poor girl who was done in at Heatherfield last night hadn't been such a tidy creature."

Dr. Ringwood stared.

" Why ? " he inquired.

" Because if she'd shirked her job and left those coffee-cups unwashed, it might have saved us a lot of bother. But when I looked over the scullery, everything had been washed and put away."

" Well . . . you don't seem to miss much," the doctor confessed. " I suppose it was what I repeated to you about Mrs. Silverdale looking queer when she came out of the drawing-room—that put you on the track ? You were thinking of drugs, even then ? "

" That was it," Sir Clinton answered. Then, after a moment he added : " And I've got a fair notion of what drug was used, too."

CHAPTER VI

THE NINE POSSIBLE SOLUTIONS

The police machinery under Sir Clinton's control always worked smoothly, even when its routine was disturbed by such unpredictable events as murders. Almost automatically, it seemed, that big, flexible engine had readjusted itself to the abnormal ; the bodies of Hassendean and the maid at Heatherfield had been taken into its charge and all arrangements had been made for dealing with them ; Heatherfield itself had been occupied by a constabulary picket ; the photographic department had been called in to take " metric photographs " showing the exact positions of the bodies in the two houses ; inquiries had ramified through the whole district as to the motor-traffic during the previous night ; and a wide-flung intelligence system was unobtrusively collecting every scrap of information which might have a bearing on this suddenly presented problem. Finally, the organism had projected a tentacle to the relief of Inspector Flamborough, marooned at the bungalow, and had replaced him by a police picket while arrangements were being made to remove Mrs. Silverdale's body and to map the premises.

" Anything fresh, Inspector ? " Sir Clinton demanded, glancing up from his papers as his subordinate entered the room.

" One or two more points cleared up, sir," Flamborough announced, with a certain satisfaction showing on his good-humoured face. " First of all, I tried the lever of the window-hasp for finger-prints. There weren't any. So that's done with. I could see you didn't lay much stress on that part of the business, sir."

The Chief Constable's nod gave acquiescence to this, and he waited for Flamborough to continue.

" I've hunted for more blood-traces about the house ; and I've found two or three small ones—a track leading from the room to the front door. There was less blood than I expected, though."

He produced a blood-soaked handkerchief.

" This was picked up near the corner of Lauderdale Avenue, sir, this morning after the fog cleared away. It has an H in one corner. You remember we found no handkerchief on Hassendean's body. Evidently he was using this one to staunch his wounds, and he probably let it drop out of the car at the place where it was found. The doctor said there might be very little external bleeding, you remember ; and the handkerchief's mopped up a fair amount of what happened to ooze out."

Sir Clinton again acquiesced, and the Inspector proceeded.

" I've taken the finger-prints from all three bodies, sir. They're filed for reference, if need be. And I've had a good look at that side-window at the bungalow. There's no doubt that someone must have been standing there ; but the traces are so poor that nothing can be done in the way of a permanent record.

" One can't even see the shape of the man's boot, let alone any fine details."

" Anything more ? " Sir Clinton inquired. " You seem to have been fairly putting your back into it."

Flamborough's face showed his appreciation of the compliment implied in the words.

" I've drafted an advertisement—worded it very cautiously of course—asking Mr. Justice to favour us with some further information, if he has any in stock. That's been sent off already ; it'll be in the *Evening Observer* to-night, and in both the morning papers to-morrow."

" Good ! Though I shouldn't get too optimistic over the results, if I were you, Inspector."

Flamborough assented to this. Putting his hand into his breast pocket he produced a paper.

" Then I've got a report from Detective-Sergeant Yarrow. I sent him down to the G.P.O. to find out about Mr. Justice's telegram. It's impossible to get a description of the sender, sir. The telegram wasn't handed in over the counter : it was dropped into a pillar box in the suburbs in a plain envelope, along with the telegraph fee ; and when it was taken to the G.P.O. they simply telegraphed it to our local office round the corner."

" H'm ! " said Sir Clinton. " There doesn't seem much likelihood of your advertisement catching much, then. Mr. Justice is obviously a shy bird."

" He is indeed, sir, as you'll see in a moment. But I'll finish Yarrow's report first, if you don't mind. When he heard this story at the G.P.O., he asked for the postman who had brought in the envelope and questioned him. It appears the thing was dropped into the pillar-box at the corner of Hill Street and Prince's Street. That's nowhere near the Lizardbridge Road, you remember—quite on the other side of the town."

" Five miles at least from the bungalow," Sir Clinton confirmed. " Yes, go on, Inspector."

" The postman made his collection, which included this envelope, at 7 a.m. this morning. The previous collection from the same box was made at 8 p.m. last night, Yarrow elicited."

" Then all we really know is that the thing was dropped into the box between 8 p.m. and 7 a.m."

" Yes, sir. Yarrow secured the original telegram form," Flamborough continued with a glance at the paper in his hand. " The envelope had been torn open carelessly and dropped into a waste-basket ; but Yarrow succeeded in getting hold of it also. There's no doubt about its identity, sir. Yarrow ascertained through whose hands the envelope and the enclosure had passed while they were in charge of the Post Office ; and he persuaded all these people to let him have their finger-prints, which he took himself on the spot. He then brought all his material back here and had the envelope and its enclosure examined for finger-prints ; and the two documents were photographed after the prints had been brought up on them with a powder."

" And they found nothing helpful, I suppose ? "

" Nothing, so far, sir. Every print that came out belonged to the postman or the sorter, or the telegraphist. There wasn't one of them that could belong to Mr. Justice."

" I told you he was a shy bird, Inspector."

The Inspector put his paper down on the desk before Sir Clinton.

" He's all that, sir. He hasn't even given us a scrap of his handwriting."

The Chief Constable leaned forward and examined the document. It was an ordinary telegram despatch form, but the message: " *Try hassendean bungalow lizardbridge road justice*," had been constructed by gumming isolated letters and groups of letters on to the paper. No handwriting of any sort had been used.

Sir Clinton scanned the type for a moment, running his eye over the official printed directions on the form as well.

" He's simply cut his letters out of another telegram blank, apparently ? "

" Yes, sir."

" Rather ingenious, that, since it leaves absolutely no chance of identification. It's useless to begin inquiring where a telegraphic blank came from, even if one could identify the particular sheet that he's been using. He's evidently got one of these rare minds than can see the obvious and turn it to account. I'd like to meet Mr. Justice."

" Well, sir, it certainly doesn't leave much to take hold of, does it ? Yarrow's done his best ; and I don't see how he could have done more. But the result's just a blank end."

Sir Clinton looked at his watch, took out his case and offered the Inspector a cigarette.

" Sit down, Inspector. We're talking unofficially now, you'll note. I think we might do worse than clear the decks in this business as far as possible before we go any further. It may save time in the end."

Inspector Flamborough thought he saw a trap in front of him.

" I'd like to hear what you think of it, sir."

The Chief Constable's smile showed that he

understood what was passing in Flamborough's mind.

" I'd hate to ask a man to do something I didn't dare to do myself," he said, with a faint twinkle in his eye. " So I'll put my cards on the table for you to look at. If the spirit moves you, Inspector, you can do the same when your turn comes."

The Inspector's smile broadened into something like a grin.

" Very good, sir. I understand that it's purely unofficial."

" On the face of it," Sir Clinton began, " two people got their deaths at the bungalow last night. Young Hassendean didn't actually die there, of course, but the shooting took place there."

Flamborough refrained from interrupting, but gave a nod of agreement.

" Deaths by violence fall under three heads, I think," the Chief Constable pursued—" accident, suicide, and homicide, including murder. Now at the bungalow you had two people put to death, and in each case the death must have been due to one or other of these three causes. Ever do permutations and combinations at school, Inspector ? "

" No, sir," Flamborough confessed, rather doubtfully.

" Well, taking the possible ways of two people dying one or other of three different deaths, there are nine different arrangements. We'll write them down."

He drew a sheet of paper towards him, scribbled on it for a moment or two, and then slid it across the table towards the Inspector. Flamborough bent over and read as follows :

Hassendean	Mrs. Silverdale
1.—Accident	Accident
2.—Suicide	Suicide
3.—Murder	Murder
4.—Accident	Suicide
5.—Suicide	Accident
6.—Accident	Murder
7.—Murder	Accident
8.—Suicide	Murder
9.—Murder	Suicide

" Now, since in that table we've got every possible arrangement which theoretically could occur," Sir Clinton continued, " the truth must lie somewhere within the four corners of it."

" Yes, *somewhere*," said Flamborough in an almost scornful tone.

" If we take each case in turn, we'll get a few notions about what *may* have happened," Sir Clinton pursued, unmoved by the Inspector's obvious contempt for the idea. " But let's be clear on one or two points to start with. The girl, so far as one can see at present, died from poison and was shot in the head after death. Young Hassendean died from pistol-shots, of which there were two. Agreed ? "

" Agreed," Flamborough conceded without enthusiasm.

" Then let's take the cases as we come to them. Case 1 : The whole thing was accidental. To fit that, the girl must have swallowed a fatal dose of poison, administered by mischance either by herself or by someone else ; and young Hassendean must either have shot himself twice by accident—which sounds unlikely—

or else some third party unintentionally shot him twice over. What do you make of that? "

" It doesn't sound very convincing, sir."

" Take Case No. 2, then : A double suicide. What about that? "

" These lovers' suicide-pacts aren't uncommon," the Inspector admitted. " That might be near the truth. And I suppose he might have put a bullet through her head before shooting himself, just in case the poison hadn't worked."

He drew a notebook from his pocket.

"Just a moment, sir. I want to make a note to remind me to see about young Hassendean's pistol license, if he had one. I think he must have had. I found a box and a half of ammunition in one of the drawers when I was searching the house after you'd gone."

Sir Clinton paused while the Inspector made his jotting.

" Now we can take the third case," he continued, as Flamborough closed his pocket-book. " It implies that Mrs. Silverdale was deliberately poisoned and that young Hassendean was shot to death intentionally, either by her before she died or by some third party."

" Three of them seems more likely than two," the Inspector suggested. " There's the man who opened the window to be fitted in somewhere, you know, and there were signs of a struggle, too."

" Quite true, Inspector. I suppose you can fit the shot in Mrs. Silverdale's head into the scheme also? "

Flamborough shook his head without offering any verbal comment on the question.

" Then we'll take Case 4," the Chief Constable pursued. " Mrs. Silverdale deliberately poisoned herself, and young Hassendean came by his end accidentally. In other words, he was shot by either Mrs. Silverdale or by a third party—because I doubt if a man could shoot himself twice over by accident."

Flamborough shook his head again, more definitely this time.

" It doesn't sound likely, sir."

Then his face changed.

" Wait a bit, though," he added quickly. " If that's what happened, she must have had a motive for suicide. Perhaps someone was on her track, somebody pretty dangerous ; and she saw the game was up. I don't profess to know how that could happen. But if the man on her heels was the fellow who did the work with the tourniquet at Heatherfield last night, she might have thought poison an easier way out of things. It's a possibility, sir."

" It leaves us hunting for the clue to a purely hypothetical mystery, though, Inspector, I'm afraid. I don't say you're wrong, of course."

" I daresay it's complicated enough already," Flamborough admitted without prejudice. " Besides, this Case 4 of yours has another flaw in it—several, in fact. Unless you take the idea I suggested, it's hard to see why the girl should have had a supply of poison handy at all. It sounds a bit wild. And you've got to assume that a third party shot young Hassendean twice by accident, if a third party came into the business at all. To my mind, that won't wash, sir. It's not good enough. Whereas if it was a case of Mrs. Silverdale shooting him by accident, there was no need for her to commit suicide because of that. No one knew she was here. She could simply have walked out of the front door and got clear away with no questions asked. And if she'd already taken poison, she wouldn't need to shoot herself in the head, would she ? "

" Grave objections," Sir Clinton admitted. It amused him to see the Inspector entering so keenly into the game. " Now we proceed to Case 5."

" Oh, Case 5 is just bunkum," the Inspector pronounced bluntly. " She gets accidentally poisoned ; then she gets accidentally shot ; then young Hassendean suicides. It's too thick altogether."

" I like the concise way you put it," Sir Clinton answered with simulated admiration. " So we go on to No. 6, eh ? She was deliberately murdered and he was accidentally shot. What about that ? "

" I'd want to see some motive for the murder, sir, before accepting that as a possible basis. And if she was deliberately poisoned, what was the good of young Hassendean dragging her off to the bungalow ? That would throw suspicion straight on to him if he poisoned her. . . ."

Flamborough broke off and seemed to think hard for a moment or two.

" That's a fresh line," he exclaimed suddenly. " I've been assuming all along that either she or young Hassendean used the poison. But it might have been a third party. I never thought of it in that light, sir."

He pondered again, while Sir Clinton watched his face.

" It might have been someone else altogether, if the poison was a slow-acting one. Someone at Heatherfield perhaps."

" There was only one available person at Heatherfield just then," Sir Clinton pointed out.

" You mean the maid, sir ? Of course ! And that

might help to account for her death, too. It might be a case of Judge Lynch, sir. Somebody squaring the account without bothering us about it."

New horizons seemed to be opening up in the Inspector's mind.

" I'll admit there's something in this method of yours, after all, sir," he conceded gracefully.

" I like your ' after all,' Inspector. But at any rate you seem to find the method suggestive, which is something, at least."

" It certainly puts ideas into one's mind that one mightn't have thought about otherwise. What about the next case ? "

" Case 7 ? That's the converse of the last one. He was shot deliberately and she died by accident. What about it ? "

" That would mean, sir, that either she took an overdose of the drug by mistake or someone gave her a fatal dose, ditto. Then either she or a third party shot young Hassendean."

" Something of the sort."

" H'm ! It's no worse than some of the other suggestions. I wonder, now. . . . She didn't look like a dope-fiend, so far as I could see ; but she might have been just a beginner and taken an overdose by accident. Her eye-pupils were pretty wide-open. That wouldn't fit in with her snuffing morphine or heroin, but she might have been a cocaine addict, for all we know. . . . This method of yours is very stimulating, sir. It makes one think along fresh lines."

" Well, have another think, Inspector. Case 8 : he suicided and she was murdered."

" That brings us up against the missing motive again, sir. I'd like to think over that later on."

" Case 9, then : He was murdered and she committed suicide. What about that ? "

" Let me take it bit by bit, sir. First of all, if he was murdered, then either she did it or a third party did it. If she did it, then she might have premeditated it, and had her dose of poison with her, ready to swallow when she'd shot young Hassendean. That's that. If a third party murdered young Hassendean, she might have suicided in terror of what was going to happen to her ; but that would imply that she was carrying poison about with her. Also, this third party—whoever he was—must have had his knife pretty deep in both of them. That's one way of looking at it. But there's another side to the thing as well. Suppose it was one of these suicide-pacts and she took the poison as her part of the bargain ; then, before he can swallow his dose, the third party comes on the scene and shoots him. That might be a possibility."

" And the third party obligingly removed the superfluous dose of poison, for some inscrutable reason of his own, eh ? "

" H'm ! It seems silly, doesn't it ? "

" Of course, unlikely things do happen," Sir Clinton admitted. " I'm no stickler for probability in crime. One so seldom finds it."

Flamborough took his notebook from his pocket and entered in it a copy of Sir Clinton's classification.

" I'll have another think about this later on," he said, as he finished writing. " I didn't think much of it when you showed it to me at first, but it certainly seems to be one way of getting a few ideas to test."

" Now let's look at the thing from another point of view," Sir Clinton suggested. " Assume that young Hassendean and Mrs. Silverdale were in the room of the bungalow. There were traces of somebody at the side-window, and someone certainly broke the glass of the front window. By the way, Inspector, when you went over young Hassendean's clothes finally last night, did you find a key-ring or anything of that sort ? "

" He had a few keys—the latchkey of Ivy Lodge, and one or two more."

" You'll need to make sure that the key of the bungalow was amongst them, because if it wasn't, then he may have had to break in—which would account for the window. But I'm pretty certain he didn't do that. He'd been up beforehand with these flowers in the afternoon, getting the place ready. It's most improbable that he hadn't the key of the front door with him."

" I'll see to it," the Inspector assured him.

" In the meantime, just let's assume that the broken window represents the work of a third party. What do you make of things on that basis ? "

" What is there to make out of them except one thing ? " Flamborough demanded. " At the side window you had somebody whom you christened Peeping Tom ; at the front window was a second person who got so excited that he broke into the room. You're not trying to make out that these two characters were filled by one person, are you, sir ? There would be no point in Peeping Tom leaving his window and walking round to the front one before breaking in. Either window was good enough for that. He'd no need to shift his ground."

" No," Sir Clinton assured him in a thoughtful tone, " I wasn't looking at it from that angle. I was merely wondering where Mr. Justice came in."

" You mean whether he was Peeping Tom or t'other ? "

" Something of that sort," the Chief Constable answered. Then, changing the subject, he added : " What bits of information are you going to hunt for next, Inspector ? "

Flamborough ran over some points in his mind and cleared his throat before speaking.

" First of all, I want to know what this poison was, where it came from, and how long it takes to act. I expect to get something from the P.M. results, and we can always send some of the organs for analysis."

Sir Clinton nodded his agreement.

" I think we'll get two people on to that part of the thing independently. Say a London man and perhaps one of the chemists at the Croft-Thornton Institute here. We'll need to see this fellow Markfield in any case, just to check the statements that Ringwood gave us, and when we're doing that we can find out if there's anyone capable of doing the analysis for us. Perhaps Markfield himself might take it on."

The Inspector, seeing that Sir Clinton was waiting for him to continue, proceeded with his list of evidence required.

" I'll put Yarrow on to the matter of young Hassendean's pistol license. That won't take long to look up, and it will help to clinch the fact that it really was his pistol that we found on the floor. I don't suppose for a moment that it was brought in from the outside. The loose ammunition in the drawer seems convincing on that point."

"I'm quite with you there," Sir Clinton admitted.

" Then I want to look into the maid's affairs and see if she had any grudge against Mrs. Silverdale. It's a pity the second maid's so ill. We can't get anything out of her for a while, I'm afraid. And I want her for another thing : to see if Mrs. Silverdale doped herself at all. But I expect, if she did, that I'll be able to pick up some hint of it somewhere or other. And of course, if the poison turns out to be a non-dope kind, that line of inquiry drops into a subsidiary place."

" Yes ? " the Chief Constable encouraged him.

" Then I'll send a man up to try the keys we found in young Hassendean's pocket on the lock of the bungalow door, just to clear up the broken window matter. That won't take long."

" And then ? "

" Well, I suppose I'll need to make a try at finding out who Peeping Tom was and also your Mr. Justice."

" Quite a lot of suggestions you seem to have extracted from my little list of possibilities, Inspector. I think you owe it an apology for the rather contemptuous way you approached it at first."

" Well, sir, it's been more suggestive than I expected, I admit."

" One thing's certain, Inspector. The solution of the affair must lie somewhere on that little table. It's simply a matter of picking out the proper case. The odds at most are eight to one and they're really less than that if one discards some of the very improbable combinations."

The desk-telephone rang sharply, and Sir Clinton listened to the message.

" That interests you, Inspector. A report's come in that Mr. Silverdale came home and has gone down to the Croft-Thornton. He mentioned where he was going to the constable in charge at Heatherfield, and he very thoughtfully suggested that as the Croft-Thornton is quite near here, it would be easy for us to interview him there if we desired to do so. The perfect little gentleman, in fact. Well, what about it, Inspector ? "

" I suppose I'd better go at once," Flamborough proposed after a glance at his watch.

" I think I'll include myself in the invitation," Sir Clinton volunteered. " And, by the way, you'd better take that fly-in-the-amber cigarette-holder with you, if they've finished with it downstairs. Young Hassendean was working at the Croft-Thornton and someone there may be able to identify it for us if it was his. I'm not anxious to trouble his relations in the matter."

" Very good, sir," Flamborough acquiesced. " You'll want your car. I'll give the order for it now."

CHAPTER VII

THE FLY IN THE AMBER

At the door of the big block of buildings which formed the Croft-Thornton Institute, Inspector Flamborough made inquiries from the porter and obtained a guide through the labyrinth of stairs and corridors.

" This is Dr. Markfield's laboratory, sir," their pilot finally informed them as he knocked on a door. " Two gentlemen to see you, sir," he announced, standing aside to allow Sir Clinton and the Inspector to enter.

As they walked into the laboratory, Trevor Markfield came towards them from one of the benches at which he had been occupied. His face betrayed his slight surprise at finding two strangers before him.

" What can I do for you ! " he inquired politely, but without any needless effusiveness.

Flamborough, in response to an almost imperceptible gesture from his superior, stepped to the front.

" This is Sir Clinton Driffield, the Chief Constable, Dr. Markfield. I'm Inspector Flamborough. We've called to see if you could give us some expert assistance in a case."

Markfield, after a glance at a water-bath on which a flask was being heated, led the way to a little office which adjoined the laboratory and closed the door behind the party.

" We shall be more private here," he said, inviting them with a gesture to take chairs. " One of my assistants will be back shortly, and I take it that your business is likely to be confidential."

The Inspector agreed with a nod.

" It's a poisoning case and we'll need some help in detecting the poison."

" That's a bit vague," Markfield commented with a smile. " There are so many kinds of poisons, you know. If it's arsenic or anything of that sort, a first-year student could spot it for you ; but if it's one of the organic lot, it'll be a stiff business most likely."

" It looks like one of the mydriatic alkaloids," Sir Clinton put in. " Atropine, or something akin to it. The eye-pupils of the body were dilated."

Markfield considered for a moment.

" I've done some alkaloid work in my time," he explained, " but I suppose in a case of this kind you ought to have the best man. Some of the alkaloids are the very devil to spot when you've only a small quantity. I'd like the fee for the case, of course," he added with a faint smile, " but the truth is that Dr. Silverdale, my chief, is an alkaloid specialist. He's worked on them for years, and he could give me points all along the line. I'll take you along to his room now."

He rose from his chair, but a gesture from Flamborough arrested him.

" I'm afraid that would hardly do, Dr. Markfield. As a matter of fact, it's Mrs. Silverdale's death that we're inquiring into ! "

Markfield could not repress an exclamation at the Inspector's statement.

" Mrs. Silverdale ? You don't mean to say that anything's happened to her ? Good God ! I knew the girl quite well. Nobody could have a grudge against her."

He glanced from one official to the other, as though doubting his ears.

" Wait a bit," he added, after a moment's pause. " Perhaps I've taken you up wrong. Do you mean Yvonne Silverdale ? "

" Yes," the Inspector confirmed.

Markfield's face showed a struggle between incredulity and belief.

" But that girl hadn't an enemy in the world, man," he broke out at last. " The thing's clean impossible."

" I've just seen her body," said the Inspector curtly.

The blunt statement seemed to have its effect.

" Well, if that's so, you can count on me for any work you want me to do. I'm quite willing to take it on."

" That's very satisfactory, Dr. Markfield," Sir Clinton interposed. " Now, perhaps you could give us help in another line as well. You seem to have been a friend of Mrs. Silverdale's. Could you tell us anything about her—anything you think might be useful to us ? "

A fresh thought seemed to pass through Markfield's mind and a faint suggestion of distrust appeared on his face.

" Well, I'm ready to answer any questions you care to put," he said, though there seemed to be a certain reluctance in his voice.

Sir Clinton's attitude indicated that it was the turn of the Inspector. Flamborough pulled out his notebook.

" First of all, then, Dr. Markfield, could you tell us when you first became acquainted with Mrs. Silverdale ? "

" Shortly after she and her husband came to Westerhaven. That's about three years ago, roughly."

" You knew her fairly well ? "

" I used to see her at dances and so forth. Lately, I've seen less of her. She picked up other friends, naturally ; and I don't dance much nowadays."

" She danced a good deal, I understand. Can you tell me any particular people who associated with her frequently in recent times ? "

" I daresay I could give you a list of several. Young Hassendean was one. She used him as a kind of dancing-partner, from all I heard ; but I go out so little nowadays that I can't speak from much direct knowledge on the point."

" What sort of person was Mrs. Silverdale, in your judgment ? "

Markfield took a little time to consider this question.

" She was French, you know," he replied. " I always found her very bright. Some people called her frivolous. She was out to enjoy herself, of course. Naturally she was a bit out of place in a backwater like this. She got some people's backs up, I believe. Women didn't like her being so smartly-dressed and all that."

" Have you any reason to suppose that she took drugs ? "

Markfield listened to this question with obvious amazement.

" Drugs ? No. She'd never touch drugs. Who's been putting that lie around ? "

Flamborough tactfully disregarded this question.

" Then from what you know of her, you would say that suicide would be improbable in her case ? "

" Quite, I should say."

" She had no worries that you know of, no domestic troubles, for instance ? "

Markfield's eyes narrowed slightly at the question.

" Hardly my business to discuss another man's affairs, is it ? " he demanded, obviously annoyed by the Inspector's query. " I don't think I'm called upon to repeat the tittle-tattle of the town."

" You mean you don't know anything personally? "

" I mean I'm not inclined to gossip about the domestic affairs of a colleague. If you're so keen on them, you can go and ask him direct."

It was quite evident that Markfield had strong views on the subject of what he called " tittle-tattle " ; and the Inspector realised that nothing would be gained by pursuing the matter. At the same time, he was amused to see that Markfield, by his loyalty to his colleague, had betrayed the very thing which he was trying to conceal. It was obvious that things had not gone smoothly in the Silverdale household, or Markfield would have had no reason for burking the question.

" You mentioned young Hassendean's name," Flamborough continued. " You know that he's been murdered, of course ? "

" I saw it in the paper this morning. He's no great loss," Markfield said brutally. " We had him here in the Institute, and a more useless pup you'd be hard put to it to find."

" What sort of person was he ? " the Inspector inquired.

" One of these bumptious brats who think they ought to have everything they want, just for the asking. He'd a very bad swelled head. Herring-gutted, too, I should judge. He used to bore me with a lot of romantic drivel until I sat on him hard once or twice. I couldn't stand him."

It was evident that young Hassendean had rasped Markfield's nerves badly.

" Had anyone a grudge against him, do you think ? "

" I shouldn't be surprised, knowing him as I did. He would have put a saint's back up with his bounce and impertinence. But if you mean a grudge big enough to lead to murder, I can't say. I saw as little of him as possible even in working hours, and I had no interest in his private affairs."

It was quite evident that nothing of real value was to be elicited along this line. The Inspector abandoned the subject of young Hassendean's personality and turned to a fresh field.

" Young Hassendean smoked cigarettes, didn't he ? "

" I've seen him smoking them."

" Is this his holder, by any chance ? "

Flamborough produced the fly-in-amber holder as he spoke and laid it on the table. As he did so, he glanced at Markfield's face and was surprised to see the swift change of expression on it. A flash of amazement followed by something that looked like dismay, crossed his features ; then, almost instantaneously, he composed himself, and only a faint trace of misgiving showed in his eyes.

" No, that isn't young Hassendean's holder," he answered.

" You recognise it ? "

Markfield bent forward to inspect the article, but it was evident that he knew it well.

" Do I need to answer these questions of yours?" he demanded, uncomfortably.

" You'll have that question put to you at the inquest,

when you're on your oath," said the Inspector sharply. " You may as well answer now and save trouble."

Markfield stared for a moment longer at the fly in the amber.

" Where did you pick this thing up ? " he demanded, without answering the Inspector's question.

But Flamborough saw that he had got on the track of something definite at last, and was not inclined to be put off.

" That's our business, sir," he said brusquely. " You recognise the thing, obviously. Whose is it ? It's no use trying to shield anyone. The thing's too conspicuous ; and if you don't tell us about it, someone else will. But it doesn't look well to find you trying to throw dust in our eyes."

Markfield could not help seeing that the Inspector attached special importance to the holder ; and he evidently recognised that further shuffling was out of the question.

" I'm not going to identify it for you," he said. " You've let slip that it's an important clue ; and I don't know it well enough to make assertions about it. I'll send for a man now who'll be able to swear definitely, one way or another. That's all I see my way to do for you."

He put his hand on a bell-push and they waited in silence until a boy came in answer to the summons.

" Send Gilling to me at once," Markfield ordered.

Then, when the boy had withdrawn, he turned to the two officials again.

" Gilling is our head mechanic. You can question him about it. He's an intelligent man."

In a few minutes the mechanic appeared at the door.

" You wanted me, sir ? " he asked.

Markfield introduced the Inspector with a gesture, and Flamborough put his questions.

" You've seen this thing before ? "

The mechanic came forward to the table and examined the holder carefully.

" Yes, sir. I made it myself."

" You're quite sure of that ? "

" No mistake about it. I know my own work."

" Tell us what you know about it," the Inspector demanded.

The mechanic thought for a moment or two.

" It was about three months ago, sir. If you want it, I can look up the exact date in my workshop notebook where I keep a record of each day's work. I made two of them for Dr. Silverdale at that time."

Flamborough shot a glance at Markfield's downcast face. It was pretty obvious now who was being shielded ; and the Inspector remembered how Markfield had fenced in the matter of the domestic troubles of the Silverdales.

" Tell us exactly what happened then," Flamborough encouraged the mechanic.

" Dr. Silverdale came to me one morning with some bits of stuff in his hand—amber-looking, same as this holder. He told me he'd been manufacturing some new stuff—a condensate like Bakelite. He wanted me to see if it could be filed and turned and so on. I remember his showing me the fly, there. He'd put it into the stuff as a joke—a fly to prove that the thing was genuine amber, and take people in when he showed the stuff to them. The condensate stuff was in sticks, two of them, about six inches long by an inch thick, so he suggested that I'd better make two cigarette-holders and see if the thing would stand being worked on a lathe without splitting or cracking. So I made the two holders for him. I remember the trouble I had to steer clear of the fly while I was shaping the thing."

"And what happened to the holders after that?"

"Dr. Silverdale used the one with no fly in it for a bit and kept the other one for show. Then he lost the plain one—he's always leaving his holders about the place on the benches—and he took to using the one with the fly in it. He's been smoking with it for a month or more, now. I remember just last week asking him whether it was wearing well, when he came into the workshop with it in his mouth."

"Have another good look at it," Flamborough suggested. "I want to be sure there's no mistake."

Gilling examined the holder once more.

"That's the one I made, sir. I could swear to it."

He hesitated a moment as if wishing to ask a question; but Flamborough, having got his information, dismissed the mechanic without more ado. When the man had gone, he turned back to Markfield.

"I don't quite like your way of doing things, Dr. Markfield. You might have given us the information at once without all this shuffling, for I could see at a glance you had recognised this cigarette-holder. If you're trying to shield your colleague from a reasonable investigation, I'll take the liberty of reminding you that one can become an accessory after the fact as well as before it."

Markfield's face grew stormy as he listened to the Inspector's warning.

"I'd have a look at the law on slander, if I were you, Inspector, before you start flinging accusations about. If you remember the facts, it'll help. I've only seen this holder at a distance when Dr. Silverdale was using it.

I've never had a good look at it until you produced it. Naturally, although I had very little doubt about whose it was, still I wasn't going to assert that it was Silverdale's. But I got you a man who could identify it properly. What more do you want? "

Flamborough's face showed that he found this defence quite unsatisfactory. Markfield's obvious fencing with him at the start had left its impression on his mind.

" Well, when you do this analysis for us, remember that you'll have to testify about it in the witness-box," he said, bluntly. " We can't have any qualifications and fine distinctions then, you know."

" I'll be quite prepared to stand over any results I get," Markfield asserted with equal bluntness. " But I don't guarantee to find a poison if it isn't there, of course."

" There *is* something there, according to the doctor," Flamborough declared. " Now I think I'd like to see Dr. Silverdale, if you can tell us where to find him."

Markfield's temper was evidently still ruffled, and he was obviously glad to be rid of the Inspector. He conducted them along a passage, pointed out a door, and then took leave of them in the curtest fashion.

They entered the room which had been shown to them; and while Flamborough was explaining who they were, Sir Clinton had leisure to examine Silverdale. He saw an alert, athletic man with a friendly manner, who looked rather younger than his thirty-five years. Whatever Silverdale's domestic troubles might have been, he showed few outward signs of them. When they disturbed him, he had been sitting before a delicate balance; and as he rose, he slid the glass front down in order to protect the instrument. Apart from his surroundings, it would have been difficult to determine his profession ; for he had an open-air skin which certainly did not suggest the laboratory. He carried himself well, and only a yellow stain of picric acid on the right-hand side of his old tweed laboratory jacket detracted from his spruceness and betrayed the chemist.

" I've been expecting you, Inspector Flamborough," he said, as soon as he realised who his visitors were. " This has been a dreadful business last night. It was a bolt from the blue to me when I got home this morning."

He paused, and looked inquiringly at the Inspector.

" Have you any notion why that unfortunate maid of mine was murdered ? It's a complete mystery to me. A dreadful business."

Flamborough exchanged a glance with the Chief Constable. As Silverdale had ignored his wife's death, it seemed to the Inspector that the news of it might be broken to him later, when the other case had been dealt with. Silverdale, of course, could hardly have picked up any hint about the affairs at the bungalow, since a knowledge of them was still confined to the police and Dr. Ringwood.

" We're rather at a loss at present," Flamborough admitted frankly. " As things stand, it looks rather like a case of a detected burglar who killed the woman when she disturbed him at his work. Had you any stock of valuables on your premises which might have attracted gentry of that sort ? "

Silverdale shook his head.

" My wife had a certain amount of jewellery, but I don't think any burglar would have found it worth while to go the length of murder for the sake of it."

" Where did Mrs. Silverdale keep her jewellery ? "

" I rather think it's kept in one of the drawers of an old chest-of-drawers in her room—the drawer that the man broke into. But she may have other things elsewhere. We had different rooms, you know ; and I never troubled to find out where she put things in her own room."

" I suppose you couldn't give us a list of your wife's jewellery ? "

" No, I really don't know what she has. I could tell you one or two things, of course ; but I couldn't guarantee to remember them all."

Flamborough switched off to a fresh line.

" This maid of yours was reliable ? I mean, she couldn't have been a confederate of the burglar by any chance ? "

Silverdale shook his head.

" Quite out of the question, I should say. That maid had been with us ever since we were married ; and before that she'd been in service with an aunt of mine who died. She'd always had a good character, and she was old enough not to do anything silly."

" An old family retainer ? I see, sir. And you never had any friction with her, I suppose ? "

" Certainly not."

Flamborough returned to his earlier line of inquiry.

" You can't think of anything else a burglar might have had his eye on in your house, sir ? Apart from the jewellery, I mean."

Silverdale seemed taken aback by the question.

" I don't quite understand, I'm afraid. What could a burglar want except jewellery or plate ? And he might take all the plate I keep away with him and not be much the richer."

Flamborough seemed unable to think of any fresh question to put on that particular subject. His face took on a new expression.

" I'm afraid we've got worse news for you, sir," he began, and in a few sentences he put Silverdale in possession of the barest outline of the bungalow tragedy. Sir Clinton, watching the manner in which the bereaved husband received the news, had to confess to himself that he could make nothing of what he saw. Silverdale's manner and words were just what might have been expected in the circumstances.

Flamborough allowed a decent interval to elapse before he came directly to business once more.

" Now, Dr. Silverdale, I'm sorry I've got to ask some awkward questions ; but I'm sure you'll give us your best help in clearing up this affair. I hate to worry you —I'm sure you understand that—but it's essential that we should get certain information at the earliest possible moment. That's my excuse."

Before Silverdale could reply, the door of the laboratory opened, and a slim, graceful girl came into the room. At the sight of the two strangers, she halted shyly. Sir Clinton caught a gleam in Silverdale's expression as he turned towards the girl : a touch of something difficult to define.

" Just a moment, Miss Deepcar, please. I'm engaged just now."

" I only came to tell you that I'd taken that mixed melting-point. It's hyoscine picrate, as you thought it was."

" Thanks," Silverdale returned. " I'll come round to your room in a few minutes. Please wait for me."

Something in the brief exchange of information

seemed to have attracted Sir Clinton's attention. He glanced at the girl as she turned to leave the room ; then he appeared to re-concentrate his mind upon Flamborough's questions.

" Now, Dr. Silverdale," Flamborough went on, " this is a very nasty business, and I don't mind admitting that we're in the dark just now. Can you think of anything which might connect the deaths of the maid and Mrs. Silverdale ? "

Silverdale stared at the floor for a time, as though turning possibilities over in his mind.

" I can't imagine how there could be any connection whatever," he said at last.

Flamborough decided to approach the most awkward part of his subject. It was impossible to tell from his manner what was coming next, but it was clear that he had something important to ask.

" Now, Dr. Silverdale, I want to be as tactful as I can ; but if I go over the score, I hope you'll take the will for the deed."

" Oh, you can be as blunt as you like," Silverdale retorted, with the first signs of impatience which he had shown. " Ask what you choose."

" Thanks," the Inspector answered with apparent relief. " Then I'll come straight to the point. What precisely were the relations existing between Mrs. Silverdale and young Hassendean ? "

Silverdale's face paled slightly and his lips tightened as this blunt response to his offer fell on his ears. He seemed to consider his reply carefully.

" I suppose you mean : ' Was she unfaithful to me with young Hassendean ? ' Then my answer would be : ' So far as my information goes, no.' She flirted with the young cub certainly ; and they behaved, to my mind, very injudiciously; but to the best of my knowledge it went no further than that. I'd have brought them up with a round turn if they'd given me cause."

"That's your candid opinion?" the Inspector demanded. "You're keeping back nothing?"

"Why, man, I'd have given . . ." Silverdale broke out. Then he stopped short in mid-sentence. "It's my candid opinion, as you put it," he ended tamely.

Flamborough, it seemed, had extracted the information he wanted. He left the subject and took up a fresh one.

"Do you recall anything important which happened in the year 1925?"

"Yes, I left London and took up my post here."

"You were married in 1923, weren't you?"

"Yes."

"Had your wife any relations in this country? She was French, wasn't she?"

"She had a brother, Octave Renard, who was in business in London. Still is, as a matter of fact. An old aunt is the only other relation I know of."

"Before you left London, had you any difficulties with Mrs. Silverdale—I mean anything like young Hassendean?"

"Nothing that came to my notice," Silverdale answered, after consulting his memory.

"Can you recall any friend of yours or of hers who had the initial B? Either in the Christian name or the surname, I mean. It might be either a man or a woman."

This question evidently surprised Silverdale.

"The initial B?" he repeated. "No. I can't recall anyone to fit that."

He seemed to be running over a list of people in his

mind, but at the end of half-a-minute he shook his head decidedly.

" No. I can't think of anyone with that initial."

Flamborough's face betrayed his dissatisfaction. He had evidently built some hopes on getting the information.

" Now, another point, Dr. Silverdale. Have you any reason to suppose that Mrs. Silverdale was addicted to drugs ? "

This time, Silverdale's surprise at the question was quite unfeigned :

" Drugs ? Of course not ! Unless you count cocktails as drugs. What on earth put that into your mind ? "

The Inspector rather shamefacedly abandoned this line of inquiry, and turned to something else.

" I'd like to hear anything you can tell me about young Hassendean, sir. He worked here in the Institute, didn't he ? "

" That depends a good deal on what precise meaning you attach to the word ' work,' Inspector. He certainly loafed about the premises, but he did as little as he could."

" Well," said Flamborough, impatiently, " can you tell me anything else about him ? Everyone I've interviewed yet has told me he was idle. I'd rather have something more to the point."

Silverdale thought for a moment or two.

" He was a nuisance from the start. When he came here first—some three years ago—he spent his time hanging round one of the girl-assistants : Miss Hailsham. He interfered with her work, and I had to speak to him about it several times. Then she got engaged to him. Some time after, my wife took him up, and he broke off his engagement to Miss Hailsham—possibly to please my wife. I remember it made things rather unpleasant here when the engagement was broken, because Miss Hailsham took it rather badly. She'd every reason to do so, though she wasn't losing much, it seemed to me."

Inspector Flamborough pricked up his ears at this information.

" Is this Miss Hailsham still an assistant here ? " he asked.

" Yes," Silverdale explained. " She's one of my private assistants. I have several girls who do routine work ; but Miss Hailsham and Miss Deepcar—the girl who came in here a moment ago—are a shade better than the usual run."

" Could you make an excuse to let me have a look at Miss Hailsham ? " Flamborough inquired.

" She's not here to-day," Silverdale answered. " Off with a sore throat, or something of that sort. But if you'll come back another time, I can take you to her room if you wish. You can pose as a visitor whom I'm showing round, if you don't want to appear officially."

" Very good, sir. I'll drop in some other day. Now, another point, if you don't mind. Mrs. Silverdale wore a signet ring. Can you tell me anything about it ? Did she get it from you or did she buy it herself ? "

" I didn't make her a present of it," Silverdale answered promptly. " I believe she got it made by some jeweller or other. I remember a few years ago she took it into her head to seal all her letters—some passing fad in the crowd she used to associate with, I suppose. But once she started doing it, she kept it up. I think she must have got the signet ring made for that purpose."

Inspector Flamborough nodded thoughtfully as though he attached some importance to this information. Then, in a casual tone he inquired :

" You weren't at home last night, of course ? Where were you ? "

" I was——"

Suddenly a thought seemed to cross Silverdale's mind and he halted abruptly in his sentence. Then he amended his statement most obviously.

" I spent the night working here."

Inspector Flamborough noted the words in his pocket-book with marked deliberation. Then he looked round the room and seemed dissatisfied with something. As though to give himself time to think before asking another question, he moved over to the window and gazed down thoughtfully into the main thoroughfare below. Whatever his reflections may have been, the result of them was singularly feeble. He turned back to Silverdale and put a final question :

" I suppose you can't think of any other point that might help us to throw light on this business, sir ? "

Silverdale shook his head decidedly.

" I'm quite in the dark about it all."

The Inspector looked him up and down deliberately for a moment.

" Well, in that case, sir, I don't think we need take up any more of your time. I'll remove the police from your house. It's been disinfected already by the sanitary people, so you can go back there any time you choose, now. Thanks for the help you've given us."

Flamborough did not speak to Sir Clinton until they had put the length of a corridor between themselves and Silverdale's laboratory.

" I think I'll drop in and see Dr. Markfield again, sir," he explained. " I'm not at all satisfied about some things."

" Do so, Inspector. I quite agree with you ! "

"I'll make an excuse about the arrangements for this analysis. Not that I'll lay much stress on Markfield's results when we get them, sir. He's made a bad impression on me over that evidence he gave us before. People shouldn't equivocate in a murder case merely to shield their friends. We've troubles enough without that sort of thing."

"Well, handle him tactfully, Inspector, or he may turn stubborn. If he takes refuge in 'I don't remember,' or anything of that sort, you'll not get much out of him." Sir Clinton observed.

"I shan't frighten him," Flamborough assured him, as they approached Markfield's room.

As they entered, Markfield looked up in surprise at seeing them once more.

"It's just occurred to me that I forgot to make arrangements about handing that stuff over to you for analysis," Flamborough said, as he went forward. "It'll be in sealed jars, of course; and I'd prefer to hand it over to you personally. I suppose I could always get hold of you either here or at your house?"

"You'd better come here. My housekeeper's away just now nursing some relation who's down with 'flu, and my house is empty except when I happen to be at home myself. You'll find me here between nine in the morning and six at night—except for lunch-time, of course. I generally clear out of here at six and dine down town."

"I suppose you have a long enough day of it," the Inspector said in a casual tone. "You don't come back here and work in the evening?"

"Sometimes, if there's something interesting that brings me back. But I haven't done that for weeks past."

" This place is shut up at night, isn't it? I mean, you don't keep a porter or a watchman on the premises? "

" No. But each of the seniors has a private key, of course. I can get in any time I wish. It's the same at the Research Station."

The Inspector seemed to be struck by an idea.

" Any valuable stuff on the premises, by any chance? "

" Nothing a thief could make much out of. There's a thousand or fifteen hundred pounds worth of platinum, dishes, electrodes, and so forth, in the safe. I believe the man on the beat is supposed to give special attention to the place and notify anything suspicious immediately ; but I've never known anything of the sort to happen."

" Rather a difficult position for our men if the staff can come and go freely at night," the Inspector pointed out. " If a constable sees a light in the window, what's he to make of it? Does Dr. Silverdale work late often? "

" I really couldn't tell you."

" You don't see much of him privately, sir? "

" Very little," Markfield answered. " Only when I run across him by accident down town, like last night."

" You met him, did you? "

" Hardly even that. I happened to drop into the Grosvenor for dinner after I left here. I can't get meals at home just now unless I cook 'em myself. As I was finishing my coffee, Silverdale came into the dining-room with Miss Deepcar and took a table in the window recess. I didn't disturb them, and I don't think they noticed me."

" Then they were just beginning dinner when you

left the place ? What time was that, can you tell me ? "

Markfield looked suspiciously at the Inspector.

" You're trying to get me to say something that you want to use against—well, someone else, shall we say ? I don't care about it, frankly. But since you could get the information from the waiter who served them, there's no harm done. I went to the Grosvenor at 6.35 or thereabouts. I was going down to the Research Station afterwards to pick up some notes, so I dined early that night. Silverdale and Miss Deepcar came in just as I was finishing dinner—that would be about a quarter past seven or thereby. I expect they were going on to some show afterwards."

" Was she in evening dress ? "

" Ask me another. I never can tell whether a girl's in evening dress or not, nowadays, with these new fashions."

Inspector Flamborough closed his notebook and took his leave, followed by Sir Clinton. When they reached the street again and had got into the waiting car, the Chief Constable turned to his subordinate.

" You collected a lot of interesting information that time."

" I noticed you left it all to me, sir ; but I think I got one or two things worth having. It's a bit disconnected ; and it'll take some thinking before it's straightened out."

" What's your main inference, as things stand ? " Sir Clinton inquired.

" Well, sir, it's a bit early yet. But I've been wondering about one thing, certainly."

" And that is ? "

" And that is whether Peeping Tom's name wasn't Thomasina," Flamborough announced gravely.

"There are two sexes, of course," Sir Clinton admitted with equal gravity. "And inquisitiveness is supposed to be more strongly developed in the female than in the male. The next thing will be to consider whether Mr. Justice shouldn't be rechristened Justitia. One ought to take all possibilities into account."

CHAPTER VIII

THE HASSENDEAN JOURNAL

When Ronald Hassendean's journal was found to consist of four bulky volumes of manuscript, Sir Clinton hastily disclaimed any desire to make its acquaintance *in extenso* and passed over to Inspector Flamborough the task of ploughing through it in detail and selecting those passages which seemed to have direct bearing on the case. The Inspector took the diary home with him and spent a laborious evening, lightened at times by flashes of cynical enjoyment when the writer laid bare certain aspects of his soul. Next day Flamborough presented himself at Sir Clinton's office with the books under his arm ; and the paper slips which he had used as markers made a formidable array as they projected from the edges of the volumes.

" Good Lord ! " exclaimed the Chief Constable in consternation. " Do you mean to say I ought to read through about a hundred and fifty passages in inferior handwriting ? Life's too short for that. Take 'em away, Inspector, and get someone to write me a *précis*."

Flamborough's lips opened into a broad smile under his toothbrush moustache.

" It's not really so bad as it looks, sir," he explained. " The white slips were put in to mark anything that seemed to bear remotely on the business ; but the passages directly relevant to the affair are indicated by red slips. I think you ought to glance through that last lot. There aren't really very many of them."

He deposited the volumes on Sir Clinton's desk so that the marking-tabs projected towards his superior. Sir Clinton eyed them without any enthusiasm.

" Well, I suppose duty calls, Inspector. I'll go over them with you, just in case you want to give me any special points drawn from your general reading in the Works of Hassendean. If you've got a morbid craving for voluminous writers, you'd better start on the *Faerie Queene*. It, also, leads up to the death of a Blatant Beast."

" I read a bit of it at school, sir. I'm keeping the rest for a rainy day."

Sir Clinton again eyed the four stout volumes with unconcealed aversion. Quite obviously he was ready to catch at anything in order to postpone the examination of them, even now that he had decided to submit to the Inspector's ruling.

" Before I start on this stuff, there are one or two points I want to get cleared up. First of all, did you get any reports in reply to our inquiries about young Hassendean's car being seen on the roads that night ? "

" No, sir. The only motor information we got was about one car that was stolen under cover of the fog. It's being looked into. Oh, yes, and there was an inquiry for the name and address of the owner of a car. It seems somebody got hit by a motor and managed to take its number. I don't think any real damage was done. It's just one of these try-on cases."

" Something more important now. Did you find out from the man on the beat whether there was a light in Silverdale's room at the Croft-Thornton on the night of the murders ? "

" How did you come to think of that, sir ? I didn't mention it to you."

" It was just a long shot, Inspector. As soon as Silverdale stated that he had been working all that night at the Croft-Thornton, I was pretty sure he was lying. So were you, I guessed. Then you walked across to the window and looked down. As I was wondering myself whether the window was visible from the street, it didn't take much mind-reading to see what you were driving at. And from your questions to Markfield later on, I couldn't help inferring that you had the constable on the beat at the back of your thoughts. Obviously you meant to check Silverdale's story by asking the constable on duty if he'd noticed a light in Silverdale's room that night. There was no light, of course ? "

" No, sir. There wasn't a light anywhere in the building, that night. I made the constable look up his notebook."

" Then you've caught Master Silverdale in a very bad lie. By the way, I suppose you noticed that girl who came into his room while we were talking to him : the Miss Deepcar who dined with him down town that night. What did you make of her ? "

" Pretty girl, sir, very pretty indeed. The quiet sort, I'd judge. One of the kind that a man might do a good deal to get hold of, if he was keen on her."

Sir Clinton's expression showed that he did not disagree with the Inspector's summing up.

" By the way," he continued, " did you take any note of what she said to Silverdale at that time ? "

" Not particularly, sir. It was all Greek to me—too technical."

"It interested me, though," Sir Clinton confessed. "I've a chemical friend—the London man who's going to act as a check on Markfield for us in the search for the poison, as a matter of fact—and he talks to me occasionally about chemistry. You don't know what a 'mixed melting-point' is, I suppose?"

"No, sir. It sounds confused," said the Inspector mischievously.

The Chief Constable treated this as beneath contempt.

"I'll explain the point," he pursued, "and then you'll know as much as I do. A pure substance melts at a higher temperature than it does when it's contaminated by even a trace of some foreign material. Suppose that you had been given a stuff which you thought was pure quinine and you had no chemicals handy to do the ordinary tests for quinine. What you'd do would be this. You'd take the melting-point of your sample first of all. Then to the sample you'd add a trace of something which you knew definitely was quinine—a specimen from your laboratory stock, say. Then you'd take the melting-point of this mixture. Suppose the second melting-point is lower than the first, then obviously you've been adding an impurity to your original sample. And since something, that you know definitely to be quinine, has acted as an impurity, then clearly the original stuff isn't quinine. On the other hand, if the addition of your trace of quinine to the sample doesn't lower the melting-point, then your original sample is proved to be quinine also. That mixing of the two stuffs and taking the melting-point is what they call 'taking a mixed melting-point.' Does that convey anything to you?"

"Not a damn, sir," Flamborough admitted crudely,

in a tone of despair. " Could you say it all over again slowly ? "

" It's hardly worth while at this stage," Sir Clinton answered, dismissing the subject. " I'll take it up again with you later on, perhaps, after we get the P.M. results. It was an illuminating conversation, though, Inspector, if my guess turns out to be right. Now there's another matter. Have you any idea when the morning papers get into the hands of the public—I mean the earliest hour that's likely in the normal course ? "

" It happens that I do know that, sir. The local delivery starts at 7 a.m. In the suburbs, it's a bit later, naturally."

" Just make sure about it, please. Ring up the publishing departments of the *Courier* and the *Gazette*. You needn't worry about the imported London papers."

" Very good, sir. And now about this journal, sir ? " the Inspector added with a touch of genial impishness in his voice.

" Evidently you won't be happy till I look at it," Sir Clinton grumbled with obvious distaste for the task. " Let's get it over, then, since you're set on the matter."

" So far as I can see, sir," Flamborough explained, " there are only three threads in it that concern us : the affair he had with that girl Hailsham ; his association with Mrs. Silverdale ; and his financial affairs—which came as a surprise to me, I must admit."

Sir Clinton glanced up at the Inspector's words ; but without replying, he drew the fat volumes of the journal towards him and began his examination of the passages to which Flamborough's red markers drew attention.

" He didn't model his style on Pepys, evidently," he said as he turned the leaves rapidly, " There seems to be about ten per cent. of ' I's ' on every page. Ah ! Here's your first red marker."

He read the indicated passage carefully.

" This is the description of his feelings on getting engaged to Norma Hailsham," he commented aloud. " It sounds rather superior, as if he felt he'd conferred a distinct favour on her in the matter. Apparently, even in the first flush of young love, he thought that he wasn't getting all that his merits deserved. I don't think Miss Hailsham would have been flattered if she'd been able to read this at the time."

He passed rapidly over some other passages without audible comment, and then halted for a few moments at an entry.

" Now we come to his meeting with Mrs. Silverdale, and his first impressions of her. It seems that she attracted him by her physique rather than by her brains. Of course, as he observes : ' What single woman could fully satisfy all the sides of a complex nature like mine ? ' However, he catalogues Mrs. Silverdale's attractions lavishly enough."

Flamborough, with a recollection of the passage in his mind, smiled cynically.

" That side of his complex nature was highly developed, I should judge," he affirmed. " It runs through the stuff from start to finish."

Sir Clinton turned over a few more pages.

" It seems as though Miss Hailsham began to have some inklings of his troubles," he said, looking up from the book. " This is the bit where he's complaining about the limitations in women's outlooks, you remember. Apparently he'd made his fiancée feel that his vision took a wider sweep than she imagined, and she seems to have suggested that he needn't spend so much time in staring at Mrs. Silverdale. It's quite characteristic that in this entry he's suddenly discovered that the Hailsham girl's hands fail to reach the standard of beauty which he thinks essential in a life-companion. He has visions of sitting in suppressed irritation while these hands pour out his breakfast coffee every day through all the years of marriage. It seems to worry him quite a lot."

" You'll find that kind of thing developing as you go on, sir. The plain truth is that he was tiring of the girl and he simply jotted down everything he could see in her that he didn't find good enough for him."

Sir Clinton glanced over the next few entries.

" So I see, Inspector. Now it seems her dancing isn't so good as he used to think it was."

" Any stick to beat a dog with," the Inspector surmised.

" Now they seem to have got the length of a distinct tiff, and he rushes at once to jot down a few bright thoughts on jealousy with a quotation from Mr. Wells in support of his thesis. It appears that this ' entanglement,' as he calls it, is cramping his individuality and preventing the full self-expression of his complex nature. I can't imagine how we got along without that word ' self-expression ' when we were young. It's a godsend. I trust the inventor got a medal."

" The next entry's rather important, sir," Flamborough warned him.

" Ah ! Here we are. We come to action for a change instead of all this wash of talk. This is the final burst-up, eh ? H'm ! "

He read over the entry thoughtfully.

" Well, the Hailsham girl seems to have astonished him when it came to the pinch. Even deducting everything for his way of looking at things, she must have been fairly furious. And Yvonne Silverdale's name seems to have entered pretty deeply into the discussion. 'She warned me she knew more than I thought she did ; and that she'd make me pay for what I was doing.' And again : 'She said she'd stick at nothing to get even with me.' It seems to have been rather a vulgar scene, altogether. 'She wasn't going to be thrown over for that woman without having her turn when it came.' You know, Inspector, it sounds a bit vindictive, even when it's filtered through him into his journal. The woman scorned, and hell let loose, eh ? I'm not greatly taken with the picture of Miss Hailsham."

"A bit of a virago," the Inspector agreed. "What I was wondering when I read that stuff was whether she'd keep up to that standard permanently or whether this was just a flash in the pan. If she's the kind that treasures grievances. . . ."

"She might be an important piece in the jigsaw, you mean ? In any case, I suppose we'll have to get her sized up somehow, since she plays a part in the story."

The Chief Constable turned back to the journal and skimmed over a number of the entries.

"Do you know," he pointed out after a time, "that young fellow had an unpleasant mind."

"You surprise me," the Inspector retorted ironically. "I suppose you've come to the place where he gets really smitten with Mrs. Silverdale's charms ? "

"Yes. There's a curious rising irritation through it all. It's evident that she led him on, and then let him down, time after time."

"For all his fluff about his complex character and so forth, he really seems to have been very simple," was Flamborough's verdict. "She led him a dance for months ; and anyone with half an eye could see all along that she was only playing with him. It's as plain as print, even in his own account of the business."

" Quite, I admit. But you must remember that he imagined he was out of the common—irresistible. He couldn't bring himself to believe things were as they were."

" Turn to the later entries," the Inspector advised ; and Sir Clinton did so.

" This is the one you mean ? Where she turned him down quite bluntly, so that even he got an inkling of how matters really stood ? "

" Yes. Now go on from there," Flamborough directed.

Sir Clinton passed from one red marker to the other, reading the entries indicted at each of the points.

" The tune changes a bit ; and his irritation seems to be on the up-grade. One gets the impression that he's casting round for a fresh method of getting his way and that he hasn't found one that will do ? Is that your reading of it ? "

" Yes," Flamborough confirmed. " He talks about getting his way ' by hook or by crook,' and one or two other phrases that come to the same thing."

" Well, that brings us up to a week ago. There seems to be a change in his tone, now. More expectation and less exasperation, if one can put it that way."

" I read it that by that time he'd hit on his plan. He was sure of its success, sir. Just go on to the next entry please. There's something there about his triumph, as he calls it."

Sir Clinton glanced down the page and as he did so his face lit up for a moment as though he had seen one of his inferences confirmed.

" This what you mean ? " he asked. " ' And only I shall know of my triumph ' ? "

" That's it, sir. High-falutin and all that ; but it points to his thinking he had the game in his hands. I've puzzled my brains a bit over what he really meant by it, though. One might read it that he meant to murder the girl in the end. That would leave him as the only living person who knew what had happened, you see ? "

" I'm not in a position to contradict that assumption," Sir Clinton confessed. " But so far as that goes, I think you'll find the point cleared up in a day or two at the rate we're going."

" You're very optimistic, sir," was all the Inspector found to reply. " Now I've left one matter to the end, because it may have no bearing on the case at all. The last year of that journal is full of groans about his finances. He seems to have spent a good deal more than he could afford, in one way and another. I've noted all the passages if you want to read them, sir. They're among the set marked with white slips."

" Just give me the gist of them," the Chief Constable suggested. " From that, I can see whether I want to wade through the whole thing or not."

" It's simple enough, sir. He's been borrowing money on a scale that would be quite big for his resources. And I gather from some of the entries that he had no security that he could produce. It seems he daren't go to his uncle and ask him to use his capital as security—I mean young Hassendean's own capital which was under his uncle's control as trustee. So he was persuaded to insure his life in favour of his creditor for a good round sum—figure not mentioned."

" So in the present circumstances the moneylender

will rake in the whole sum insured, after paying only a single premium ? "

" Unless the insurance company can prove suicide."

Sir Clinton closed the last volume of the journal.

" I've heard of that sort of insurance racket before. And of course you remember that shooting affair in Scotland thirty years ago when the prosecution made a strong point out of just this very type of transaction. Have you had time to make any inquiries along that line yet ? "

Flamborough was evidently glad to get the opportunity of showing his efficiency.

" I took it up at once, sir. In one entry, he mentioned the name of the company : the Western Medical and Mercantile Assurance Co. I put a trunk call through to their head office and got the particulars of the policy. It's for £5,000 and it's in favour of Dudley Amyas Guisborough & Co.—the moneylender."

" Sounds very aristocratic," the Chief Constable commented.

" Oh, that's only his trade sign. His real name's Spratton."

" No claim been made yet ? "

" No, sir. I don't suppose he's hurrying. The inquest was adjourned, you remember ; and until they bring in some verdict excluding suicide, Spratton can't do much. There's a suicide clause in the policy, I learned. But if it pans out as a murder, then Spratton's £5,000 in pocket."

" In fact, Inspector, Mr. Justice is doing a very good bit of work for Dudley Amyas Guisborough & Co."

Flamborough seemed struck by an idea.

" I'll go and pay a call on Mr. Spratton, I think. I'll do it now."

" Oh, he's a local light, is he ? "

" Yes, sir. He was mixed up in a case last year. You won't remember it, though. It never came to much. Just an old man who fell into Spratton's hands and was driven to suicide by the damnable rapacity of that shark. Inspector Ferryside had to look into the matter, and I remember talking over the case with him. That's how it sticks in my memory."

" Well, see what you can make of him, Inspector. But I shan't be disappointed if you come back empty-handed. Even if he were mixed up in this affair, he'll have taken good care not to leave a straight string leading back to his front door. If it was a case of murder for profit, you know, there would be plenty of time to draw up a pretty good scheme beforehand. It wouldn't be done on the spur of the moment."

CHAPTER IX

THE CREDITOR

Inspector Flamborough's orderly mind found something to respect in the businesslike appearance of the moneylender's premises. As he waited at the counter of the outer office while his card was submitted to the principal, he was struck by the spick-and-span appearance of the fittings and the industry of the small staff.

" Quite impressive as a fly-trap," he ruminated. " Looks like a good solid business with plenty of money to spend. And the clerks have good manners, too. Spratton's evidently bent on making a nice impression on new clients."

He was not kept waiting more than a minute before the clerk returned and ushered him into a room which had very little of the office in its furnishings. As he entered, a clean-shaven man in the late thirties rose from an arm-chair beside the fire. At the first glance, his appearance seemed to strike some chord in the Inspector's memory ; and Flamborough found himself pursuing an elusive recollection which he failed to run to ground.

The moneylender seemed to regard the Inspector's visit as a perfectly normal event. His manner was genial without being effusive.

" Come in, Inspector," he invited, with a gesture towards one of the comfortable chairs. " Try a cigarette ? "

He proffered a large silver box, but Flamborough declined to smoke.

" And what can I do for you ? " Spratton inquired pleasantly, replacing the box on the mantelpiece. " Money's very tight these days."

" I'm not a client," Flamborough informed him, with a slightly sardonic smile. " Sorry to disappoint you."

The moneylender's eyes narrowed, but otherwise he showed no outward sign of his feelings.

" Then I'm rather at a loss to know what you want," he confessed, without any lapse from his initial geniality. " I run my business strictly within the four corners of the Act. You've no complaint about that ? "

The Inspector had no intention of wasting time.

" It's this affair of young Hassendean," he explained. " The young fellow who was murdered the other day. You must have seen the case in the papers. I understand he was a client of yours."

A flash of intelligence passed over the moneylender's face, but he suppressed it almost instantly.

" Hassendean ? " he repeated, as though cudgelling his memory. " I've some recollection of the name. But my business is a large one, and I don't profess to carry all the details in my head."

He stepped over to the bell and rang it. When a clerk appeared in answer to the summons, the moneylender turned to give an order :

" I think we had some transactions with a Mr. Hassendean—Mr. Ronald Hassendean, isn't it ? " he glanced at Flamborough for confirmation, and then continued : " Just bring me that file, Plowden."

It did not take the Inspector long to make up his mind that this by-play was intended merely to give

Spratton time to find his bearings ; but Flamborough waited patiently until the clerk returned and placed a filing-case on the table. Spratton turned over the leaves for a few moments, as though refreshing his memory.

" This fellow would have made a good actor," Flamborough reflected with a certain admiration. " He does it deuced well. But who the devil does he remind me of ? "

Spratton's nicely-calculated interlude came to an end, and he turned back to the Inspector.

" You're quite right. I find that he had some transactions with us ! "

" They began about eleven months ago, didn't they ? "

The moneylender nodded in confirmation.

" I find that I lent him £100 first of all. Two months after that—he not having repaid anything—I lent him £200. Then there was a further item of £300 in April, part of which he seems to have paid back to me later on in order to square up for the interest which he hadn't paid."

" What security had you for these loans ? "

Again the moneylender's eyes narrowed for a moment ; but his manner betrayed nothing.

" Up to that time, I was quite satisfied with his prospects."

And after that he borrowed more from you ? "

" Apparently." Spratton made a pretence of consulting the file. " He came to me in June for another £500, and of course the interest was mounting up gradually."

" He must have been making the money fly," Flamborough suggested with a certain indifference. " I wish I could see my way to splash dibs at that rate. It would be a new experience. But when it came to figures of that size, I suppose you expected something better in the way of security ? ”

Despite the Inspector’s casual tone, the moneylender seemed to suspect a trap.

“ Well, by that time he was in my books for well over a thousand.”

He appeared to feel that frankness would be best.

“ I arranged matters for him,” he continued. “ He took out a policy on his life with the Western Medical and Mercantile. I have the policy in my safe if you wish to see it.”

“ Of course you allowed a reasonable margin for contingencies, I suppose ? ” Flamborough inquired sympathetically.

“ Oh, naturally I expected him to go on borrowing, so I had to allow a fair margin for contingencies. The policy was for £5,000.”

“ So you’re about £4,000 in pocket, now that he’s dead,” Flamborough commented enviously. “ Some people are lucky.”

“ Against that you’ve got to offset the bad debts I make,” Spratton pointed out.

Flamborough could not pretend to himself that he had managed to elicit much of importance during his call ; but he had no excuse for prolonging the interview. He rose to his feet.

“ I don’t suppose we shall need any of these facts if it comes to trying anyone,” he said, as he prepared to leave. “ If we do, you’ll have plenty of warning, of course.”

The moneylender opened a door which allowed a direct exit into the corridor, and Flamborough went out. As he walked along the passage, he was still racking his memory to discover who Spratton resembled ; and at last, as he reached the pavement outside, it flashed into his mind.

" Of course ! It's the Chief ! Put a moustache on to that fellow and dye his hair a bit and he might pass for Driffield in the dusk. He's not a twin-brother ; but there's a resemblance of sorts, undoubtedly."

He returned to headquarters feeling that he had wasted his time over the moneylender. Except that he had now seen the man in the flesh and had an opportunity of sizing him up, he was really no further forward than he had been before ; for the few actual figures of transactions which he had obtained were obviously of little interest in themselves.

As he entered the police station, a constable came forward.

"There's a gentleman here, Inspector Flamborough. He's called about the Silverdale case and he wants to see you. He's a foreigner of the name of Renard."

" Very well. Send him along to me," Flamborough ordered.

In a few moments, the constable ushered in a small man with a black moustache and a shock of stiffly-brushed hair which gave him a foreign appearance. The Inspector was relieved to find that he spoke perfect English, though with a slight accent.

" My name is Octave Renard," he introduced himself. " I am the brother of Mrs. Yvonne Silverdale."

Flamborough, with a certain admiration for the fortitude of the little man in the tragic circumstances, made haste to put him at his ease by expressing his sympathy.

" Yes, very sad," said the little Frenchman, with an obvious effort to keep himself under control. " I was very fond of my sister, you understand. She was so gay, so fond of life. She enjoyed herself every moment of the day. And now——"

A gesture filled out the missing phrase.

Flamborough's face betrayed his commiseration ; but he was a busy man, and could ill afford to waste time.

" You wished to see me about something ? "

" All I know is what was printed in the newspapers," Renard explained. " I would like to learn the truth of the case—the real facts. And you are in charge of the case, I was told. So I come to you."

Flamborough, after a moment's hesitation, gave him an outline of the bungalow tragedy, softening some of the details and omitting anything which he thought it undesirable to make public. Renard listened, with an occasional nervous twitch which showed that his imagination was at work, clothing the bare bones of the Inspector's narrative with flesh.

" It is a bad business," he said, shaking his head mournfully as Flamborough concluded. " To think that such a thing should have happened just when she had had her great stroke of good-fortune ! It is incredible, the irony of Fate."

The Inspector pricked up his ears.

" She'd had a piece of good luck, lately, you say, Mr. Renard ? What was that ? "

" You do not know ? " the little man inquired in surprise. " But surely her husband must have told you ? No ? "

Flamborough shook his head.

" That is strange," Renard continued. " I do not quite understand that. My sister was the favourite of her aunt. She was down in her will, you understand ?

And my aunt was a very wealthy woman. Pots of money, as you English say. For some time my aunt has been in feeble health. She has been going downhill for the last year or more. A heart trouble, you understand. And just a fortnight ago, puff !—she went out like that. Like a blown-out candle."

" Yes ? " the Inspector prompted.

" Her will was in the keeping of her lawyer and he communicated the contents to myself and my sister. We were trustees, you see. I had a little bequest to myself ; but the principal sum went to my sister. I was surprised ; I had not thought that my aunt had so much money—mostly in American stocks and shares. In your English money it came to about £12,000. In francs, of course, it is colossal—a million and a half at least."

" Ah ! " interjected Flamborough, now keenly interested. " And your sister knew of this ? "

" She learned it from me just two days before her death. And you understand, there was no grief with it. My aunt had suffered terribly in the last few months. Angina pectoris, very painful. We were quite glad to see her suffering at an end."

Flamborough felt that this fresh piece of information needed consideration before he ventured on to the ground which had been disclosed.

" Are you staying in Westerhaven, Mr. Renard ? " he inquired.

" Yes, for a few days yet, I expect," the little man answered. " I have some legal matters in my hands which need my presence on the spot. As my sister is now dead, there is the disposal of this money to be considered. I find difficulties which I had not expected."

" And your address during your stay will be ? "

" I am at the Imperial Hotel. You can always find me there."

" Well, Mr. Renard, I'd like to have a talk with you later on, if I may. Just at present, I'm very busy. Perhaps you could spare a few minutes when my hands are free."

" I shall be delighted," Renard acquiesced. " Whenever you wish to see me, send a message. I am much worried, you understand ? " he concluded, with a quiver in his voice which pierced through the official coating of Flamborough and touched the softer material inside.

CHAPTER X

INFORMATION RECEIVED

For the next day or two, Sir Clinton's interest in the Hassendean case appeared to have faded out ; and Inspector Flamborough, after following up one or two clues which eventually proved useless, was beginning to feel perturbed by the lack of direct progress which the investigation showed. Rather to his relief, one morning the Chief Constable summoned him to his office. Flamborough began a somewhat apologetic account of his fruitless investigations ; but Sir Clinton cut him short with a word or two of appreciation of his zeal.

" Here's something more definite for you to go on," he suggested. " I've just had a preliminary report from the London man whom we put on to search for the poison. I asked him to let me have a private opinion at the earliest possible moment. His official report will come in later, of course."

" Has he spotted it, sir ? " the Inspector inquired eagerly.

" He's reached the same conclusion as I did—and as I suppose you did also," Sir Clinton assured him.

Flamborough looked puzzled.

" I didn't spot it myself," he confessed diffidently. " In fact, I don't see how there was anything to show definitely what stuff it was, barring dilatation of the eye-pupils, and that might have been due to various drugs."

" You should never lose an opportunity of exercising your powers of inference, Inspector. I mustn't rob you of this one. Now put together two things : the episode of the mixed melting-point and the phrase about his ' triumph ' that young Hassendean wrote in his journal. Add the state of the girl's pupils as a third point—and there you are ! "

Flamborough pondered for a while over this assortment of information, but finally shook his head.

" I don't see it yet, sir."

" In that case," Sir Clinton declared, with the air of one bestowing benevolence, " I think we'd better let it dawn on you slowly. You might be angry with yourself if you realised all of a sudden how simple it is."

He rose to his feet as he spoke.

" I think we'll pay a visit to the Croft-Thornton Institute now, and see how Markfield has been getting along with his examination. We may as well have a check, before we begin to speculate too freely."

They found Markfield in his laboratory, and Sir Clinton came to business at once.

" We came over to see how you were getting on with that poison business, Dr. Markfield. Can you give us any news ? "

Markfield indicated a notebook on his desk.

" I've got it out, I think. It's all there ; but I haven't had time to write a proper report on it yet. It was——"

" Hyoscine ? " Sir Clinton interrupted.

Markfield stared at him with evident appreciation.

" You're quite right," he confirmed, with some surprise. " I suppose you've got private information."

The Chief Constable evaded the point.

" I'm asking this question only for our own information ; you won't be asked to swear to it in court. What amount of hysocine do you think was in the body, altogether? I mean, judging from the results you obtained yourself."

Markfield considered for a moment.

"I'm giving you a guess, but I think it's fairly near the mark. I wouldn't, of course, take my oath on it. But the very smallest quantity, judging from my results, would be somewhere in the neighbourhood of seven or eight milligrammes."

"Have you looked up anything about the stuff—maximum dose, and so forth?" Sir Clinton inquired.

"The maximum dose of hyoscine hydrobromide is down in the books as six-tenths of a milligramme—about a hundredth of a grain in apothecaries' weights."

"Then she must have swallowed ten or twelve times the maximum dose," Sir Clinton calculated, after a moment or two of mental arithmetic.

He paused for a space, then turned again to Markfield.

"I'd like to see the hyoscine in your store here, if you can lay your hands on it easily."

Markfield made no objection.

"If you'd come in yesterday, the bottle would have been here, beside me. I've taken it back to the shelf now."

"I suppose you borrowed it to do a mixed melting-point?" Sir Clinton asked.

"Yes. When there's only a trace of a stuff to identify, it's the easiest method. But you seem to know something about chemistry?"

"About enough to make mistakes with, I'm afraid. It simply happened that someone described the mixed melting-point business to me once; and it stuck in my mind. Now suppose we look at this store of yours."

Markfield led them along a passage and threw open a door at the end.

" In here," he said.

" You don't keep it locked ? " Sir Clinton inquired casually, as he passed in, followed by the Inspector.

" No," Markfield answered in some surprise. " It's the general chemical store for this department. There's no point in keeping it locked. All our stuffs are here, and it would be a devilish nuisance if one had to fish out a key every time one wanted some chloroform or benzene. We keep the duty-free alcohol locked up, of course. That's necessary under the Customs' regulations."

Sir Clinton readily agreed.

" You're all trustworthy people, naturally," he admitted, " It's not like a place where you have junior students about who might play thoughtless tricks."

Markfield went over to one of the cases which lined the room, searched along a shelf, and took down a tiny bottle.

" Here's the stuff," he explained, holding it out to the Chief Constable. " That's the hydrobromide, of course —a salt of the alkaloid itself. This is the compound that's used in medicine."

Now that he had got it, Sir Clinton seemed to have little interest in the substance. He handed it across to Flamborough who, after looking at it with would-be sagacity, returned it to Markfield.

" There's just one other point that occurs to me," the Chief Constable explained, as Markfield returned the poison-bottle to its original place. " Have you, by any chance, got an old notebook belonging to young Hassendean on the premises ? Anything of the sort would do."

The Inspector could make nothing of this demand and his face betrayed his perplexity as he considered it. Markfield thought for a few moments before replying, evidently trying to recall the existence of any article which would suit Sir Clinton's purpose.

"I think I've got a rough notebook of his somewhere in my room," he said at last. "But it's only a record of weighings and things like that. Would it do?"

"The very thing," Sir Clinton declared, gratefully. "I'd be much obliged if you could lay your hands on it for me now. I hope it isn't troubling you too much."

It was evident from Markfield's expression that he was as much puzzled as the Inspector; and his curiosity seemed to quicken his steps on the way back to his room. After a few minutes' hunting, he unearthed the notebook of which he was in search and laid it on the table before Sir Clinton. Flamborough, familiar with young Hassendean's writing, had no difficulty in seeing that the notes were in the dead man's hand.

Sir Clinton turned over the leaves idly, examining an entry here and there. The last one seemed to satisfy him, and he put an end to his inspection. Flamborough bent over the table and was mystified to find only the following entry on the exposed leaf:

Weight of potash bulb	= 50.7789 grs.
Weight of potash bulb + CO_2	= 50.9825 grs.
Weight of CO_2	= 0.2046 grs.

"By the way," said Sir Clinton casually, "do you happen to have one of your own notebooks at hand—something with the same sort of thing in them?"

Markfield, obviously puzzled, went over to a drawer

and pulled out a notebook which he passed to the Chief Constable. Again Sir Clinton skimmed over the pages, apparently at random, and then left the second book open beside the first one. Flamborough, determined to miss nothing, examined the exposed page in Markfield's notebook, and was rewarded by this :—

Weight of U-tube	=	24.7792 gms.
Weight of U-tube + H_2O	=	24.9047 gms.
Weight of H_2O	=	0.1255 gms.

" Damned if I see what he's driving at," the Inspector said savagely to himself. " It's Greek to me."

" A careless young fellow," the Chief Constable pronounced acidly. " My eye caught three blunders in plain arithmetic as I glanced through these notes. There's one on this page here," he indicated the open book. " He seems to have been a very slapdash sort of person."

" An unreliable young hound ! " was Markfield's slightly intensified description. " It was pure influence that kept him here for more than a week. Old Thornton, who put up most of the money for building this place, was interested in him—knew his father, I think—and so we had to keep the young pup here for fear of rasping old Thornton's feelings. Otherwise. . . ."

The gesture accompanying the aposiopesis expressed Markfield's idea of the fate which would at once have befallen young Hassendean had his protector's influence been withdrawn.

The Chief Constable appeared enlightened by this fresh information.

" I couldn't imagine how you came to let him have the run of the place for so long," he confessed. " But, of course, as things were, it was evidently cheaper to keep him, even if he did no useful work. One can't afford to alienate one's benefactors."

After a pause, he continued, reverting apparently to an earlier line of thought :

" Let's see. You made out that something like twelve times the normal dose of hyoscine had been administered ? "

Markfield nodded his assent, but qualified it in words :

" That's a rough figure, remember."

" Of course," Sir Clinton agreed. " As a matter of fact, the multiple I had in my mind was 15. I suppose it's quite possible that some of the stuff escaped you and that your figure is an under-estimate ? "

" Quite likely," Markfield admitted frankly. " I gave you the lowest figure, naturally—a figure I could swear to if it came to the point. As it's a legal case, it's safer to be under than over the mark. But quite probably, as you say, I didn't manage to isolate all the stuff that was really present ; and I wouldn't deny that the quantity in the body may have run up to ten milligrammes or even slightly over it."

" Well, it's perhaps hardly worth bothering about," the Chief Constable concluded. " The main thing is that even at the lowest estimate she must have swallowed enough of the poison to kill her in a reasonably short time."

With this he seemed satisfied, and after a few questions about the preparation and submission of Markfield's official report, he took his leave. As he turned away, however, a fresh thought seemed to strike him.

" By the way, Dr. Markfield, do you know if Miss Hailsham's here this morning ? "

" I believe so," Markfield answered. " I saw her as I came in."

" I'd like to have a few words with her," Sir Clinton suggested.

" Officially ? " Markfield demanded. " You're not going to worry the girl, are you ? If it's anything I can tell you about, I'd be only too glad, you know. It's not very nice for a girl to have the tale going round that she's been hauled in by the police in a murder case."

The Chief Constable conceded the point without ado.

" Then perhaps you could send for her and we could speak to her in here. It would be more private, and there need be no talk about it outside."

" Very well," Markfield acquiesced at once. " I think that would be better. I'll send for her now."

He rang a bell and despatched a boy with a message. In a few minutes a tap on the door sounded, and Markfield ushered Norma Hailsham into the room. Inspector Flamborough glanced at her with interest, to see how far his conception of her personality agreed with the reality. She was a girl apparently between twenty and twenty-five, dressed with scrupulous neatness. Quite obviously, she spent money freely on her clothes and knew how to get value for what she spent. But as his eyes travelled up to her face, the Inspector received a more vivid impression. Her features were striking rather than handsome, and Flamborough noted especially the squarish chin and the long thin-lipped flexible mouth.

" H'm ! " he commented to himself. " She might flash up in a moment, but with that jaw and those lips she wouldn't cool down again in a hurry. I was right when I put her down as a vindictive type. Shouldn't much care to have trouble with her myself."

He glanced at Sir Clinton for tacit instructions, but apparently the Chief Constable proposed to take charge of the interview.

" Would you sit down, Miss Hailsham," Sir Clinton suggested, drawing forward a chair for the girl.

Flamborough noticed with professional interest that by his apparently casual courtesy, the Chief Constable had unobtrusively manœuvred the girl into a position in which her face was clearly illuminated by the light from the window.

" This is Inspector Flamborough," Sir Clinton went on, with a gesture of introduction. " We should like to ask you one or two questions about an awkward case we have in our hands—the Hassendean business. I'm afraid it will be painful for you ; but I'm sure you'll give us what help you can."

Norma Hailsham's thin lips set in a hard line at his first words, but the movement was apparently involuntary, for she relaxed them again as Sir Clinton finished his remarks.

" I shall be quite glad to give any help I can," she said in a level voice.

Flamborough, studying her expression, noticed a swift shift of her glance from one to the other of the three men before her.

" She's a bit over-selfconscious," he judged privately. " But she's the regular look-monger type, anyhow ; and quite likely she makes play with her eyes when she's talking to any man."

Sir Clinton seemed to be making a merit of frankness :

" I really haven't any definite questions I want to ask

you, Miss Hailsham," he confessed. " What we hoped was that you might have something to tell us which indirectly might throw some light on this affair. You see, we come into it without knowing anything about the people involved, and naturally any trifle may help us. Now if I'm not mistaken, you knew Mr. Hassendean fairly well ? "

" I was engaged to him at one time. He broke off the engagement for various reasons. That's common knowledge, I believe."

" Could you give us any of the reasons ? I don't wish to pry, you understand ; but I think it's an important point."

Miss Hailsham's face showed that he had touched a sore place.

" He threw me over for another woman—brutally."

" Mrs. Silverdale ? " Sir Clinton inquired.

" Yes, that creature."

" Ah ! Now I'd like to put a blunt question. Was your engagement, while it lasted, a happy one ? I mean, of course, before he was attracted to Mrs. Silverdale."

Norma Hailsham sat with knitted brows for a few moments before answering.

" That's difficult to answer," she pointed out at last. " I must confess that I always felt he was thinking more of himself than of me, and it was a disappointment. But, you see, I was very keen on him ; and that made a difference, of course."

" What led to the breaking of your engagement ? "

" You mean what led up to it ? Well, we were having continual friction over Yvonne Silverdale. He was neglecting me and spending his time with her. Naturally, I spoke to him about it more than once. I wasn't going to be slighted on account of that woman."

There was no mistaking the under-current of animosity in the girl's voice in the last sentence. Sir Clinton ignored it.

" What were your ideas about the relations between Mr. Hassendean and Mrs. Silverdale ? "

Miss Hailsham's thin lips curled in undisguised contempt as she heard the question. She made a gesture as though averting herself from something distasteful.

" It's hardly necessary to enter into *that*, is it ? " she demanded. " You can judge for yourself."

But though she verbally evaded the point, the tone in which she spoke was sufficient to betray her private views on the subject. Then with intense bitterness mingled with a certain malicious joy, she added :

" She got what she deserved in the end. I don't pretend I'm sorry. I think they were both well served."

Then her temper, which hitherto she had kept under control, broke from restraint :

" I don't care who knows it ! They deserved all they got, both of them. What business had she—with a husband of her own—to come and lure him away ? She made him break off his engagement to me simply to gratify her own vanity. You don't expect me to shed tears over them after that ? One can forgive a good deal, but there's no use making a pretence in things like that. She hit me as hard as she could, and I'm glad she's got her deserts. I warned him at the time that he wouldn't come off so well as he thought ; and he laughed in my face when I said it. Well, it's my turn to laugh. The account's even."

And she actually did laugh, with a catch of hysteria in the laughter. It needed no great skill in psychology to see that wounded pride shared with disappointed passion in causing this outbreak.

Sir Clinton checked the hysteria before it gained complete hold over her.

" I'm afraid you haven't told us anything that was new to us, Miss Hailsham," he said, frigidly. " This melodramatic business gets us no further forward."

The girl looked at him with hard eyes.

" What help do you expect from me ? " she demanded. " I'm not anxious to see him avenged—far from it."

Sir Clinton evidently realised that nothing was to be gained by pursuing that line of inquiry. Whether the girl had any suspicions or not, she certainly did not intend to supply information which might lead to the capture of the murderer. The Chief Constable waited until she had become calmer before putting his next question :

" Do you happen to know anything about an alkaloid called hyoscine, Miss Hailsham ? "

" Hyoscine ? " she repeated. " Yes, Avice Deepcar's working on it just now. She's been at it for some time under Dr. Silverdale's direction."

Flamborough, glancing surreptitiously at Markfield, noted an angry start which the chemist apparently could not suppress. Put on the alert by this, the Inspector reflected that Markfield himself must have had this piece of information, and had refrained from volunteering it.

" I meant as regards its properties," Sir Clinton interposed. " I'm not an expert in these things like you chemical people."

" I'm not an alkaloid expert," Miss Hailsham objected. " All I can remember about it is that it's used in Twilight Sleep."

" I believe it is, now that you mention it," Sir Clinton

agreed, politely. " By the way, have you a car, Miss Hailsham ? "

" Yes. A Morris-Oxford four-seater."

" A saloon ? "

" No, a touring model. Why do you ask ? "

" Someone's been asking for information about a car which seems to have knocked a man over on the night of the last fog. You weren't out that night, I suppose, Miss Hailsham ? "

" I was, as it happened. I went out to a dance. But I'd a sore throat ; and the fog made it worse ; so I came away very early and got home as best I could. But it wasn't my car that knocked anyone down. I never had an accident in my life."

" You might have been excused in that fog, I think, even if you had a collision. But evidently it's not your car we're after. What was the number of the car we heard about, Inspector ? "

Flamborough consulted his notebook.

" GX.9074, sir."

" Say that again," Markfield demanded, pricking up his ears.

" GX.9074 was the number."

" That's the number of my car," Markfield volunteered.

He thought for some time, apparently trying to retrace his experiences in the fog. At last his face lighted up.

" Oh, I guess I know what it is. When I was piloting Dr. Ringwood that night, a fellow nearly walked straight into my front mudguard. I may have hurt his feelings by what I said about his brains, but I swear I didn't touch him with the car."

" Not our affair," Sir Clinton hastened to assure him.

" It's a matter for your insurance company if anything comes of it. And I gathered from Dr. Ringwood that you didn't exactly break records in your trip across town, so I doubt if you need worry."

" I shan't," said Markfield, crossly. " You can refer him to me if he comes to you again."

" We'd nothing to do with the matter," Sir Clinton pointed out. " He was told he'd get the owner's address from the County Council. I expect he got into a calmer frame of mind when he'd had time to think."

He turned to Miss Hailsham, who seemed to have recovered complete control over herself during this interlude.

" I think that's all we need worry you with, Miss Hailsham. I'm sorry that we put you to so much trouble."

As a sign that the interview was at an end, he moved over to open the door for her.

" I certainly don't wish you success," she said icily, as she left the room.

" Well, I think that's all we have to do here, Inspector," Sir Clinton said as he turned back from the open door. " We mustn't take up any more of Dr. Markfield's time. I don't want to hurry you too much," he added to Markfield, " but you'll let us have your official report as soon as you can, won't you ? "

Markfield promised with a nod, and the two officials left the building. When they reached headquarters again, Sir Clinton led the way to his own office.

" Sit down for a moment or two, Inspector," he invited. " You may as well glance over the London man's report when you're about it. Here it is—not for actual use, of course, until we get the official version from him."

He passed over a paper which Flamborough unfolded.

"By the way, sir," the Inspector inquired before beginning to read, "is there any reason for keeping back this information? These infernal reporters are all over me for details; and if this poison affair could be published without doing any harm, I might as well dole it out to them to keep them quiet. They haven't had much from me in the last twenty-four hours, and it's better to give them what we can."

Sir Clinton seemed to attach some importance to this matter, for he considered it for a few seconds before replying.

"Let them have the name of the stuff," he directed at last. "I don't think I'd supply them with any details, though. I'm quite satisfied about the name of the drug, but the dose is still more or less a matter of opinion, and we'd better not say anything about that."

Flamborough glanced up from the report in his hand.

"Markfield and the London man both seem to put the dose round about the same figure—eight milligrammes," he said.

"Both of them must be super-sharp workers," Sir Clinton pointed out. "I don't profess to be a chemist, Inspector, but I know enough about things to realise that they've done a bit of a feat there. However, let's get on to something more immediately interesting. What did you make of the Hailsham girl?"

"What did I make of her?" Flamborough repeated, in order to gain a little time. "I thought she was more or less what I'd expected her to be, sir. A hard vixen with a good opinion of herself—and simply mad with rage at being jilted: that's what I made of her. Revengeful, too. And a bit vulgar, sir. No decent girl would talk like that about a dead man to a set of strangers."

" She hadn't much to tell us that was useful," Sir Clinton said, keeping to the main point. " And I quite agree with you as to the general tone."

Flamborough turned to a matter which had puzzled him during their visit to the Institute :

" What did you want young Hassendean's notebook for, sir ? I didn't quite make that out."

" Why, you saw what I got out of it : arithmetical errors which proved conclusively that he was a careless worker who didn't take any trouble at all to verify his results."

" I had a kind of notion that you got more out of it than that, sir, or you wouldn't have asked to see Markfield's notebook as well. It doesn't take someone else's notebook to spot slips in a man's arithmetic, surely."

Sir Clinton gazed blandly at his subordinate :

" Now that you've got that length, it would be a pity to spoil your pleasure in the rest of the inference. Just think it out and tell me the result, to see if we both reach the same conclusion independently. You'll find a weights-and-measures conversion table useful."

" Conversion table, sir ? " asked the Inspector, evidently quite at sea.

" Yes. ' One metre equals 39·37 inches,' and all that sort of thing. The sort of stuff one used at school, you know."

" Too deep for me, sir," the Inspector acknowledged ruefully. " You'll need to tell me the answer. And that reminds me, what made you ask whether the dose could have been fifteen times the maximum ? "

The Chief Constable was just about to take pity on

his subordinate when the desk-telephone rang sharply. Sir Clinton picked up the receiver.

" . . . Yes. Inspector Flamborough is here."

He handed the receiver across to the Inspector, who conducted a disjointed conversation with the person at the other end of the wire. At length Flamborough put down the instrument and turned to Sir Clinton with an expression of satisfaction on his face.

"We're on to something, sir. That was Fossaway ringing up from Fountain Street. It seems a man called there a few minutes ago and began fishing round to know if there was any likelihood of a reward being offered in connection with the bungalow case. He seemed as if he might know something, and they handed him over to Detective-Sergeant Fossaway to see what he could make of him. Fossaway's fairly satisfied that there's something behind it, though he could extract nothing whatever from the fellow in the way of definite statements."

" Has Fossaway got him there still ? "

" No, sir. He'd no power to detain him, of course ; and the fellow turned stubborn in the end and went off without saying anything definite."

" I hope they haven't lost him."

" Oh, no, sir. They know him quite well."

" What sort of person is he, then ? "

" A nasty type, sir. He keeps one of these little low-down shops where you can buy a lot of queer things. Once we nearly had him over the sale of some post-cards, but he was too clever for us at the last moment. Then he was up in an assault case : he'd been wandering round the Park after dark, disturbing couples with a flash-lamp. A thoroughly low-down little creature. His name's Whalley."

Sir Clinton's face showed very plainly his view of the activities of Mr. Whalley.

" Well, so long as they can lay their hands on him any time we need him, it's all right. I think we'll persuade him to talk. By the way, was this lamp-flashing stunt of his done for æsthetic enjoyment, or was he doing a bit of blackmailing on the quiet ? "

" Well, nobody actually lodged a complaint against him ; but there's no saying whether people paid him or not. His record doesn't make it improbable that he might do something in that line, if he could manage to pull it off."

" Then I'll leave Mr. Whalley to your care, Inspector. He sounds interesting, if you can induce him to squeak."

CHAPTER XI

THE CODE ADVERTISEMENT

On the following morning, Inspector Flamborough was summoned to the Chief Constable's room and, on his arrival, was somewhat surprised to find his superior poring over a copy of the *Westerhaven Courier*. It was not Sir Clinton's habit to read newspapers during office hours ; and the Inspector's eyebrows lifted slightly at the unwonted spectacle.

"Here's a little puzzle for you, Inspector," Sir Clinton greeted him as he came in. "Just have a look at it."

He folded the newspaper to a convenient size and handed it over, pointing as he did so to an advertisement to which attention had been drawn by a couple of crosses in pen and ink. Flamborough took the paper and scanned the advertisement :

> DRIFFIELD. AAACC. CCCDE. EEEEF. HHHHH. IIIIJ. NNNNO. OOOOO. RRSSS. SSTTT. TTTTT. TTUUW. Y.

"It doesn't seem exactly lucid, sir," he confessed, as he read it a second time. "A lot of letters in alphabetical order and divided into groups of five—bar the single letter at the end. I suppose it was your name at the front that attracted your eye ? "

"No," Sir Clinton answered. "This copy of the paper came to me through the post, marked as you see it. It came in by the second delivery. Here's the wrapper. It'll probably suggest something to you."

Flamborough looked at it carefully.

" Ordinary official stamped wrapper. There's no clue there, since you can buy 'em by the hundred anywhere."

Then a glance at the address enlightened him.

" Same old game, sir? Letters clipped from telegraph forms and gummed on to the wrapper. It looks like Mr. Justice again."

" The chances are in favour of it," Sir Clinton agreed, with a faint tinge of mockery in his voice at the Inspector's eager recognition of the obvious. " Well, what about it? "

Flamborough scanned the advertisement once more, but no sign of comprehension lightened his face.

" Let's clear up one point before we tackle the lettering," Sir Clinton suggested. " That's to-day's issue of the *Courier*; so this advertisement was received at the newspaper office yesterday. Since the thing reached me by the second post, this copy of the paper may have been bought in the normal way—first thing in the morning—and posted at once."

" That's sound, sir. It's among the ordinary advertisements—not in the ' Too Late For Classification ' section."

" It may be a hoax, of course," Sir Clinton mused, " but the telegram-form business would hardly occur to a practical joker. I think one can take it as a genuine contribution until it's proved to be a fake. Now what do you make of it? "

The Inspector shook his head.

" Cyphers are not my long suit, sir. Frankly, it seems

to me just a jumble, and I don't think I'd make it anything else if I tried."

Sir Clinton reflected for a minute or two in silence, his eyes fixed on the advertisement.

"I've a notion that this is only Chapter I, Inspector. There's more to come, in all probability. If it's Mr. Justice, he's not the man to waste time. By the way, did you give the reporters the information you were talking about yesterday?"

"Yes, sir. It was printed in last night's *Evening Herald*, and I think both the *Courier* and the *Gazette* have got it this morning."

Sir Clinton was still scrutinising the advertisement.

"I'm like you, Inspector—no great shakes on cyphers. But this affair looks to me more like the letters of a plain message arranged in ordinary alphabetical order. I think that most likely we shall get the key from the writer in some form or other before long. In the meantime, though, we might have a dash at interpreting the affair, if we can."

Flamborough's face showed that he thought very poorly of the chances of success.

"Ever read Jules Verne or Poe?" Sir Clinton demanded. "No? Well, Poe has an essay on cryptography in its earlier stages—nothing like the stuff you'll find in Gross or Reiss, of course, and mere child's play compared with the special manuals on the subject. But he pointed out that in cypher-solving you have to pick the lock instead of using the normal key. And Jules Verne puts his finger on the signature of a cypher-communication as a weak point, if you've any idea who the sender is. That's assuming, of course, that there is a signature at all to the thing."

The Inspector nodded his comprehension of this.

" You mean, sir, that 'Justice' would be the signature here, like in the wire we got? "

" We can but try," Sir Clinton suggested. " Not that I'm over-hopeful. Still, it's worth a shot. Suppose we hook out the letters of 'Justice' and see what that leaves us. And we may as well disregard the groups of five for the moment and simply collect the remaining letters under A, B, C, etc."

He tore a sheet of paper into small squares and inscribed one letter of the message on each square.

" Now we take out 'Justice,' " he said, suiting the action to the word, " and simply leave the rest in alphabetical groups."

The Inspector, following the operation, found himself faced with the arrangement :

AAA CCCC D EEEE F HHHHH III NNNN
OOOOOO RR SSSS TTTTTTTTT U W Y
JUSTICE.

" It doesn't seem much clearer, sir," Flamborough pointed out with a certain tinge of enjoyment in his tone. It was not often that he had a chance of crowing over his superior.

" Wait a moment, Inspector. Just let's reflect for a bit. At any rate, the letters of 'Justice' are there ; and that's always better than a complete blank end. Now consider what Mr. Justice might be burning to tell us about in his unobtrusive way. He had time to see the news printed in last night's *Herald* before he composed this little affair. Let's suppose that he got some fresh ideas from that—since this communication falls pat after the publication and he hasn't bothered us for days before that. The crucial thing was the identification of the hyoscine. We'll see if we can get the word out here."

He sifted out the letters rapidly ; and the jumble then took the form :

HYOSCINE AAA CCC D EEE F HHHH II
NNN OOOOO RR SSS TTTTTTTTT U W
JUSTICE.

" It fits, so far," Sir Clinton said, surveying his handiwork doubtfully, " but we might have got a couple of words like that out of a random jumble of fifty-six letters. It's encouraging, but far from convincing, I admit."

He glanced over the arrangement with knitted brows.

" There seem to be a devil of a lot of T's in the thing, if we're on the right track. Now what do you associate with hyoscine in your mind, Inspector ? Quick, now ! Don't stop to think."

" The Croft-Thornton Institute," said the inspector, promptly.

" Bull's eye, I believe," the Chief Constable ejaculated. " You could hardly jam more T's together in English than there are in these three words. Let's sift 'em out."

The Inspector bent eagerly forward to see if the necessary letters could be found. Sir Clinton separated the ones which he required for the three words, and the arrangement stood thus :

HYOSCINE THE CROFT-THORNTON
INSTITUTE AAA CC D E HH OO SS TT
W JUSTICE.

" I think this is getting outside the bounds of mere chance," Sir Clinton adjudged, with more optimism in his tone. " Now we might go a step further without straining things, even if it's only a short pace. Let's make a guess. Suppose that it's meant to read : " Hyoscine *at* the Croft-Thornton Institute." That leaves us with the jumble here :

AA CC D E HH OO SS T W

" What do you make of that, Inspector ? "

" The start of it looks like ACCEDE—no, there's only one E," Flamborough began, only to correct himself.

" It's not ACCEDE, obviously, Let's try ACCESS and see if that's any use."

The Chief Constable shifted the letters while the Inspector, now thoroughly interested, watched for the result.

" If it's ACCESS then it ought to be ACCESS TO," Sir Clinton suggested. " And that leaves A, D, HH, O, W."

One glance at the six letters satisfied him.

" It's panned out correctly, Inspector. There isn't a letter over. See ! "

He rearranged the lettering, and the inspector read the complete message :

WHO HAD ACCESS TO HYOSCINE AT THE CROFT-THORNTON INSTITUTE. JUSTICE.

" The chances of an anagram working out so sensibly as that are pretty small," Sir Clinton said, with satisfaction. " It's a few million to one that we've got the correct version. H'm ! I don't know that Mr. Justice has really given us much help this time, for the Croft-Thornton was an obvious source of the drug. Still, he's doing his best, evidently ; and he doesn't mean to let us overlook even the obvious, this time. I'm prepared to bet that we get the key to this thing by the next post. Mr. Justice wouldn't leave the matter to the mere chance of our working the thing out. Still it's some satisfaction to feel that we've done without his assistance.

Flamborough occupied himself with copying the cypher and its solution into his notebook. When he had finished, Sir Clinton lit a cigarette and handed his case to the Inspector.

"Let's put officialism aside for a few minutes," the Chief Constable proposed. "No notes, or anything of that sort. Now I don't mind confessing, Inspector, that we aren't getting on with this business at all well. Short of divination, there seems no way of discovering the truth, so far as present information goes. And we simply can't afford to let this affair go unsolved. Your Whalley person seems to be our best hope."

The Inspector evidently found a fresh train of thought started in his mind by Sir Clinton's lament.

"I've been thinking over that set of alternatives you put down on paper the other day, sir," he explained. "I think they ought to be reduced from nine to six. It's practically out of the question that young Hassendean was shot twice over by pure accident ; so it seems reasonable enough to eliminate all that class from your table."

He put his hand in his pocket and produced a sheet of paper which had evidently been folded and unfolded fairly often since it had been first written upon.

"If you reject accident as a possibility in Hassendean's case," he continued, "then you bring the thing within these limits here."

He put his paper down on the table and Sir Clinton read the following :

HASSENDEAN	MRS. SILVERDALE
A—Suicide	Suicide
B—Murder	Murder
C—Suicide	Accident
D—Murder	Accident
E—Suicide	Murder
F—Murder	Suicide

" Now I think it's possible to eliminate even further than that, sir, for this reason. There's a third death—the maid's at Heatherfield—which on the face of it is connected in some way with these others. I don't see how you can cut the Heatherfield business away from the other two."

" I'm with you there, Inspector," Sir Clinton assured him.

Flamborough, obviously relieved to find that he was not going to be attacked in the flank, pursued his exposition with more confidence.

" Who killed the maid ? That's an important point. It wasn't young Hassendean, because the maid was seen alive by Dr. Ringwood immediately after young Hassendean had died on his hands. It certainly wasn't Mrs. Silverdale, because everything points to her having died even before young Hassendean left the bungalow to go home and die at Ivy Lodge. Therefore, there was somebody afoot in the business that night who wouldn't stick at murder to gain his ends, whatever they were."

" Nobody's going to quarrel with that, Inspector."

" Very good, sir," Flamborough continued. " Now, with that factor at the back of one's mind, one might review these six remaining cases in the light of what we do know."

" Go ahead," Sir Clinton urged him, covertly amused to find the Inspector so completely converted to the method which at first he had decried.

" Case A, then," Flamborough began. " A double suicide. Now I don't cotton much to that notion, for this reason. If it was suicide, then one or other of them must have had possession of hyoscine in quantity sufficient to kill both of them. So I judge from the quantity found in her body. Now no hyoscine was in young Hassendean's system. His eyes were quite normal and there was no trace of the stuff in the stomach, as they found when they sent to your London friend on the question. From what I've seen of young Hassendean's diary, and from what we've picked up about him from various sources, he wasn't the sort of person to go in for needless pain. If he'd shot himself at all, it would have been in the head. And if he'd had hyoscine at hand, he wouldn't have shot himself at all. He'd have swallowed a dose of the poison instead, and gone out painlessly."

" Correct inference, I believe," Sir Clinton confirmed. " I don't say it's certain, of course."

" Well, then, what holds in Case A, ought to hold also in the other two cases—C and E—where it's also a question of young Hassendean's suicide. So one can score them off as well."

" Not so fast," Sir Clinton interrupted. " I don't say you're wrong ; but your assumption doesn't cover the cases. In Case A you assumed that Mrs. Silverdale committed suicide—ergo, she had hyoscine in her possession. But in Case C, the assumption is that she died by accidental poisoning ; and before you can eliminate suicide on young Hassendean's part, you've got to prove that he had the hyoscine in his possession.

I'm not saying that he hadn't. I'm merely keeping you strictly to your logic."

Flamborough considered this for a few moments.

" Strictly speaking, I suppose you're right, sir. And in Case E, I'd have to prove that he poisoned her wilfully, in order to cover the case of his having hyoscine in his possession. H'm ! "

After a pause, he took up the table afresh.

" Let's go back to Case B, then : a double murder. That brings in this third party—the person who did for the maid at Heatherfield, we'll say ; and the fellow who broke the window. There were signs of a struggle in that room at the bungalow, you remember. Now it seems to me that Case B piles things on too thick, if you understand what I mean. It means that Mrs. Silverdale was murdered by poison and that young Hassendean was shot to death. Why the two methods when plain shooting would have been good enough in both cases ? Take the obvious case—it's been at the back of my mind, and I'm sure it's been at the back of yours too, that Silverdale surprised the two of them at the bungalow and killed them both. Where does the poison come in ? To my mind we ought to put a pencil through Case B. It's most improbable."

Rather to his relief, Sir Clinton made no objection. The Inspector drew his pencil through the first two lines of the table, then let it hover over the last line.

" What about Case F, sir ? She suicided and he was murdered. If she suicided, it was a premeditated affair —otherwise they wouldn't have had the hyoscine at hand. But if it was one of these lovers' suicide-pacts, they'd have had a dose ready for him as well—and there wasn't a trace of the stuff spilt on the floor or anywhere about the bungalow. Score out Case F, sir ? "

" I've no objections to your putting your pencil through it if you like, Inspector, though my reasons are rather different from the ones you give."

Flamborough looked up suspiciously, but gathered from Sir Clinton's face that there was nothing further to be expected.

" Well, at least that's narrowed down the possibilities a bit," he said with relief. " You started out with nine possible solutions to the affair—covering every conceivable combination. Now we're down to three."

He picked up his paper and read out the residual scheme, putting fresh identifying letters to the three cases :

HASSENDEAN	MRS. SILVERDALE
X—Suicide	Accident
Y—Murder	Accident
Z—Suicide	Murder

" You agree to that, sir ? " Flamborough demanded.

" Oh, yes ! " Sir Clinton admitted, in a careless tone. " I think the truth probably lies somewhere among those three solutions. The bother will be to prove it."

At this moment a constable entered the room, bringing some letters and a newspaper in a postal wrapper.

" Come by the next post, as I expected," the Chief Constable remarked, picking up the packet and removing the wrapper with care. " The usual method of addressing, you see : letters cut from telegraph forms and gummed on to the official stamped wrapper. Well, let's have a look at the news."

He unfolded the sheet and glanced over the advertisement pages in search of a marked paragraph.

"Ingenious devil, Inspector," he went on. "The other advertisement was in the *Courier*, this is a copy of to-day's *Gazette*. That makes sure that no one reading down a column of advertisements would be struck by a resemblance and start comparisons. I begin to like Mr. Justice. He's thorough, anyhow. . . . Ah, here we are ! Marked like the other one. Listen, Inspector :

"CLINTON : Take the letters in the following order.
55. 16. 30. 17. 1. 9. 2. 4. 5. 10. 38. 39. 43. 31.
18. 56. 32. 40. 6. 21. 26. 11. 3. 44. 45. 19. 12. 7.
36. 33. 15. 46. 47. 20. 34. 37. 27. 48. 35. 28. 22.
29. 41. 49. 23. 50. 53. 51. 13. 25. 54. 42. 52.
24. 8. 14.

Now that was why he split up his letters into groups of five in the first advertisement—to make it easy for us to count. I really like this fellow more and more. A most thoughtful cove."

He placed the two advertisements side by side on the table.

"Just run over this with me, Inspector. Call the first A number 1, the second A number 2, and so on. There are fifty-six letters in all, so number 55 is the W. Number 16 is the first letter in the fourth quintette—H. Number 30 is the last letter in the sixth quintette—O. So that spells WHO. Just go through the lot and check them please."

Flamborough ploughed through the whole series and ended with the same solution as Sir Clinton had obtained earlier in the morning : "WHO HAD ACCESS TO HYOSCINE AT THE CROFT-THORNTON INSTITUTE ?"

" Well, it's pleasant to hit the mark," the Chief Constable confessed. " By the way, you had better send someone down to the *Courier* and *Gazette* Offices to pick up the originals of these advertisements. But I'm sure it'll be just the same old telegram stunt ; and the address which has to be given as a guarantee of good faith will be a fake one."

CHAPTER XII

THE SILVERDALE WILLS

"This is Mr. Renard, sir."

Flamborough held open the door of Sir Clinton's office and ushered in the little Frenchman. The Chief Constable glanced up at the interruptors.

"Mrs. Silverdale's brother, isn't it?" he asked courteously.

Renard nodded vigorously, and turned toward the Inspector, as though leaving explanations to him. Flamborough threw himself into the breach:

"It appears, sir, that Mr. Renard isn't entirely satisfied with the state of things he's unearthed in the matter of his sister's will. It's taken him by surprise; and he came to see what I thought about it. He'd prefer to lay the point before you, so I've brought him along. It seems just as well that you should hear it at first-hand, for it looks as though it might be important."

Sir Clinton closed his fountain pen and invited Renard to take a seat.

"I'm at your disposal, Mr. Renard," he said briskly. "Let's hear the whole story, if you please, whatever it is. Inspector Flamborough will make notes, if you don't mind."

Renard took the chair which Sir Clinton indicated.

"I shall be concise," he assured the Chief Constable. "It is not a very complicated affair, but I should like to have it thrashed out, as you English say."

He settled himself at ease and then plunged into his tale.

" My sister, Yvonne Renard, as you know, married Mr. Silverdale in 1923. I was not altogether pleased with the alliance, not quite satisfied, you understand ? Oh, there was nothing against Mr. Silverdale ! But I knew my sister, and Silverdale was not the right man for her : he was too serious, too intent on his profession. He had not the natural gaiety which was needed in a husband for Yvonne. Already I was in doubt, at the very moment of the marriage. There were incompatibilities, you understand. . . . ? "

Sir Clinton's gesture assured him that he had made himself sufficiently clear.

" I have nothing to say against my brother-in-law, you follow me ? " Renard went on. " It was a case of ' Marry in haste and repent at leisure,' as your English proverb says. They were unsuited to each other, but that was no fault of theirs. When they discovered each other—their real selves—it is clear that they decided to make the best of it. I had nothing to say. I was sorry that my sister had not found a husband more suited to her temperament ; but I am not one who would make trouble by sympathising too much."

" I quite understand, Mr. Renard," Sir Clinton intervened, with the obvious intention of cutting short this elaborate exposition of the self-evident.

" Now I come to the important point," Renard went on. " At the time of the marriage, or shortly afterwards —I do not know your English law about testaments very well—my brother-in-law transferred part of his property in stocks and shares to my sister. It was some question of Death Duties, I was told. If he died first, then she would have had to pay on his whole estate ;

but by transferring some of his property to her, this could be avoided. In case of his death, she would have to pay only on what he had retained in his own name. It is, I understand, a usual precaution in the circumstances."

"It's often done," Sir Clinton confirmed. "By the way, Mr. Renard, can you give me some idea of how much he transferred to her on their marriage?"

"I cannot give you the precise figures," Renard explained. "I have seen the lawyer's accounts, of course; but they were involved, and I have no good memory for figures. It was only a few hundred pounds—a mere drop in the bucket, as you would say in English. My brother-in-law is not a rich man, not by any means. But the sum itself is of little importance. It is the sequel which is of more interest, as you shall see."

He leaned forward in his chair as though to fix Sir Clinton's attention.

"When my brother-in-law transferred this little property to my sister, they each made their testament. That, I believe, was on the advice of a lawyer. By his will, my brother-in-law left all his property to my sister. He had no relations, so far as I have learned; and that seemed very fair. The second will, my sister's, was in identical terms, so far as the principal clauses went. All her property in stocks, shares, and money, went to my brother-in-law. There was a little provision at the end which left to me a few small souvenirs, things of sentimental value only. It seemed very fair in the circumstances. I suggest nothing wrong. How could there be anything wrong?"

"It seems a normal precaution in the circumstances," Sir Clinton assured him. "Naturally, if she died first, he would expect to get his own property back again—less the Death Duties, of course."

"It was a very small affair," Renard emphasised. "If I had been consulted, I should certainly have advised it. But I was not consulted. It was no business of mine, except that I was made a trustee. I am not one who mixes himself up with affairs which do not concern him."

"Where is this leading to, Mr. Renard ?" Sir Clinton asked patiently. "I don't see your difficulty as yet, I must confess."

"There is no difficulty. It is merely that I wish to lay some further information before you. Now, I proceed. My aunt had been ill for a long time. A disease of the heart, it was : angina pectoris. She was bound to die in a spasm, at a moment's notice. One expected it, you understand ? And less than three weeks ago, she had the spasm which we had so long anticipated, and she died."

Sir Clinton's face expressed his sympathy, but he made no attempt to interrupt.

"As I told Inspector Flamborough when I saw him last," Renard continued, "the figure of her fortune came as a surprise to me. I had no idea she was so rich. She lived very simply, very parsimoniously, even. I had always thought of her as hard-up, you understand ? Figure to yourself my astonishment when I learned that she had accumulated over £12,000 ! That is a great sum. Many people would do almost anything to acquire £12,000."

He paused for a moment as though in rapt contemplation of the figures.

"Her testament was very simple," he proceeded. "My sister Yvonne was her favourite. My aunt had always put her in front of me. I make no complaint, you understand? Someone must be preferred. I had a little bequest under my aunt's testament; but Yvonne secured almost the whole of my aunt's fortune. That was how things stood a fortnight ago."

He hitched himself in his chair as though preparing for a revelation.

"My sister and I were the trustees under my aunt's testament. The lawyer who had charge of the will communicated with me and forwarded a copy of the document. These legal documents are not easy to understand. But I soon saw that my sister had acquired the whole of my aunt's capital in stocks and shares—about a million and a half francs. I am not very good at legal affairs. It took me some time to understand what all this meant; but I thought it out. It is really quite simple, very easy. My sister had gained £12,000 under my aunt's will; but if she died without any change in the circumstances, then under the will which she signed after her marriage, my brother-in-law would inherit the whole of that money. Figure to yourself, he had never even seen my aunt, and all that £12,000 would pour into his lap. And I, who had been almost like a son to my aunt, I would get nothing! I make no complaint, of course."

Sir Clinton's face betrayed nothing whatever of his views on the question. He merely waited in silence for Renard to continued his story.

"When I understood the position," Renard resumed, "I sat down and wrote a letter to my sister. 'Here is the state of affairs,' I said. 'Our good aunt is dead, and she has named you as her heiress. A whole million and a half francs! To me she has left some little things, enough at least to buy a suit of mourning. I have no complaints to make : our good aunt had the right to dispose of her money as she chose.' That was how I began, you understand ? Then I went on thus : 'Things are for the best for the present,' I said, 'but one must think of the future as well. Recall the will which you made at the time of your marriage. All is to go to your husband, should anything happen to you. Now,' I wrote, 'that seems to me hardly as it should be. If you should die—a motor accident might happen any day—then all the money of our aunt would pass into the hands of your husband, this husband with whom you have so little in common and who had no relations with our good aunt. And I, who am your nearest in kin, would receive not one penny. Think of that,' I wrote, 'and consider whether it would be fair. Is the fortune of our family to pass into the hands of strangers and we ourselves to be left without a share in it ? ' "

Renard looked from the Inspector to Sir Clinton and back to the Inspector, as though seeking for sympathy. Apparently finding nothing very satisfying in their expressions, he continued his tale.

" I put it to her that this state of affairs was not as it should be. I did not plead for myself, of course. That is not my way. I tried to show her that as things stood, injustice would be done if she should happen to die. And I urged her very strongly to make a fresh will. 'See,' I wrote, 'how things would fall out. To you, it would mean nothing, very naturally. You would be far beyond all cares. But this money would be left. Would you desire that it should fall into the hands of this husband of yours, with whom you cannot find anything in common ? Or would you not prefer that it should be left to your brother who has always been good to you ? ' That is how I put it to her. I asked her to take swift action and to call in a lawyer who could aid her to draw up a fresh will which would be fair to both her husband and myself. I desired to be fair, you understand ? merely to be fair. He would have received back his own stocks and shares which he had given to her at the time of their marriage. I would have gained the fortune which descended from my aunt. That seemed reasonable, surely."

" Yes," Sir Clinton confirmed, " it sounds quite reasonable in the circumstances. And what happened ? "

" I have been to see the lawyers," Renard went on. " Figure to yourself what I discovered. My poor Yvonne was not a woman of affairs. She had no business-like habits. If a thing seemed likely to give her trouble, she would put it aside for as long as she could, before dealing with it. Affairs bored her. It was her temperament, like that. So when she received my letter, she put it aside for some days. One cannot blame her. It was not in her nature to go to great trouble over a thing like that. Besides, death was not in her thoughts. One day was as good as another."

He paused, as though wishing to heighten the interest of his narrative ; for it was evident that he had produced but little impression on Sir Clinton.

" She had a good heart, my poor sister. She understood the position well enough, it seems. And she had no wish to see her good brother left out in the cold, as you English put it. But she delayed and delayed in the affair. And in the end she delayed too long."

Again he hitched himself forward in his chair, as though he were approaching something important.

" I went to the lawyers. What did I find ? This. My poor Yvonne had not forgotten her good brother. She had the intention of setting things right. One day she rang up the lawyers on the telephone and made an appointment with them for the following afternoon. She informed them that she proposed to alter her will ; but of course, over the telephone, she said nothing about her wishes on the point. That is to be understood. But she said she would jot down the points to be embodied in the new will and bring that paper with her. That is all the lawyers know. That is all I know myself. For before the next afternoon, when she had made her appointment with the lawyers—my poor Yvonne was dead ! Is it not distressing ? Twelve thousand pounds ! A million and a half francs ! And they slip through my fingers just by a few hours. But I make no complaint, of course. I do not grumble. It is not my way. These things happen, and one has to bear them."

If he had expected to read any sympathy in Sir Clinton's face, he must have been disappointed. The Chief Constable betrayed nothing of the feelings in his mind.

" Was it not most inopportune ? " Renard continued " Or most opportune indeed, for Silverdale, that things fell out as they have done. A coincidence, of course. Life is full of these things. I have seen too many to be astonished, myself. But is it not most apt that she should die just at that juncture ? Another day of life, and the twelve thousand pounds goes into one pocket ; a death, and the money falls into other hands. I am something of a philosopher. One has to be, in this world. And these strange chances have an attraction for my mind. I know there is nothing behind them, nothing whatever, you understand ? And yet, is it not most striking that things fall out as they do ? "

The Chief Constable declined to be drawn into a general discussion on the Universe.

" I am afraid it is scarcely a matter for the police, Mr. Renard. Wills hardly fall into our province, you know, unless a case of forgery turns up ; and in this case there's nothing of that sort. The only advice I could give you would be to consult a lawyer, but as you've already had the legal position made clear, I don't see that there's anything to be done."

Inspector Flamborough took his cue and, without more ado he hinted to Renard very plainly that enough time had been spent on the matter. At length the little Frenchman withdrew, leaving the two officials together.

" I don't much care for his way of telling his story, sir," Flamborough remarked, " but I'm not sure, if I were in his shoes, that I wouldn't feel much the same as he seems to do. It must be a bit galling to lose £12,000 by a few hours' delay. And he's quite reasonably suspicious, evidently."

Sir Clinton refused to be drawn.

" Don't let's be too much influenced by the stop press news, Inspector. Renard's evidence is the latest we have ; but that adds nothing to its value, remember. Look at the case as a whole and try to reckon up the people who could conceivably gain anything by the crime. Then you can assess the probabilities in each case—apart altogether from the order in which the facts have come to light."

The Inspector had evidently considered the matter already from this stand-point. He hardly paused before offering his views.

" Well, sir, if you ask me, Silverdale had at least two sound motives for committing murder. By getting his wife out of the way, he opened the road to a marriage with the Deepcar girl, whom he's obviously keen on. Also, if Renard's story's true, the death of his wife at that particular juncture put £12,000 into his pocket, which he'd have lost if Mrs. Silverdale had lived a day or two longer."

" One has to admit that he hadn't evidence to get a divorce, which would have been an obvious alternative to murder," Sir Clinton acknowledged. " And the cash affair makes the death of Mrs. Silverdale peculiarly opportune. It's no use burking the plain fact that either money or a woman might tempt a man to murder ; and when you've got both of them together, one can't brush them aside cavalierly. But go on with your list, Inspector."

" There's that money-lender, Spratton," Flamborough pursued. " If young Hassendean's death can be proved to be a murder, then Spratton lifts some thousands out of the pocket of the insurance company in return for the payment of a single premium. That's a motive, certainly."

" It's a sound motive for *proving* that it was a case of murder and not suicide ; and it's a possible motive for murder, I admit. But the position of a gentleman who commits a murder for gain and can only collect the money by proving that murder was done . . . Well, it sounds a bit complicated, doesn't it ? "

" Unless he can be sure of fixing the murder on someone else, sir."

" It's a bit difficult in practice to produce a frame-up of that description, isn't it ? "

The Inspector refrained from betraying any opinion on this point.

" Then there's the Hailsham girl, sir. She's a

vindictive type ; and she quite obviously had the worst kind of grudge against both of them. Revenge might have been at the back of the business for all one can tell. I don't say it's likely ; but I'm considering possibilities, not necessarily probabilities."

" I don't think Miss Hailsham can reckon me among her admirers," Sir Clinton confessed. " But that's hardly evidence against her in a murder case. We'd need something a bit more concrete."

" She admitted that she left the dance early that night and took her car home, sir. She hasn't got a clean alibi for the time the murder was committed."

" So I noticed when she told her story. But the absence of an alibi doesn't establish murderous intent, you know. Go ahead."

" Well, sir, there's the Deepcar girl. She's keen on Silverdale. It's always a motive."

" Save me from being mixed up in any murder case that you have charge of, Inspector. My character wouldn't escape, I see. You'll need to have something better than that before you start arresting anyone."

" I'm not talking about arresting anyone, sir," the Inspector replied in an injured tone. " I'm just reviewing possible motives."

" Quite true. Can't one make a feeble joke without rasping your susceptibilities ? Now is that the end of your list ? "

" I think so, sir."

" Ah ! You didn't think of including someone with the initial ' B,' then ? You remember the ' B ' on the bracelet ? "

The Inspector seemed rather startled.

"You mean this fellow B. might have been a discarded lover of Mrs. Silverdale's who was out for revenge like the Hailsham girl? I hadn't thought of that. It's possible, of course."

"Now let's turn to a fresh side of the case," Sir Clinton suggested. "One thing's certain; hyoscine played a part in the affair. What about Mr. Justice's pertinent inquiry: 'Who had access to hyoscine at the Croft-Thornton Institute?'"

"Every blessed soul in the place, so far as I could see," the Inspector confessed, rather ruefully. "Silverdale, Markfield, young Hassendean, and the two girls: they all had equal chances of helping themselves from that bottle in the store. I don't think that leads very far. That hyoscine was common property so far as access to it went. Anyone might have taken some."

"Then push the thing a little further. Out of all that list, who had an opportunity of administering hyoscine to Mrs. Silverdale—directly or indirectly—on the night she died?"

"Directly or indirectly?" Flamborough mused. "There's something in that perhaps. On the face of it, only three people could have administered the drug directly, since there were only three people at Heatherfield in a fit state to do it. I take it that she swallowed the stuff at Heatherfield, sir, because I found no trace of a paper which might have held it, either at the bungalow or on the bodies of young Hassendean and Mrs. Silverdale."

"That's sound, I believe," Sir Clinton acquiesced. "She swallowed the stuff at Heatherfield before going out. Now who are your three suspects?"

"Mrs. Silverdale herself might have taken it, sir, either on purpose or by mistake."

" But she had no access to hyoscine that we know of."

" No, sir, but both Silverdale and young Hassendean had. She may have taken it in mistake for a headache powder or something of that sort. And it might have been added to a headache powder by either Silverdale or young Hassendean."

" That's a good enough suggestion, Inspector. But I didn't see any sign of a powder paper in her room when I searched it ; and you remember she came straight downstairs and went out of the house, according to the maid's evidence. Any other view ? "

" Then it must have been administered in the coffee, sir, by either young Hassendean or the maid."

" The maid ? Where would she get hyoscine ? "

" From Silverdale, sir. It's just occurred to me. Silverdale wanted a divorce ; but he couldn't get evidence because his wife was simply playing with young Hassendean and keeping well within the limits. But if she were drugged, then young Hassendean might seize the chance that was offered to him, and if Silverdale was prepared beforehand, he'd have his evidence at the cost of watching them for an hour or two."

" So Silverdale gave the maid the drug to put in one of the cups of coffee and ordered her to give that cup to Mrs. Silverdale, you think ? "

" It's possible, sir. I don't put it higher. That maid was a simple creature—look how the doctor pumped her on the pretence of getting medical information that night. She was devoted to Silverdale ; he told us that himself. She'd swallow any talk he chose to hand out to her. Suppose he faked up some yarn about Mrs. Silverdale needing a sedative but refusing to take it. The maid would believe that from Silverdale, and she'd put the hyoscine into the cup quite innocently. If the worst came to the worst, and the cups got mixed, then young Hassendean would get the dose instead."

" It's asking a bit too much, I'm afraid. Remember it was a heavy over-dose that was given."

" Everybody's liable to make a mistake, sir."

" True. And I suppose you'd say that after the murder at the bungalow Silverdale awoke to the fact that the maid's evidence about the hyoscine would hang him, probably ; so he went back and murdered her also."

" It was someone well known to her who did her in, sir. That's clear enough."

" In the meantime, you've left aside the possibility that young Hassendean may have administered the stuff. How does that strike you ? "

" It's possible, sir," the Inspector admitted cautiously. " But there's no evidence for it."

" Oh, I shouldn't like to go so far as that," Sir Clinton said, chaffingly. " I'll tell you what evidence there is on the point. There's Hassendean's own diary, first of all. Then there's what we found in young Hassendean's laboratory notebook."

" But that was just some stuff about weighing potash-bulbs, whatever they may be."

" Quite correct. That was what it was."

" Well, I'm no chemist, sir. It's off my beat."

" There's no chemistry in it. I gave you the key to it at the time. Then there's other evidence. Young Hassendean was a careless worker. Everyone agreed on that ; and his notebook confirmed it. Next, there's what Miss Hailsham said about hyoscine, which is more or less common knowledge, nowadays, of course. And there's young Hassendean's interference in the serving of coffee at Heatherfield, that night. Finally, there's what the maid said about Mrs. Silverdale's appearance when she was going out of the house. Put all these points together, and I'll engage to satisfy a jury that young Hassendean administered the hyoscine to Mrs. Silverdale in her coffee, with a definite purpose—but not murder—in view."

"I'll need to think over all that, sir. You seem pretty sure about it."

"I'm practically certain. Now look at the business from another stand-point. Who had a grudge against the two victims, either separately or together?"

"Silverdale, obviously."

"Obviously, as you say. That's if you take them together, of course. Now for a final problem. Who is Mr. Justice? He seems to be in the know, somehow. If we could lay hands on him, we might be near the centre of things. He knew before anyone else that something had happened at the bungalow. He knew about the hyoscine at the Institute—although as Silverdale's a fairly well-recognised authority on alkaloids, that might have been just a shot aimed on chance. Anyhow, look at it as you choose, Mr. Justice has information, and he seems to have a motive. Who is he, can you guess?"

"Somebody who won't come out into the open until he's dragged there, evidently. It might be an unwilling accomplice, sir."

"That's possible. Anyone else?"

"It might be Spratton. He's got an interest in establishing that it was a case of murder and not suicide."

"Obviously true. Anyone else?"

"I can't think of anyone else who would fit the

case, sir. By the way, I've got the originals of these advertisements—the code ones. I sent down to the newspaper offices and got hold of them."

He produced two sheets of paper from his pocket-book and handed them to the Chief Constable. Sir Clinton glanced over them.

" H'm ! The first one—the letters—is built up as usual from telegram forms. The one with the numbers is fitted together from numbers printed in a newspaper ; it might have been clipped from one of these lists of the results of drawings of bonds for redemption—Underground Electric Railways, and that kind of thing. These advertisements have columns and columns of figures out of which he'd be able to pick what he wanted easily enough. Now what about this address that he's put down—the usual guarantee of good faith at the bottom. It's fictitious, of course ? "

" Yes, sir. There's no such place."

" It's in writing. It looks like a girl's writing. This is a dangerous game for Mr. Justice ; but I suppose if he'd put all the advertisement in clipped-out letters the newspaper people might have got suspicious and refused to print it. What about this handwriting, Inspector ? "

Flamborough's expression showed that he felt he had done his work thoroughly.

" I managed to get hold of specimens of the writing of Miss Hailsham and Miss Deepcar. It isn't either of them. Then I tried to get it recognised—and I succeeded, sir. Miss Hailsham recognised it at once. It's Mrs. Silverdale's own writing ! "

" A forgery, then ? That's very neat of Mr. Justice. I feel inclined to take off my hat to that fellow. He thinks of everything."

"Well, it's a blank end for us, so far as I can see, sir."

Sir Clinton seemed to be so lost in admiration of Mr. Justice's ingenuity that he failed to notice Flamborough's dissatisfaction. When he spoke again, it was on a different topic.

"What about your friend, Mr. Whalley, Inspector? It seems to me we ought to have him up and put him through it as quick as possible. Quite obviously he knows something."

"I've tried to get hold of him, sir. But he's left the town and I can't get on his track. He's gone off to some race-meeting or other, I expect. He often goes off like that and leaves no address. I'll lay hands on him as soon as he comes back to Westerhaven."

"He's an essential witness, I suspect; so don't let him slip through your fingers. You'd better ask for assistance from the local police in likely places."

"Very good, sir."

"And now, Inspector, how are you getting along with the game of eliminations? How low have you brought the possibles out of the original nine solutions?"

Flamborough produced his often-unfolded scrap of paper and scanned it once more.

"If one accepts what you said a minute or two ago, sir, then the drugging of Mrs. Silverdale was meant to be plain drugging and wasn't wilful murder. So the last case drops out."

He put his pencil through the line of writing.

"That leaves only two alternatives:

Hassendean	Mrs. Silverdale
X—Suicide..........	Accident
Y—Murder..........	Accident

And young Hassendean, from all accounts, was hardly the lad to suicide by shooting himself twice in the body —too painful for him. So it really looks rather like Case Y. Certainly it's coming down to brass tacks quicker than I thought it would."

CHAPTER XIII

THE MURDER OF THE INFORMER

As he entered Sir Clinton's office on the following morning, Inspector Flamborough blurted out bad news without any preliminary beating about the bush.

" There's been another murder, sir," he announced, with a tinge of what seemed grievance in his tone.

Sir Clinton looked up from the mass of papers upon his desk.

" Who is it, this time ? " he demanded curtly.

" It's that fellow Whalley, sir—the man who seemed to have some information about the bungalow affair."

The Chief Constable leaned back in his chair and gazed at Flamborough with an expressionless face.

" This is really growing into a wholesale trade," he said, drily. " Four murders in quick succession, and we've nothing to show for it. We can't go on waiting until all the population of Westerhaven, bar one individual, is exterminated ; and then justify ourselves by arresting the sole survivor on suspicion. The public's getting restive, Inspector. It wants to know what we do for our money, I gather."

Inspector Flamborough looked resentful.

" The public'll have to lump it, if it doesn't like it," he said crudely. " I've done my best. If you think I ought to hand the thing over to someone else, sir, I'll be only too glad to do so."

" I'm not criticising you, Inspector," Sir Clinton

reassured him. " Not being a member of the public—for this purpose, at least—I know enough to appreciate your difficulties. There's no burking the fact that whoever's at the back of this affair is a sharper man than the usual clumsy murderer. He hasn't left you much of a chance to pick up usable clues."

" I've followed up every one that he did leave," Flamborough argued. " I don't think I've been exactly idle. But I can't arrest Silverdale merely because I picked up his cigarette-holder in suspicious surroundings. Confound the public ! It doesn't understand the difference between having a suspicion and being able to prove a case."

" Let's hear the details of this latest affair," Sir Clinton demanded, putting aside the other subject.

" I've been trying to get hold of this fellow Whalley for the last day or two, sir, so as to follow up that line as soon as possible," the Inspector began. " But, as I told you, he's been away from Westerhaven—hasn't been seen anywhere in his usual haunts. I've made repeated inquiries at his lodgings, but could get no word of him except that he'd gone off. He'd left no word about coming back ; but he obviously did mean to turn up again, for he left all his traps there and said nothing about giving up his bedroom."

" You didn't get on his track elsewhere ? "

" No, I hardly expected it. He's a very average-looking man and one couldn't expect people to pick him out of a crowd at a race-meeting by his appearance."

Sir Clinton nodded as a permission to the Inspector to continue his narrative.

" This morning, shortly before seven o'clock," Flamborough continued, " the driver of a milk-lorry on the Lizardbridge Road noticed something in the ditch by the roadside. It was about half an hour before sunrise, so I expect he still had his lamps alight. It's pretty dark, these misty mornings. Anyhow, he saw something sticking up out of the ditch and he stopped his lorry. Then he made out that it was a hand and arm ; so he got down from his seat and had a closer look. I expect he took it for a casual drunk sleeping things off quietly. However, when he got up to the side of the road, he found the body of a man in the ditch, face downward.

" This milkman was a sensible fellow, it seems. He felt the flesh where he could get at it without moving the body ; and the coldness of it satisfied him that he'd got a deader on his hands. So instead of muddling about and trampling all over the neighbourhood, he very sensibly got aboard his lorry again and drove in towards town in search of a policeman. When he met one, he and the constable went back on the lorry to the dead man ; and the constable stood on guard whilst the milkman set off with the lorry again to give the alarm."

" Did you go down yourself, by any chance, Inspector ? "

" Yes, sir. The constable happened to recognise Whalley from what he could see of him—I told you he was pretty well known to our men—and knowing that I'd been making inquiries about the fellow, they called me up, and I went down at once."

" Yes ? "

" When I got there, sir," the Inspector continued, " it didn't take long to see what was what. It was a case of the tourniquet again. Whalley had been strangled, just like the maid at Heatherfield. Quite obvious symptoms: face swollen and congested; tongue swollen, too; eyes wide open and injected a bit, with dilated pupils; some blood on the mouth and nostrils. And when I had a chance of looking for it, there was the mark of the tourniquet on his neck sure enough."

Flamborough paused, as though to draw attention to his next point.

"I hunted about in the ditch, of course. And there, lying quite openly, was the tourniquet itself. Quite a complicated affair this time; he's evidently improved his technique."

"Well, what about it?" Sir Clinton demanded rather testily, as though impatient of the Inspector's comments.

"Here it is, sir."

Flamborough produced the lethal instrument with something of a flourish.

"You see, sir, it's made out of a banjo-string threaded through a bit of rubber tubing. The handles are just bits of wood cut from a tree-branch, the same as before; but the banjo-string and the rubber tube are a vast improvement on the bit of twine he used last time, at Heatherfield. There'd be no chance of the banjo-string breaking under the strain; and the rubber tube would distribute the pressure and prevent the wire cutting into the flesh as it would have done if it had been used bare."

Sir Clinton picked up the tourniquet and examined it with obvious interest.

"H'm! I don't say you've much to go on, but there's certainly more here than there was in the other tourniquet. The banjo-string's not much help, of course; one can buy 'em in any musical-instrument shop. But the rubber tubing might suggest something to you."

Inspector Flamborough scrutinised it afresh.

" It's very thick-walled, sir, with a much smaller bore than one would expect from the outside diameter."

Sir Clinton nodded.

" It's what they call ' pressure-tubing ' in a chemical laboratory. It's used when you're pumping out vessels or working under reduced pressures generally. That's why it's made so thick-walled : so that it won't collapse flat under the outside air-pressure when you've pumped all the gas out of the channel in the middle."

" I see," said the Inspector, fingering the tubing thoughtfully. " So it's the scrt of thing one finds in a scientific place like the Croft-Thornton Institute ? "

" Almost certainly," Sir Clinton agreed. " But don't get too sure about your rubber tubing. Suppose someone is trying to throw suspicion on one of the Croft-Thornton staff, wouldn't this be an excellent way of doing it ? One can buy pressure-tubing in the open market. It's not found exclusively in scientific institutes, you know."

Flamborough seemed a shade crestfallen at the loss of what he had evidently regarded as a promising line.

" Oh, indeed ? " he said. " I suppose you're right, sir. Still it's a bit uncommon, isn't it ? "

" Not what you'd expect the ordinary criminal to hit on straight off, I suppose you mean ? But this fellow isn't an ordinary criminal. He's got plenty of brains. Now doesn't it strike you as strange that he should go to the trouble of leaving this tourniquet for your inspection ? He could have slipped it into his pocket easily enough and it wouldn't have bulged much."

" Well, sir, a glance at the body would show anyone that something of the sort had been used. He wasn't giving much away by leaving the thing itself, was he ? "

Sir Clinton did not seem altogether satisfied with the Inspector's view.

"The less a murderer leaves behind, the more difficult it is to catch him, Inspector. That's a truism. Now this fellow is no fool, as I've frequently remarked to you. Hence one might have anticipated that he'd leave as few traces as possible. But here he presents us with the actual weapon, and a weapon that has fairly salient peculiarities of its own. Queer, isn't it?"

"Then you think it's a non-scientific murderer using scientific appliances so as to suggest that the crime was done by someone in the scientific line—Silverdale, I mean?"

Sir Clinton was silent for a moment or two, then he said thoughtfully:

"What I'm not sure about is whether it's a pure bluff or a double bluff. It looks like one or the other."

The Inspector obviously had difficulty in interpreting this rather cryptic utterance. At last he saw his way through it.

"I think I see what you mean, sir. Suppose it's not Silverdale that did the murder. Then somebody—knowing that this kind of tubing's common in Silverdale's laboratory—may have left it on purpose for us to find, so that we'd be bluffed into jumping to the conclusion—as I admit I did—that Silverdale did the trick. That would be a simple bluff. Or again, supposing it's Silverdale who's the murderer, then he may have left the tubing on purpose, because he'd say to himself that we'd never believe that he'd be such a fool as to chuck a thing like that down beside the body—and hence we'd pass him over in our suspicions. Is that it, sir?"

"It sounds devilish involved, as you put it, Inspector;

but I have a sort of dim perception that you've grasped my meaning," Sir Clinton answered. "My own impression is simply that we musn't let this tourniquet lead us too far, for fear we go completely astray. If we get on the right track, I've no doubt it'll fit neatly enough to the rest of the evidence ; but it's not the sort of thing I'd care about staking a lot on by itself. Now suppose we come out of these flowery by-paths and get back to the main thoroughfare of the facts."

The Inspector refused to be damped by his superior. Indeed, he had the air of a player holding good cards, and not caring who knew it.

"It was hard frost last night, sir, as you'll remember ; so there were no foot-prints on the road, or anything of that sort. But the grass by the side of the ditch is fairly long ; and when I examined it, it was clear enough that there hadn't been any struggle on it. They may have struggled on the road, of course ; but the grass was quite undisturbed."

"Then the body hadn't been dragged off the road into the ditch? It must have been lifted and pitched in?"

"So I think, sir. The grass border between road and ditch is quite narrow—just room to stand on it comfortably. One could hoist a body over it without too much trouble."

"And from the look of the body you think it had been thrown in?"

"Yes, sir. It was huddled up anyhow in the ditch, just as it might have fallen if it had been dropped in with a thud."

"Single-handed business, then, you believe?"

"Well, sir, I think if two people had been handling him—one taking his shoulders and another taking his feet—he'd have fallen more tidily. He certainly looked as if he's been bundled in anyhow. I'd put it down as a single-handed job from the look of it."

" I suppose you examined the pockets, and so forth?" Sir Clinton asked.

" Of course, sir. But there was nothing in *them* of any use to us."

The Inspector's voice betrayed that he had something still in reserve. Now he brought it forward.

" I examined his hands, sir ; and in the right one, I found something important. The hand was clenched, and when I got it open at last, this fell out."

He produced a button with a shred of cloth attached to it, which he laid on the desk before Sir Clinton. The Chief Constable picked it up, examined it closely, and then, pulling out a pocket magnifying glass, made a still more minute inspection.

" Very interesting, Inspector. What do you make of it ? "

" Obviously it was torn off the murderer's clothes during the struggle, sir. And I've seen something like it before. You see that canary-coloured stain on the bit of cloth and also on the threads that hold the button to the fabric ? "

" Dyed with picric acid, by the look of it, I should say. Is that what you mean ? "

" Yes, sir. And the pattern of the cloth's another point."

" You mean it looks like a button torn off the old jacket that Silverdale was wearing, that day we saw him at the Croft-Thornton Institute—his laboratory coat ? "

" That's undoubtedly what it is, sir. I remember that stain perfectly. And as soon as I saw it, I remembered the pattern of the cloth."

" And your view is ? "

" I think that when Silverdale set out to murder Whalley he was afraid that some blood from the face might get on to his coat. So he put on his old laboratory jacket. If it got spotted, he could destroy it and rouse no suspicions. It was only an old coat that he might think was worn out. Quite a different thing from destroying some of his ordinary clothes. That would have been suspicious. But an old coat—no one would wonder if he got rid of it and brought another one down to the laboratory to replace it."

" It sounds deuced plausible, Inspector, I must admit. But——"

" But what, sir ? "

" Well," Sir Clinton answered thoughtfully, " it leaves us again with the choice between the single and the double bluff, you see, even if one goes no further with one's inquiries."

The Inspector pondered over the point for a few seconds, but at the end of his cogitation he seemed unimpressed. Apparently, however, he thought it wise to change the subject.

" In any case, sir, I think Whalley's part in the bungalow affair is pretty plain now. I told you he was the sort of fellow who was out for easy money, no matter how dirty it might be. By the way, he was the man who inquired about the number of that motor which he said knocked him spinning—an obvious try-on to get damages, although he wasn't hurt at all. You can see he'd do anything to make money and save himself from honest work. If you remember that, it's easy enough to see the part he played at the bungalow. He was the person you christened Peeping Tom."

" Anything further about him that you can think of, Inspector ? I don't say you're wrong, of course."

" Well, sir, if Silverdale expected to take his wife in *flagrante delicto*, he'd need an independent witness, wouldn't he ? Possibly Whalley was the man he picked out for the work."

" Do you think he was the sort of witness that was wanted ? I'm not so sure of his suitability myself."

" It wasn't exactly a nice job, sir," the Inspector pointed out. " Silverdale would hardly care to take one of his close friends to inspect an affair of that sort. And of course a woman——"

He broke off suddenly, as though struck by a fresh idea. Sir Clinton ignored the last phrase of the Inspector.

" Assume that Whalley was the witness, then, what next ? "

" Assume that Silverdale posted Whalley at the second window and went round to the first one—at the front. Then, to make the thing complete, he breaks in through the window and jumps into the room. Young Hassendean has his pistol and mistakes the state of affairs—thinks that Silverdale means to thrash him or worse. He pulls out his pistol and there's a struggle for the possession of it. The pistol goes off accidentally, and the bullet hits Mrs. Silverdale in the head by pure chance. Then the struggle goes on, and in the course of it, young Hassendean gets shot twice over in the lung."

The Chief Constable looked at his subordinate with quite unaffected respect.

" It looks as if you'd come very near the truth there," he admitted. " Go on."

" The rest's fairly obvious, if you grant what's gone before. Whalley's seen the whole affair from his post at the window. He sneaks off into the dark and gets out of Silverdale's reach. If he hadn't, then Silverdale would probably have shot him at sight to destroy the chance of evidence against him. But when Whalley has time to think things over, he sees he's got a gold-mine in the business. If he can blackmail Silverdale, he's got a steady income for life. But I expect he weakened and tried to play for safety. He blackmailed Silverdale; then he came to us, so that he could say he'd been to the police, meaning to give information. Then he went back to Silverdale, and in some way he let out that he'd given us a call. That would be enough for Silverdale. Whalley would have to go the way the maid went. And so he did."

Sir Clinton had listened intently to the Inspector's reconstruction of the episode.

"That's very neat indeed, Inspector," he adjudged at the close. "It's quite sound, so far as it goes, and so far as one can see. But, of course, it leaves one or two points untouched. Where does the murder of the maid come into the business?"

Flamborough reflected for a moment or two before answering.

"I'm not prepared to fill that gap just at this moment, sir. But I'll suggest something. Renard told us that Mrs. Silverdale was going to draw up a note of the terms of her new will. It's on the cards that Silverdale knew about that—she may have mentioned it to him. He'd want to get that note and destroy it at any cost, before there was any search of his house or any hunting through Mrs. Silverdale's possessions."

"He might have thought it worth while, I admit. But I'd hardly think it important enough to lead to an unnecessary murder. Besides, it wasn't necessary for Silverdale to murder the maid at all. It was his own house. He could search where he chose in it and nobody could object. The maid wouldn't see anything strange in that."

" It was pretty clear that the maid knew her murderer, anyhow," the Inspector pointed out. " Everything points to that. I admit I'm only making a guess, sir. I can't bring any evidence against Silverdale on that count yet. For all one can tell, she may have seen something—blood on his coat from the shots, or something of that sort. Then he'd have to silence her."

Sir Clinton made no comment on the Inspector's suggestion. Instead, he turned to a fresh aspect of the case.

" And where does Mr. Justice come into your theory of the affair ? He wasn't your friend Whalley. That's evident."

The Inspector rubbed his nose thoughtfully, as though trying to gain inspiration from the friction.

" It's a fact, sir, that I can't fit Mr. Justice into my theory at present. He wasn't Whalley, and that's a fact. But hold on a moment ! Suppose that Whalley wasn't Silverdale's witness at all. Come to think of it, Whalley was hardly the sort that one would pick out for the job, if one had been in Silverdale's shoes."

" I'm quite convinced of that, at any rate, Inspector. You needn't waste breath in persuading me."

" Yes, but there's another possibility that's been overlooked, sir," Flamborough interrupted eagerly. " I've been assuming all along that Silverdale was the only person at the opened window. But suppose he'd brought someone along with him. Both of them might have been looking through the front window, whilst Whalley was at the side window, quite unknown to them at the time."

" Now you're getting positively brilliant, Inspector,"

Sir Clinton commended. " I think you've got at least half the truth there, beyond a doubt. "

" Who could Silverdale's witness have been ? " the Inspector pursued, as if impatient of the interruption. " What about the Deepcar girl ? "

" Think again," Sir Clinton advised him drily. " Do you really suppose that Silverdale—who seems in love with the girl—would have picked her out for business of that sort ? It's incredible, Inspector."

The first flush of enthusiasm at his discovery passed from Flamborough's thoughts at the tone of the Chief Constable's voice.

" I suppose you're right, sir," he had to admit. " But there's another girl who'd have enjoyed the job—and that's the Hailsham girl. She'd have given a good deal just for the pleasure of seeing those two humiliated. She'd have gloated over the chance of giving that particular evidence in court and squaring accounts with young Hassendean and Mrs. Silverdale. It would have been all jam to her, sir. You can't deny that."

Sir Clinton conceded the point without ado.

" I won't deny it," he said curtly. " But you needn't let your mind run exclusively on the female population of Westerhaven in a matter of this sort. A man would be a much more convenient witness for Silverdale to take with him. Why leave Silverdale's male friends out of account ? "

" If you're thinking of Markfield, sir, we'll not get much out of him, I'm afraid," Flamborough pronounced. " So far, except when he couldn't help it, he's done his level best to refuse any information about Silverdale and his doings—if he hasn't actually served out misleading statements to us. I don't much care for Dr. Markfield's way of going about things."

Sir Clinton crossed the room and took down his hat from its peg.

" Well, let's sample his methods once more, Inspector. We'll go round now to the Croft-Thornton and look into the question of the jacket. You can bear the burden of the interview, if you like ; but I should prefer to hear what goes on. And you might press Silverdale a little more sharply about his doings on the night of the bungalow affair. We may as well give him a chance of second thoughts, though really I don't expect anything from him at this stage."

CHAPTER XIV

THE JACKET

Sir Clinton and the Inspector found Markfield at work in his laboratory when they reached the Croft-Thornton Institute. Flamborough wasted no time in preliminaries, but plunged at once into the business which had brought him there.

" What do you make of that, Dr. Markfield ? " he demanded, producing the shred of cloth with the button attached and showing them to the chemist.

Markfield examined the object carefully, but his face showed only a certain bewilderment when he looked up at the Inspector again.

" It seems to be a button and a bit of cloth with a picric acid stain on it," he pointed out with a tinge of irony. " Do you want me to make an expert examination of it ? If so, you'd better tell me some more about it, so that I'll know what you want with it."

Flamborough stared at him for a moment or two, as though trying to read something in his expression, but Markfield seemed in no way put out.

" I'm not a mind-reader, Inspector," he pointed out. " You'll need to explain clearly what you expect me to do ; and I'll have to be told whether I can cut bits out of your specimen for chemical analysis."

Flamborough saw that his attempt to draw Markfield was not going to be so easy as he had hoped.

" Have a good look at the thing first of all," he suggested. " Can you remember anything like it ? "

Markfield stolidly examined the object once more.

" It's a button and a piece of cloth," he said at last. " Of course I've seen buttons before, and bits of cloth are not uncommon. I should think that this stain is a picric acid one, but that's a matter for further examination before I could say anything definite. Is that what you wanted ? "

Flamborough kept his temper with difficulty.

" What I want to know, Dr. Markfield, is whether you have recently seen anything that you could associate with that thing—any garment from which it might have been torn, or anything of that sort."

Markfield's eyes narrowed and he glanced with obvious unfriendliness at the Inspector.

" It's a coat-button, by the look of it. I'm no specialist in buttons, I admit. It might have come off any lounge suit, so far as I can see."

" I'd advise you not to fence with us too long, Dr. Markfield," Flamborough suggested. " Look at the cloth. Does that remind you of anything that's familiar to you ? "

Markfield's face betrayed his obvious annoyance.

" I suppose you've identified it already for yourselves. Why come to me ? Presumably you mean that it's a bit torn off Dr. Silverdale's laboratory coat. Well, I can't swear to that. It may be, for all I know. Why not compare it with the coat, and if the coat's torn, you've got your evidence, whatever it may be. I don't see why you drag me into the thing at all."

Flamborough's voice grew hard as he answered :

" There's one thing I want you to bear in mind, Dr. Markfield. A man may very easily become an accessory after the fact in a murder case ; and the penalty runs as high as penal servitude for life. I'm not at all satisfied with the way in which you seem to have determined to evade some of the questions I've had to put to you ; and I'd like to remind you that you may be running risks. It would be far better if you'd deal frankly with us instead of shuffling."

The covert threat seemed to have its effect on Markfield. He looked sulky, but he appeared to make up his mind to alter his tactics.

" Well, ask your questions, then," he snapped. " But put them on matters of fact. I'm not going to say what I *think* about this and what I *suppose* about that. I'll tell you anything that I *know* definitely, if you ask about it."

Flamborough wasted no time before taking up the challenge.

" Very good, Dr. Markfield. We'll stick to facts, if you like. Now once upon a time you saw Dr. Silverdale acting in some private theatricals, I believe. I learned that from Dr. Ringwood. That's correct, isn't it ? "

" Yes. We were members of a small amateur show at one time."

" In any of his parts, did Dr. Silverdale play the banjo ? "

Markfield reflected for a moment.

" I think he did."

" He's an expert banjo-player ? "

" He plays the banjo," Markfield corrected. " I'm not going to give you my opinion about his playing. That's not a question of fact ; it's a mere matter of taste."

Flamborough let this pass without comment.

" He plays the banjo, anyhow. That's what I want to get at."

He stepped across the laboratory to where a little glass apparatus was attached to a tap at a sink and examined the rubber tubing attached.

" What's this thing here ? " he demanded.

" A water-pump," Markfield answered, as though not quite following the Inspector's train of thought.

" And this rubber tubing, what sort of stuff is it ? "

" Pressure-tubing. What about it ? "

" Does Dr. Silverdale use anything of that sort ? "

" Everybody in the place uses it. Whenever one wants quick filtering one uses a water-pump with pressure-tubing connections."

" Miss Deepcar and Miss Hailsham use it, then ? "

" I should think there are a dozen or two of these pumps in this department alone. They're ordinary fittings in every chemical laboratory. If I may ask, Inspector, what are you getting at ? "

Flamborough switched off to a fresh line without making any direct reply.

" Is Miss Deepcar here to-day ? "

" I don't think so. I believe she's out of town—been away for a couple of days. I'll send a message to find out definitely if you want to know."

Flamborough shook his head.

" Don't trouble. I can find out for myself."

" I heard that she would be back the day after to-morrow," Markfield volunteered. " But you'd better find out for yourself of course."

Again the Inspector turned to a fresh line.

" Do you know anything about a man Whalley—Peter Whalley ? " he demanded.

"Whalley ? " Markfield repeated as though trying to recall the name. " Whalley ? Oh, yes. He came to me with some story about having been hit by my car on a foggy night. I didn't believe him. I knew I'd hurt no one with the car, though once I came near it that night. Mr. Whalley got no change out of me."

" He didn't go any further in the matter, then ? "

" I heard no more about it. The thing was so obviously a try-on that I didn't even advise my insurance company about it."

Flamborough reflected for a few moments, obviously trying to think of fresh questions which he could put ; but apparently he had come to the end of his stock.

" We'll go along to Dr. Silverdale's room," he said, leading the way to the door. " You had better come with us, Dr. Markfield. You'll do as a witness, perhaps."

" I'm not very keen," Markfield retorted grumblingly.

However, he followed Sir Clinton and the Inspector along the corridors to Silverdale's laboratory. The room was empty, but the door was unlocked and the Inspector opened it and stepped inside. A glance round the place revealed Silverdale's laboratory jacket hanging on a peg ; and Flamborough went over and took it down.

" Now we'll see," he said, laying it on the table and spreading it out for examination. " Ah, I thought there was no mistake."

He pointed to the right-hand side, where it was obvious that one of the buttons had been wrenched away, taking a piece of the cloth with it.

" Now we'll see if it fits," Flamborough continued, producing the fragment of fabric found in Whalley's hand and adjusting it to the tear in the coat. " That's clear enough. You see now the stains on the two bits correspond exactly."

Markfield leaned over and satisfied himself that the Inspector's statement was accurate.

" What is this bit of cloth ? " he asked.

Flamborough, however, had found something further, and Markfield got no answer to his question.

" Look there," the Inspector ejaculated, indicating a a small brownish stain on the breast of the jacket. " That's blood, clear enough."

Markfield seemed about to repeat his demand for information when steps sounded in the corridor outside. Flamborough picked up the coat, moved swiftly across the room, and hung the garment on its original peg. As he turned away unconcernedly from the spot, the door opened and Silverdale entered the laboratory. He seemed taken aback by the presence of the police and looked from one to another in the group without speaking. Then he came forward.

" Do you want me ? " he asked, in a colourless voice.

Markfield seemed rather ashamed at being caught there in the company of the two officials. He was about to say something when Flamborough robbed him of the opportunity.

" I've come to put one or two questions, Dr. Silverdale," the Inspector began. "First of all, have you had any dealings lately with a man named Peter Whalley ? "

Silverdale was obviously taken aback.

" Whalley ? " he repeated. " I know nothing about anyone of that name. Who is he ? "

Flamborough seemed to discount this statement, but he did not persist along that direct line.

" Can you tell us what you were doing last night ? " he demanded.

Silverdale reflected for a time before answering.

" I left here about six o'clock—between six and six-thirty. Then I walked down to the Central Hotel and had dinner. I suppose I left the hotel again about a quarter to eight. I walked home, as it was a clear night; and I did some work until about half-past eleven. After that I went to bed and read for a while before going to sleep."

Flamborough jotted something in his notebook before going further.

"I suppose you could produce some witnesses in support of that?" he asked.

Silverdale appeared to consult his memory.

"I met Miss Hailsham as I was leaving here," he explained. "That would give you the approximate time, if she remembers it. The waiter at the Central could probably satisfy you that I was there—it's the tall one with the wart on his cheek who looks after the tables at the north window. After that, you'll have to take my word for it."

"What about your maids at Heatherfield?"

"I haven't anyone on the premises. No maid would take the place owing to the murder. I merely sleep there and take my meals at an hotel. A charwoman comes in during the day and cleans the place."

"Ah," said the Inspector, thoughtfully. "Then you can't prove that you were actually at home after, say, half-past eight? By the way, you hadn't a visitor by any chance?"

Silverdale shook his head.

"No, I was quite alone."

Flamborough made another note; and then continued his interrogation.

"I want you to cast your mind back to the night when Mrs. Silverdale came by her death. I asked you once before what you were doing that night, but you put me off. I think you'd find it more advisable to be frank, now that I'm putting the question again."

Silverdale's face showed some conflict of emotions, and he evidently considered the matter for almost a minute before answering.

" I've nothing further to add," he said at last.

" I'll put it plainly, so that there can be no mistake," Flamborough emphasised. " Can you give us any account of your movements on the night that your maid was murdered at Heatherfield ? "

Silverdale tightened his lips and shook his head.

" I've no information to give you," he said at length.

" I may as well tell you, Dr. Silverdale," said Flamborough warningly, " that we have a certain amount of information drawn from other sources. We may know more than you think. Wouldn't it be best to be frank with us ? "

Silverdale shook his head definitely without making any vocal reply. Flamborough concealed his disappointment, though his face grew darker. He put his hand into his waistcoat pocket and drew out something.

" Do you recognise that, Dr. Silverdale ? "

Silverdale examined it.

" Yes, that's a cigarette-holder of mine. I recognise it by the fly in it."

" When did you discover that you had lost it ? "

Silverdale was obviously at a loss.

" I can't tell you. Ten days ago or so, I should think."

" Was it before or after the murder of your maid that you missed it ? Think carefully."

" I can't remember," Silverdale explained. " I didn't note it down in a diary or anything of that sort, of course. I use two or three holders. I leave them in the pockets of different suits. Naturally if one of them goes a-missing, I simply use one of the others ; and perhaps the missing one may turn up later. I can't give you any exact date when this one went astray."

Flamborough returned the holder to his pocket.

" You play the banjo, don't you, Dr. Silverdale ? "

Silverdale seemed completely astounded by this question.

" I used to do so," he admitted, " but I haven't played for quite a long time. The banjo isn't much in request nowadays."

" Have you bought strings for your instrument recently ? "

" No. I haven't. Last time I used it, two of the strings snapped, and I never troubled to replace them."

" Just so," Flamborough said, as though attaching no great importance to the point. " Now there's another thing I'd like to ask about. I think that's your laboratory coat hanging on the peg over there ? "

Silverdale glanced across the room and nodded.

" When did you wear that coat last ? " Flamborough demanded.

" Last night," Silverdale answered, after a slight hesitation.

" You mean you took it off when you left the Institute to go out to dinner ? "

" Yes. This morning I've been up at the Research Station, so I've had no occasion to change my jacket."

Flamborough crossed the room, took down the coat, and spread it out on the table once more.

" Can you explain this ? " he questioned, putting his hand on the tear.

Silverdale stared at the rent in the cloth with dismay gathering on his face. He looked like a man who finds himself surrounded by enemies in unknown strength.

"I can't account for it," he said curtly, with whitened lips.

"Or for this blood-stain on it, I suppose?" Flamborough demanded, putting his finger on the spot.

Silverdale's discomposure became even more obvious. It was clear that he felt himself in a most dangerous position; and his denials betrayed his nervousness.

"I've no idea how it came there. I noticed nothing of the sort when I took the coat off last night. Neither the tear nor that stain. I can't account for it at all."

"You're sure you can't?" the Inspector persisted.

"I can't," Silverdale repeated.

Much to the Inspector's annoyance, Markfield broke into the interrogation.

"Why are you so sure that Dr. Silverdale has anything to do with the matter?" he interjected in a sardonic tone. "It's not impossible that someone borrowed his jacket last night after he'd gone. Several of us were on the premises after he left, I know."

Flamborough, glancing up, surprised an expression on Sir Clinton's face which indicated that his opinion of Markfield had risen on account of this interposition; and the Inspector felt his irritation against Markfield increasing once more.

"I'm not asking for your assistance now, Dr. Markfield," he pointed out, chillingly. "I want to know what Dr. Silverdale knows about the matter. You can hardly speak as an authority on that point, can you?"

Markfield made no reply; but his smile was a comment in itself and did nothing to soothe the Inspector's ruffled feelings.

"I'll have to take this coat, Dr. Silverdale," Flamborough explained in an official tone. "It's a piece of evidence which we must have in our charge."

Then, as an afterthought, he added :

" A man Whalley has been murdered. The case didn't get into the morning newspapers. You'll see it in the evening news."

His voice took on a sub-tinge of warning :

" If you think the better of your attitude, you'd be well advised to come to us at once and tell us what you can. It's hardly necessary to tell you that your silence on these points is bound to raise suspicions ; and if you can clear things up, you may save yourself a good deal of trouble."

Markfield seemed to take a cynical pleasure in destroying the Inspector's effects. Instead of leaving him the last word, he closed the interview himself.

" They used to say a man was innocent until he was proved guilty, Inspector," he remarked ironically, " but I see you've interchanged the adjectives nowadays. It must save a lot of trouble to the police."

CHAPTER XV

SIR CLINTON'S DOUBLE

Two days after the interview with Markfield and his colleague at the Croft-Thornton Institute, Inspector Flamborough came into Sir Clinton's office, obviously in a state of faint trepidation.

" I've arrested Silverdale this morning, sir," he announced in a voice which betrayed that he was not quite sure whether this step would meet his superior's approval.

The Chief Constable exhibited neither surprise nor disapproval at the news.

" I shouldn't care to say that you've got a complete case against him, Inspector. Not yet, at any rate. But he's got himself to thank for his troubles ; and now I expect things will begin to move a bit quicker in the case. Mr. Justice will be calling up his last reserves."

Flamborough seemed to feel that his action needed some justification, though Sir Clinton had asked for none.

" Well, sir, it seems to me we had to forestall a possible bolt on Silverdale's part. There's quite enough evidence to justify his detention on suspicion in the meantime."

" There's just one point I'd like to know about," Sir Clinton said, disregarding the Inspector's statement. " You've got four deaths to choose from. Which of them are you going to select as your main case ? You can hardly put him on trial for all four simultaneously. There's nothing against it legally, but you'd confuse the jury, I'm afraid."

"I thought the bungalow business would be best, sir. There's a fair chance of establishing a motive in it ; whereas in the Heatherfield affair there's only conjecture as to what he was after ; and in the Whalley case we simply haven't got enough evidence apart from the jacket, unless we can prove that Silverdale was the bungalow murderer. And if we can prove that, then there's no need to enter into the Whalley case at all."

Sir Clinton acquiesced with a nod.

"The bungalow affair is the key to the whole series," he admitted without qualification.

There was a knock at the door and a constable entered.

"A young lady wants to see you, sir," he announced as he crossed the room and handed a card to the Chief Constable. "She insisted that she must see you personally. There's a woman with her."

"Send her up," Sir Clinton ordered, after a glance at the card.

When the constable had left the room, Sir Clinton flicked the tiny oblong of pasteboard across his desk to the Inspector who picked it up.

"Miss Avice Deepcar," he read. "What the deuce can she be wanting here ? "

"Calm yourself, Inspector. The next instalment will be published in a moment or two. You'd better wait here while she interviews me."

When Avice Deepcar entered the office, Flamborough was puzzled by her manner. She seemed to be agitated, but it was not the sort of agitation he had expected. When she spoke, it sounded as if she were both indignant and perturbed.

" You're Sir Clinton Driffield, aren't you ? " she demanded, scanning the Chief Constable closely.

The Chief Constable confessed to his identity.

" Then I'll come straight to the point," Avice said. " What is the meaning of your visiting my house last night, terrorising my maid, and making a search through my private papers ? I'm going to see my solicitor about it—I don't believe it's legal. But in the meantime, I want to know why you did it."

Flamborough was completely taken aback by this charge. He stared open-mouthed at his superior. Sir Clinton occasionally did things which mystified him ; but this seemed something completely out of the common.

" He must have got a search-warrant without saying anything about it to me," the Inspector reflected. " But why on earth didn't he take me with him, even if he wanted to go through her papers personally ? "

Sir Clinton's face had become an inscrutable mask.

" Perhaps you wouldn't mind being a little more explicit, Miss Deepcar," he suggested. " I'm not quite sure that I understand your grievance."

Avice Deepcar's face showed that she had nothing but contempt for this apparent quibbling.

" If you think it worth while, I'll give you details," she said, disdainfully. " But you're not thinking of denying it, are you ? I've got a witness to prove the facts, you know."

With a gesture, Sir Clinton invited her to tell her story.

" I've been away from home for a day or two," Avice began. " This morning, I came back to Westerhaven by the eleven o'clock train and drove to my house in a taxi. I left my maid alone in the house while I was away ; and when I got home again, I found her in a great state of excitement. It seems that last night you came to the door, showed her your card, and told her that you had come to search the house on some matter connected with these awful murders. Naturally she was greatly shocked ; but there was nothing for it but to let you in. You went over the whole place, searched in every corner of the house, opened every drawer, poked your nose into all my private possessions—in fact, you behaved as if I were a criminal under suspicion."

She paused, as though to rein in her temper after this sudden outpouring. Indignation had brought a slight flush to her cheeks, and her quickened breathing betrayed the agitation she was trying to keep under control. Mechanically she changed the position of her feet and smoothed down her skirt ; and Flamborough's sharp eye noted a trembling in her hand as she did so. Sir Clinton maintained his silence and gazed at her as though he expected further information.

" My maid was very much put about, naturally," she went on. " She asked you again and again what was at the back of it all ; but you gave her no explanation whatever. When you'd completed your search of my house, you sat down with a pile of correspondence you'd collected—you see I know all about it—and you began to read through my private letters. Some of them you put aside ; others you laid down in a pile on my desk. When you'd finished reading them all, you took away the ones you'd selected and left the rest on the desk. Then you left the house, without offering the slightest explanation of this raid of yours. I shan't stand that, you know. You've no right to do things of that sort—throwing suspicion on me in this way, without the faintest ground for it. Naturally, my maid has been babbling about it and everyone knows the police have been on the premises. It's put me in a dreadful position ; and you'll have to give me an explanation and an apology. It's no use trying to deny the facts, you know. I can prove what I've said. And I want my letters back at once—the ones you stole. . . . You've no right to them, and I simply won't put up with this kind of thing."

She broke off once more, evidently afraid that she was letting her feelings get the better of her. For a moment or two Sir Clinton made no reply. He seemed to be considering something carefully before he spoke.

" I suppose you know, Miss Deepcar," he said at last, " that Dr. Silverdale is under arrest."

The girl's expression changed in an instant. Something like fear replaced her earlier anger.

" Dr. Silverdale ? Arrested ? " she demanded, with a tremor in her voice. " What do you mean ? "

" He was arrested yesterday in connection with the affair at the bungalow."

Avice Deepcar's eyes showed her amazement at the news.

" The affair at the bungalow ? " she repeated. " But he had nothing to do with that ! He couldn't have had."

All her indignation seemed to have been swept away by this fresh information. She had the appearance of someone upon whom a wholly unexpected peril has descended. Sir Clinton seemed satisfied by the effect of his words ; but without giving her time for thought, he pursued his narrative.

" Several things have turned up which seem to implicate him in that affair, and when we tried to extract some information from him about his movements on the night of the bungalow murder, he refused to say anything. He wouldn't tell us where he had been at that time."

Avice Deepcar clasped and unclasped her hands mechanically for a second or two. It was obvious that she was thinking swiftly and coming to some decision upon which much might turn.

" He won't say where he was ? " she demanded in a trembling voice. " Why not ? "

Sir Clinton made a vague gesture with his hand.

" I can hardly tell you his motive. Perhaps he hasn't an alibi. I've told you what we know."

He looked keenly at the girl before him, evidently expecting something ; and he was not disappointed.

" I can tell you where he was at that time," Avice said at last. " Probably you won't believe me, but this is true, at any rate. He and I dined together in town that evening and after dinner we went home to my house. We had a lot to talk over. We reached my house about half-past eight. And then we began to talk things over. We had such a lot to discuss that the time passed without our noticing it ; and when at last he got up to go, it was between one and two in the morning. So you see he couldn't possibly have been at the bungalow."

Sir Clinton interjected a question :

" Why didn't Dr. Silverdale tell us all this frankly when he was questioned about his movements during that night ? "

Avice Deepcar flushed at the direct attack, but she evidently had made up her mind to make a clean breast of the whole business.

" I told you that Dr. Silverdale was with me that night from dinner-time until the early hours of the morning. As it happened, my maid was away that day and did not return until the next afternoon. You must have a pretty good idea of what people would have said about me if they got to know I'd been alone with Dr. Silverdale in my house. I shouldn't have cared, really ; because there was nothing in it. We were simply talking. But I expect that when you questioned him he thought of my position. He's a married man—at least he was a married man then—and some people would have twisted the whole business into something very unpleasant for me, I'm sure. So I think, knowing him well, that he very likely didn't want to give me away. He knew he'd had nothing to do with the murders, and I expect he imagined that the real murderer would be detected without his having to give any precise account of his doings on that night. If I'd known that he was running the risk of arrest, of course, I'd have insisted on his telling what really happened ; but I've been out of town and I'd no idea things had got to this pitch."

Flamborough intervened as she paused for a moment.

" Your maid was away that night ? Then you've got no one else who could give evidence that Dr. Silverdale was with you during that crucial period ? "

Avice seemed to see a fresh gulf opening before her.

" No," she admitted, with a faint tremor in her voice. " We were quite alone. No one saw us go into the house and no one saw him leave it."

" H'm ! " said Flamborough. " Then it rests on your own evidence entirely ? There's no confirmation of it ? "

" What confirmation do you need ? " Avice demanded. " Dr. Silverdale will tell you the same story. Surely that's sufficient ? "

Before Flamborough could make any comment on

this, Sir Clinton turned the interview back to its original subject.

" I should like to be clear about the other matter first, if you please, Miss Deepcar. With regard to this police raid on your house, as you called it, can you tell me something more about it ? For instance, you say that I produced my card. Was that card preserved ? "

" No," Avice admitted. " My maid tells me that you only showed it to her ; you didn't actually hand it over to her."

" Then anybody might have presented it ? "

" No," Avice contradicted him. " My maid recognised you. She'd seen your photograph in a newspaper once, some months ago, and she knew you from that."

" Ah ! Indeed ! Can you produce this maid ? She's not out of town at present or anything like that ? "

" I can produce her in a few moments," Avice retorted with obvious assurance. " She's waiting for me somewhere in this building at the present time."

Sir Clinton glanced at Flamborough and the Inspector retired from the room. In a very short time he returned, bringing with him a middle-aged woman, who glanced inquisitively at Sir Clinton as she entered.

" Now, Marple," Avice Deepcar demanded, " do you recognise anyone here ? "

Mrs. Marple had no hesitation in the matter.

" That's Sir Clinton Driffield, Miss. I know his face quite well."

Flamborough's suspicion that his superior had been moving in the background of the case were completely confirmed by this evidence ; but he was still further surprised to catch a gleam of sardonic amusement passing across the face of the Chief Constable.

" You recognise me, it seems ? " he said, as though

half in doubt as to what line to take. " You won't mind my testing your memory a little? Well, then, what kind of suit was I wearing when I came to your house ? "

Mrs. Marple considered carefully for a moment or two before replying :

" An ordinary suit, sir ; a dark one rather like the one you've got on just now."

" You can't recall the colour ? "

" It was a dark suit, that's all I can remember. You came in the evening, sir, and the light isn't good for colours."

" You didn't notice my tie, or anything like that ? "

" No, sir. You'll remember that I was put about at the time. You gave me a shock, coming down on me like that. It's the first time I ever had to do with the police, sir ; and I was all on my nerves' edge with the idea that you'd come after Miss Avice, sir. I couldn't hardly get to believe it, and I was all in a twitter."

Sir Clinton nodded sympathetically.

" I'm sorry you were so much disturbed. Now have a good look at me where the light's bright enough. Do you see anything that strikes you as different from the appearance I had that night ? "

He moved across to the window and stood patiently while Mrs. Marple scanned him up and down deliberately.

" You haven't got your eyeglass on to-day, sir."

" Ah ! Did you say eyeglass or eyeglasses ? "

" Eyeglass, sir. I remember you dropped it out of your eye when you began to read Miss Avice's letters."

" Apart from the eyeglass, then, I'm much the same ? "

" You've got quit of your cold now, sir. You were quite hoarse that night you came to the house—as if you'd got a touch of sore throat or something like that."

" That's true. I've no cold now. Anything more ? "

Mrs. Marple subjected him to another prolonged scrutiny.

" No, sir. You're just like you were that night."

" And you recognised me from some newspaper portrait, it seems ? "

" Yes, sir. I saw your picture in the evening paper once. It was just a head-and-shoulders one ; but I'd have recognised you from it even if you hadn't shown me your card."

Sir Clinton reflected for a moment.

" Can you remember what was on that card ? " he asked.

Mrs. Marple consulted her memory.

" It said : ' Sir Clinton Driffield (and some letters after the name), Chief Constable.' Then in the left-hand corner was the address : ' Police Headquarters, Westerhaven.' "

Sir Clinton caught Flamborough's eye and they exchanged glances. The Inspector had little difficulty in seeing that his first impression had been wrong. It was not the Chief Constable who had ransacked Avice Deepcar's house.

Sir Clinton took out his card-case and handed a card to Mrs. Marple.

" It wasn't that card I showed you, was it ? "

Mrs. Marple scanned the card for a moment.

" Oh, no, sir. This one reads quite different."

Sir Clinton nodded and took back the card.

" I think that's really all I want to know, Mrs. Marple. Perhaps Inspector Flamborough may want to ask you a question or two later on."

Avice Deepcar seemed by no means satisfied at this close to the interview.

"That's all very fine, Sir Clinton," she said, "but you seem to think you've satisfied me. You haven't. You can't invade my house in this way and then pass the whole thing off as if it were part of your routine. And you can't carry away a pile of my private letters and keep them without my consent. I insist on having them back. If you don't, I'll see my solicitor at once about the matter. And may I remind you again that you owe me some apology for your proceedings?"

Sir Clinton seemed in no way ruffled.

"Of course I apologise for anything I've done which may have inconvenienced you, Miss Deepcar. I'm quite sincere in saying that I very much regret that you should have been worried in this way. Nothing that I have done has been meant to throw any suspicion on you, I can assure you. As to the letters, I think your best plan will be to consult your solicitor as you suggest. Ask him to ring me up at once, and I'll try to settle the matter as soon as we can. I've no wish to cause you any trouble—none whatever."

Avice glanced suspiciously from him to the Inspector. It was evident that this solution did not satisfy her; but obviously she realised that nothing would be gained by attempting to argue the point.

"Very well," she said at last, "I'll go straight to my solicitor now. You'll hear from him very shortly."

Sir Clinton held the door open for her and she passed out of the room, followed by Mrs. Marple. After a few seconds, the Chief Constable turned to Flamborough.

"What do you make of it all, Inspector?"

"Well, sir, that Mrs. Marple seems to me honest enough, but not very bright."

Sir Clinton nodded in assent.

"She recognised her visitor from his resemblance

to some blurred newspaper portrait ; and she recognised me from my resemblance to her visitor. That's your idea ? "

" It looks like it. I never saw you wearing a single eyeglass, sir. And it occurs to me that a single eyeglass helps to change the normal expression of a face owing to the wrinkling that you make in holding it in your eye. Also if it's an unfamiliar thing, one would drop it when one began to read documents, so as not to be hampered by it."

" True. I suppose that satisfies you—along with the faked visiting-card which was meant to impress her with the fact that a high official had descended on her—that I personally wasn't mixed up in the business. I've the best of reasons for knowing that myself, of course, since I know I was elsewhere at the time. But what do you make of the raid ? "

" Documents were what the man was after, obviously, sir."

" It seems clear enough that he expected to get hold of something compromising amongst her correspondence. If you ask me, Inspector, Mr. Justice doesn't seem to stick at much in his self-appointed task."

" I was pretty sure it was some of his work, sir. The Deepcar girl and Silverdale had a common interest in getting Mrs. Silverdale out of the way ; there's no doubt about that. And some people are perfect fools in what they put down on paper. It's quite on the cards that Mr. Justice thought he might find something useful amongst Silverdale's letters to Avice Deepcar."

" He evidently found something which he thought worth taking away, at any rate," Sir Clinton pointed out. " I had a notion that once you arrested Silverdale, things would begin to move faster. If Mr. Justice has got hold of any evidence, it'll be in our hands before long, I'm prepared to bet."

"He's saving us some trouble, if there *is* anything in writing," the Inspector said, with a grin. "We would hardly have raided the Deepcar house on such a long chance as that; and he's done the job for us."

"A most useful and altruistic person, evidently," Sir Clinton commented ironically. "Now what about the rest of the affair, Inspector? If you accept Miss Deepcar's evidence, then the bottom's out of your case against Silverdale. He couldn't be with her and at the bungalow simultaneously."

"Why should we accept her evidence at all?" Flamborough demanded crossly. "She had as much interest in getting Mrs. Silverdale out of the way as Silverdale himself had. Their interests are absolutely at one in the affair. It's more than an even chance that she was his accomplice in the business—standing ready with this tale of hers to prove an alibi for him. I don't reckon her statement was worth that!"

He snapped his fingers contemptuously.

"There's something else, sir," he continued. "This Mrs. Marple wasn't at the house that night. What evidence is there that Silverdale and the Deepcar girl ever went home at all after they'd dined down town? There's no corroboration of that story. Why not assume that the Deepcar girl was an actual accomplice on the spot? She and Silverdale may have driven out to the bungalow after dinner, and she may have stood at the window during the whole affair. There's nothing against that, if you discount her story. My reading of the Deepcar girl is that she may be surface-shy, so to speak, but she's got good strong fibre in her character underneath. Look how she faced up to you not ten minutes ago. Not much shyness about that."

" I think I'd have been a bit stirred up myself, Inspector, if you came along in my absence and pawed over all my private possessions. One isn't necessarily a scoundrel if one turns peevish over a thing of that sort."

The Inspector let the point pass.

" Have you any notion who this Mr. Justice can be, sir ? "

" I've a pretty fair notion, but it's only a notion. Who stands to profit by the affair ? "

Some recollection seemed to cross the Inspector's mind.

" Spratton, of course, sir. And now I come to think of it, if you shaved off your moustache, he's very like you in face and build. If Spratton's going to collect his insurance on young Hassendean, then murder's got to be proved."

" Well," said Sir Clinton lightly. " I trust Mr. Spratton will get what he deserves in the matter."

CHAPTER XVI

WRITTEN EVIDENCE

Inspector Flamborough had to wait a couple of days before his unknown ally, Justice, made any further move. It so happened that Sir Clinton was not at headquarters when the post brought the expected communication; and the Inspector had plenty of time to consider the fresh evidence, unbiased by his superior's comments. As soon as the Chief Constable reappeared, Flamborough went to him to display the latest document in the case.

"This came by the midday post, sir," he explained, laying some papers on the table. "It's Mr. Justice again. The results of his raid on the Deepcar house, it seems."

Sir Clinton picked up the packet and opened out the papers. Some photographic prints attracted his attention, but he laid them aside and turned first to a plain sheet of paper on which the now familiar letters from telegraph forms had been gummed. With some deliberation he read the message.

> "I enclose photographs of part of the correspondence which has recently taken place between Dr. Silverdale and Miss Deepcar.
>
> "JUSTICE."

Sir Clinton gazed at the sheet for a moment or two, as though considering some matter unconnected with the message. At last he turned to the Inspector.

" I suppose you've tried this thing for finger-prints ? No good, eh ? I can still smell a faint whiff of rubber from it—off his gloves, I suppose."

Flamborough shook his head in agreement with Sir Clinton's surmise.

" Nothing on it whatever, sir," he confirmed.

The Chief Constable laid down the sheet of paper and took up one of the photographs. It was of ordinary half-plate size and showed a slightly reduced copy of one page of a letter.

> that things cannot go on any
> longer in this way.
> The plan we talked over last
> seems the best. When I have given
> Hassendean hints about the use of
> hyoscine, he will probably see for
> himself how to get what he wants.
> After that, it merely means watching
> them, and I am sure that we shall soon
> have her out of our way. It will be
> very easy to make it seem intentional
> on their part ; and no one is likely
> to look further than that.

Flamborough watched the Chief Constable's face as he read the message, and as soon as he saw that Sir Clinton had completed his perusal of it, the Inspector put in his word.

" I've checked the writing, sir. It's Silverdale's beyond any doubt."

The Chief Constable nodded rather absent-mindedly and took up another of the prints. This showed a largely-magnified reproduction of the first two lines of the document ; and for a minute or so Sir Clinton subjected the print to a minute scrutiny with a magnifying glass.

" It's an original, right enough," Flamborough ventured to comment at last. " Mr. Justice has been very thorough, and he's given us quite enough to prove that it isn't a forgery. You can see there's no sign of erasing or scraping of any sort on the paper of the original ; and the magnification's big enough to show up anything of that sort."

" That's true," Sir Clinton admitted. " And so far as one can see, the lines of the writing are normal. There are none of those halts-in-the-wrong-place that a forger makes if he traces a manuscript. The magnification's quite big enough to show up anything of that sort. I guess you're right, Inspector, it's a photograph of part of a real document in Silverdale's own handwriting."

" The rest of the things make that clear enough," Flamborough said, indicating several other prints which showed microphotographic reproductions of a number of other details of the document. " There's no doubt whatever that these are all genuine bits of Silverdale's handwriting. There's been no faking of the paper or anything like that."

Sir Clinton continued his study of the photographs, evidently with keen interest ; but at last he put all the prints on his desk and turned to the Inspector.

" Well, what do you make of it ? " he demanded.

" It seems clear enough to me," Flamborough answered. " Look at the contents of that page as a whole. It's as plain as one could wish. Silverdale and the Deepcar girl have had enough of waiting. Things can't go on any longer in this way. They've been discussing various ways of getting rid of Mrs. Silverdale. 'The plan we talked over last seems the best.' That's the final decision, evidently. Then you get a notion of what the plan was. Silverdale was going to prime Hassendean with information about hyoscine, and practically egg him on to drug Mrs. Silverdale so as to get her into his power. Then when the trap was ready, Silverdale and the Deepcar girl were to be on the alert to take advantage of the situation. And the last sentence makes it clear enough that they meant to go the length of murder and cover it up by making it look like a suicide-pact between young Hassendean and Mrs. Silverdale. That's how I read it, sir."

Sir Clinton did not immediately endorse this opinion. Instead, he picked up the full copy of the manuscript page and studied it afresh as though searching for something in particular. At last he appeared to be satisfied ; and he slid the photograph across the desk to the Inspector.

" I don't wish to bias you, Inspector, so I won't describe what I see myself. But will you examine the word ' probably ' in that text and tell me if anything whatever about it strikes you as peculiar—anything whatever, remember."

Flamborough studied the place indicated, first with his naked eye and then with the magnifying glass.

" There's no sign of any tampering with the paper that I can see, sir. The surface is intact and the ink lines run absolutely freely, without the halts and shakes one would expect in a forgery. The only thing I do notice is that the word looks just a trifle cramped."

"That's what I wanted. Note that it's in the middle of a line, Inspector. Now look at the word ' shall ' in the fifth line from the bottom of the page."

" One might say it was a trifle cramped too," Flamborough admitted.

" And the ' it ' in the third line from the foot ? "

" It looks like the same thing."

Flamborough relapsed into silence and studied the photograph word by word while Sir Clinton waited patiently.

" The word ' the ' in the phrase ' about the use of hyoscine ' seems cramped too ; and the ' to ' at the start of the last line suffers in the same way. It's so slight in all these cases that one wouldn't notice it normally. I didn't see it till you pointed it out. But if you're going to suggest that there's been any erasing and writing in fresh words to fit the blank space, I'll have to disagree with you, sir. I simply don't believe there's been any thing of the sort."

" I shan't differ from you over that," Sir Clinton assured him blandly. " Now let's think of something else for a change. Did it never occur to you, Inspector, how much the English language depends on the relative positions of words ? If I say : ' It struck you,' that means something quite different from : ' You struck it.' And yet each sentence contains exactly the same words."

" That's plain enough," Flamborough admitted, " though I never thought of it in that way. And," he added in a dubious tone, " I don't see what it's got to do with the case, either."

" That's a pity," Sir Clinton observed with a sympathy which hardly sounded genuine. " Suppose we think it over together. Where does one usually cramp words a trifle when one is writing ? "

" At the end of a line," Flamborough suggested. " But these crampings seem to be all in the middle of the lines of that letter."

" That's what seems to me interesting about them," Sir Clinton explained drily. " And somehow it seems to associate itself in my mind with the fact that Mr. Justice hasn't supplied us with the original document, but has gone to all the trouble of taking photographs of it."

" I wondered at that, myself," the Inspector confessed. " It seems a bit futile, true enough."

" Try a fresh line, Inspector. We learned on fairly good authority that Mr. Justice took away a number of letters from Miss Deepcar's house. And yet he only sends us a single page out of the lot. If the rest were important, why doesn't he send them. If they aren't important, why did he take them away ? "

" He may be holding them up for use later on, sir."

Sir Clinton shook his head.

" My reading of the business is different. I think this is Mr. Justice's last reserve. He's throwing his last forces into the battle now."

" There seems to be something behind all this," Flamborough admitted, passing his hand over his hair as though to stimulate his brain by the action, " but I can't just fit it all together as you seem to have done, sir. You can say what you like, but that handwriting's genuine ; the paper's not been tampered with ; and I can't see anything wrong with it."

Sir Clinton took pity on the inspector's obvious anxiety.

" Look at the phrasing of the whole document, Inspector. If you cared to do so, you could split it up into a set of phrases something after this style : ' that things cannot go on any longer in this way. . . . The plan we talked over last seems the best. . . . When I have given . . . Hassendean . . . hints . . . about the . . . use of . . .

hyoscine . . . he will probably see for himself how . . . to get what he wants. . . . After that, it merely means . . . watching them . . . and I am sure that . . . we shall soon have . . . her . . . out of our way. . . . It will be very easy . . . to make it seem . . . intentional . . . on their part . . . and no one is likely . . . to look further than that.' Now, Inspector, if you met any one of these phrases by itself, would you infer from it inevitably that a murder was being planned ? 'Things cannot go on any longer in this way.' If you consider how Mrs. Silverdale was behaving with young Hassendean, it's not astonishing to find a phrase like that in a letter from Silverdale to the girl he was in love with. 'The plan we talked over last seems the best.' It might have been a day's outing together that he was talking about for all one can tell. 'He will probably see for himself how my wife is playing with him.' And so forth."

"Yes, that's all very well," Flamborough put in, "but what about the word 'hyoscine ?' That's unusual in love-letters."

"Miss Deepcar was working on hyoscine under Silverdale's directions, remember. It's quite possible that he might have mentioned it incidentally."

"Now I think I see what you mean, sir. You think that this document that Mr. Justice has sent us is a patchwork—bits cut out of a lot of different letters and stuck together and then photographed ? "

"I'm suggesting it as a possibility, Inspector. See how it fits the facts. Here are a set of phrases, each one innocuous in itself, but with a cumulative effect of suggestion when you string them together as in this document. If the thing is a patchwork, then a number of real letters must have been used in order to get fragments which would suit. So Mr. Justice took a fair selection of epistles with him when he raided Miss Deepcar's house. Further, in snipping out a sentence here and there from these letters, he sometimes had to include a phrase running on from one line to another in the original letter ; but when he came to paste his fragments together, the original hiatus at the end of a line got transferred to the middle of a line in the final arrangement made to fit the page of the faked letter. That's what struck me to begin with. For example, suppose that in the original letter you had the phrase : ' he will probably see for himself how' ; and the original line ended with ' probably.' That word might be a bit cramped at the end of the line. But in reconstructing the thing, ' probably ' got into the middle of the line, and so you get this apparently meaningless cramping of the word when there was space enough for it to be written uncramped under normal conditions. Just the same with the other cases you spotted for yourself. They represent the ends of lines in the original letters, although they all occur in the middle of lines in the fake production."

" That sounds just as plausible as you like, sir. But you've got the knack of making things sound plausible. You're not pulling my leg, are you ? " the Inspector demanded suspiciously. " Besides, what about there being no sign of the paper having been tampered with ? "

" Look at what he's given us," Sir Clinton suggested. " The only case where he's given a large-scale reproduction of a whole phrase is at the top of the letter : ' Things cannot go on any longer in this way.' That's been complete in the original, and he gives you a large-scale copy of it showing that the texture of the paper is intact. Of course it is, since he cut the whole bit out of the letter *en bloc*. When it comes to the microphotographs, of course he only shows you small bits of the words and so there's no sign of the cutting that was needed at the end of each fragment. And in the photograph of the full text, there's no attempt to show you fine details. He simply pasted the fragments in their proper order on to a real sheet of note-paper, filled up the joins with Chinese White to hide the solutions of continuity, and used a process plate which wouldn't show the slight differences in the shades of the whites where the Chinese White overlay the white of the note-paper. If you have a drawing to make for black-and-white reproduction in a book, you can mess about with Chinese White as much as you like, and it won't show up in the final result at all."

Flamborough, with a gesture, admitted the plausibility of Sir Clinton's hypothesis.

"And you think that explains why he didn't send us the original document, sir?"

"Since I'm sure he hadn't an original to send, it's hard to see how he could have sent it, Inspector."

Flamborough did not contest this reading of the case. Instead, he passed to a fresh aspect of the subject.

"Mr. Justice is evidently ready to go any length to avenge somebody—and that somebody can hardly have been young Hassendean, judging from what we've heard about his character."

Sir Clinton refused the gambit offered by the Inspector.

"Mr. Justice is a very able person," he observed, "even though he does make a mistake now and again, as in this last move."

"You said you'd some idea who he was, sir?" Flamborough said with an interrogative note in his voice.

The Chief Constable showed no desire to be drawn. He glanced rather quizzically at his subordinate for a moment before speaking.

" I'll give you the points which strike me in that connection, Inspector ; and then you'll be just as well placed as I am myself in the matter of Mr. Justice. First of all, if you compare the time of publication of the morning newspapers with the time, at which Mr. Justice's telegram was collected from the pillar-box, I think it's fairly evident that he didn't depend on the journalists for his first information about the affair. Even the Ivy Lodge news wasn't printed until after he had despatched his message."

" That's true, sir," Flamborough admitted.

His manner showed that he expected a good deal more than this tittle of information.

" Therefore he must have had some direct information about the bungalow business. Either he was on the spot when the affair occurred, or else he was told about it almost immediately by someone who was on the spot."

" Admitted," the inspector confirmed.

" Then he obviously—or is it ' she obviously,' Inspector ?—saw the importance of hyoscine as a clue as soon as any word about it got into the newspapers. Immediately, in comes the code advertisement, giving us—rather unnecessarily I think—the tip to inquire at the Croft-Thornton Institute."

Flamborough's face showed that he felt Sir Clinton was merely recapitulating very obvious pieces of evidence.

" Then there was the writing on the advertisements which he sent to the papers—Mrs. Silverdale's writing rather neatly forged, if you remember."

" Yes," said the Inspector, showing by his tone that at this point he was rather at sea.

" Then there was the fact that he managed to choose his time most conveniently for his raid on Miss Deepcar's house."

" You mean he made his visit when only the maid was at home, sir ? "

" Precisely. I rather admire his forethought all through the business. But there's more in it than that, if you think it over, Inspector ? "

" Well, sir, if your reading's correct, he wanted some of Silverdale's letters to serve as a basis for these photographs."

" Something even more obvious than that, Inspector. Now, with all that evidence in front of you, can't you build up some sort of picture of Mr. Justice ? You ought to be able to come fairly near it, I think."

" Somebody fairly in the swim with the Silverdale crowd, at any rate. I can see that. And someone who knew the Croft-Thornton by hearsay, at any rate. Is that what you mean, sir ? "

Sir Clinton betrayed nothing in his expression, though the Inspector scrutinised his face carefully ; but he added something which Flamborough had not expected.

" Final points. The date on the fragment of an envelope that I found in the drawer in Mrs. Silverdale's room was 1925. The date inside that signet-ring on her finger was 5–11–25. And there was the initial ' B ' engraved alongside the date."

Inspector Flamborough quite obviously failed to see the relevancy of these details. His face showed it in the most apparent way.

" I don't see what you're getting at there, sir," he

said rather shamefacedly. " These things never struck me ; and even now I don't see what they've got to do with Mr. Justice."

If he expected to gain anything by this frank confession, he was disappointed. Sir Clinton had evidently no desire to save his subordinate the trouble of thinking, and his next remark left Flamborough even deeper in bewilderment.

" Ever read anything by Dean Swift, Inspector ? "

" I read *Gulliver's Travels* when I was a kid, sir," Flamborough admitted, with the air of deprecating any investigation into his literary tastes.

" You might read his *Journal to Stella* some time. But I guess you'd find it dull. It's a reprint of his letters to Esther Johnson. He called her ' Stella,' and it's full of queer abbreviations and phrases like ' Night, dear MD. Love Pdfr.' It teems with that sort of stuff. Curious to see the human side of a man like Swift, isn't it ? "

" In love with her, you mean, sir ? "

" Well, it sounds like it," Sir Clinton replied cautiously. " However, we needn't worry over Swift. Let's see if we can't do something with this case, for a change."

He glanced at his watch.

" Half-past five. We may be able to get hold of her."

He picked up the telephone from his desk and asked for a number while Flamborough waited with interest to hear the result.

" Is that the Croft-Thornton Institute ? " Sir Clinton demanded at length. " Sir Clinton Driffield speaking. Can you ask Miss Hailsham to come to the telephone ? "

There was a pause before he spoke once more.

" Miss Hailsham ? I'm sorry to trouble you, but can you tell me if there's a microphotographic camera in the Institute ? I'd like to know."

Flamborough, all ears, waited for the next bit of the one-sided conversation which was reaching him.

" You have two of them ? Then I suppose I might be able to get permission to use one of them, perhaps, if we need it. . . . Thanks, indeed. By the way, I suppose you're just leaving the Institute now. . . . I thought so. Very lucky I didn't miss you by a minute or two. I mustn't detain you. Thanks again. Good-bye."

He put down the telephone and turned to Flamborough.

" You might ask Miss Morcott to come here, Inspector."

Flamborough, completely puzzled by this move, opened the door of the adjoining room and summoned Sir Clinton's typist.

" I want you to telephone for me, Miss Morcott," the Chief Constable explained. " Ring up Dr. Trevor Markfield at his house. When you get through, say to his housekeeper : ' Miss Hailsham speaking. Please tell Dr. Markfield that I wish to see him to-night and that I shall come round to his house at nine o'clock.' Don't say any more than that, and get disconnected before there's any chance of explanations."

Miss Morcott carried out Sir Clinton's orders carefully and then went back to her typing. As soon as the door closed behind her, the Inspector's suppressed curiosity got the better of him.

" I don't quite understand all that, sir. I suppose you asked about the photomicrographic affair just to see if these prints could have been made at the Croft-Thornton ? "

" I hadn't much doubt on that point. Photomicrographic apparatus isn't common among amateur photographers, but it's common enough in scientific institutes. No, I was really killing two birds with one stone : finding out about the micro-camera and making sure that Miss Hailsham was leaving the place for the night and wouldn't have a chance to speak to Markfield before she went."

" And what about her calling on Markfield to-night, sir ? "

" She'll have to do it by proxy, I'm afraid. We'll represent her, however inefficiently, Inspector. The point is that I wanted to be sure that Markfield would be at home when we called ; and I wished to avoid making an appointment in my own name lest it should put him too much on his guard. The time's come when we'll have to persuade Dr. Markfield to be a bit franker than he's been, hitherto. I think I see my way to getting out of him most of what he knows ; and if I can succeed in that, then we ought to have all the evidence we need."

He paused, as though not very sure about something.

" He's been bluffing us all along the line up to the present, Inspector. It's a game two can play at ; and you'll be good enough to turn a deaf ear occasionally if I'm tempted out of the straight path. And whatever happens, don't look over-surprised at anything I may say. If you can contrive to look thoroughly stupid, it won't do any harm."

CHAPTER XVII

MR. JUSTICE

Just before entering the road in which Markfield lived, Sir Clinton drew up his car ; and as he did so, a constable in plain clothes stepped forward.

" Dr. Markfield's in his house, sir," he announced. " He came home just before dinner-time."

Sir Clinton nodded, let in his clutch, and drove round the corner to Markfield's gate. As he stopped his engine, he glanced at the house-front.

" Note that his garage is built into the house, Inspector," he pointed out. " That seems of interest, if there's a door from the house direct into the garage, I think."

They walked up the short approach and rang the bell. In a few moments the door was opened by Markfield's housekeeper. Rather to her surprise, Sir Clinton inquired about the health of her relation whom she had been nursing.

" Oh, she's all right again, sir, thank you. I got back yesterday."

She paused a moment as though in doubt, then added :

" I'm not sure if Dr. Markfield is free this evening, sir. He's expecting a visitor."

" We shan't detain him if his visitor arrives," Sir Clinton assured her, his manner leaving no doubt in her mind as to the advisability of his own admission.

The housekeeper ushered them into Markfield's sitting-room, where they found him by the fire, deep in a book. At the sound of Sir Clinton's name he looked up with a glance which betrayed his annoyance at being disturbed.

" I'm rather at a loss to understand this visit," he said stiffly, as they came into the room.

Sir Clinton refused to notice the obviously grudging tone of his reception.

" We merely wish to have a few minutes' talk, Dr. Markfield," he explained pleasantly. " Some information has come into my hands which needs confirmation, and I think you'll be able to help us."

Markfield glanced at the clock.

" I'm in the middle of an experiment," he said gruffly. " I've got to run it through, now that it's started. If you're going to be long. I'd better bring the things in here and then I can oversee it while I'm talking to you."

Without waiting for permission, he left the room and came back in a couple of minutes with a tray on which stood some apparatus. Flamborough noticed a conical flask containing some limpid liquid, and a stoppered bottle. Markfield clamped a dropping funnel, also containing a clear liquid, so that its spout entered the conical flask ; and by turning the tap of the funnel slightly, he allowed a little of the contents to flow down into the flask.

" I hope the smell doesn't trouble you," he said, in a tone of sour apology. " It's the triethylamine I'm mixing with the tetranitromethane in the flask. Rather a fishy stink it has."

He arranged the apparatus on the table so that he could reach the tap conveniently without rising from his chair ; then, after admitting a little more of the liquid from the funnel into the flask, he seated himself once more and gave Sir Clinton his attention.

" What is it you want to know ? " he demanded abruptly.

Sir Clinton refused to be hurried. Putting his hand into his breast-pocket, he drew out some sheets of type-writing which he placed on the table before him, as though for future reference. Then he turned to his host.

" Some time ago, a man Peter Whalley came to us and made a statement, Dr. Markfield."

Markfield's face betrayed some surprise.

" Whalley ? " he asked. " Do you mean the man who was murdered on the Lizardbridge Road ? "

" He was murdered, certainly," Sir Clinton confirmed. " But as I said, he made a statement to us. I'm not very clear about some points, and I think you might be able to fill in one or two of the gaps."

Markfield's face showed a quick flash of suspicion.

" I'm not very sure what you mean," he said, doubtfully, " If you're trying to trap me into saying things that might go against Silverdale, I may as well tell you I've no desire to give evidence against him. I'm sure he's innocent ; and I don't wish to say anything to give you a handle against him. That's frank enough, isn't it ? "

" If it relieves your mind, I may as well say I agree with you on that point, Dr. Markfield. So there's no reason why you shouldn't give us your help."

Markfield seemed slightly taken aback by this, but he did his best to hide his feelings.

" Go on, then," he said. " What is it you want ? "

Sir Clinton half-opened the paper on the table, then took away his hand as though he needed no notes at the moment.

" It appears that on the night of the affair at the bungalow, when Mrs. Silverdale met her death, Peter Whalley was walking along the Lizardbridge Road, coming towards town," Sir Clinton began. " It was a foggy night, you remember. He'd just passed the bungalow gate when he noticed, ahead of him, the headlights of a car standing by the roadside ; and he appears to have heard voices."

The Inspector listened to this with all his ears. Where had Sir Clinton fished up this fresh stock of information, evidently of crucial importance ? Then a recollection of the Chief Constable's warning flashed through his mind and he schooled his features into a mask of impassivity. A glance at Markfield showed that the chemist, though outwardly uninterested, was missing no detail of the story.

" It seems," Sir Clinton went on, " that the late Mr. Whalley came up to the car and found a man and a girl in the front seat. The girl seemed to be in an abnormal state ; and Mr. Whalley, from his limited experience, inferred that she was intoxicated. The man, Whalley thought, had stopped the car to straighten her in the seat and make her look less conspicuous ; but as soon as Whalley appeared out of the night, the man started the car again and drove slowly past him towards the bungalow."

Sir Clinton mechanically smoothed out his papers, glanced at them, and then continued :

" The police can't always choose their instruments, Dr. Markfield. We have to take witnesses where we can get them. Frankly, then, the late Mr. Whalley was not an admirable character—far from it. He'd come upon a man and a girl alone in a car, and the girl was apparently not in a fit state to look after herself. An affair of this sort would bring two ideas into Mr. Whalley's mind. Clothing them in vulgar language, they'd be : ' Here's a bit o' fun, my word ! ' and ' What is there in it for me ? ' He had a foible for trading on the weaknesses of his fellow-creatures, you understand ? "

Markfield nodded grimly, but made no audible comment.

" The late Mr. Whalley, then, stared after the car ; and, to his joy, no doubt, he saw it turn in at the gate of the bungalow. He guessed the place was empty, since there hadn't been a light showing in it when he passed it a minute or two before. Not much need to analyse Mr. Whalley's ideas in detail, is there ? He made up his mind that a situation of this sort promised him some fun after his own heart, quite apart from any little financial pickings he might make out of it later on, if he were lucky. So he made his best pace after the car."

Sir Clinton turned over a page of the notes before him and, glancing at the document, knitted his brows slightly.

" The late Mr. Whalley wasn't a perfect witness of course, and I'm inclined to think that at this point I can supply a missing detail in the story. A second car came on the scene round about this period—a car driving in towards town—and it must have met the car with the man and the girl in it just about this time. But that's not in Mr. Whalley's statement. It's only a surmise of my own, and not really essential."

Inspector Flamborough had been growing more and more puzzled as this narrative unfolded. He could not imagine how the Chief Constable had accumulated all this information. Suddenly the explanation crossed his mind.

" Lord ! He's bluffing ! He's trying to persuade

Markfield that we know all about it already. These are just inferences of his ; and he's put the double bluff on Markfield by pretending that Whalley's statement wasn't quite full and that he's filling the gap with a guess of his own. What a nerve ! " he commented to himself.

" By the time the late Mr. Whalley reached the bungalow gate," Sir Clinton pursued, " the man had got the girl out of the car and both of them had gone into the house. Mr. Whalley, it seems, went gingerly up the approach, and, as he did so, a light went on in one of the front rooms of the bungalow. The curtains were drawn. The late Mr. Whalley, with an eye to future profit, took the precaution of noting the number of the motor, which was standing at the front door."

Flamborough glanced at Markfield to see what effect Sir Clinton was producing. To his surprise, the chemist seemed in no way perturbed. With a gesture as though asking permission, he leaned over and ran a little of the liquid from the funnel into the flask, shook the mixture gently for a moment or two, and then turned back to Sir Clinton. The Inspector, watching keenly, could see no tremor in his hand as he carried out the operations.

" The late Mr. Whalley," Sir Clinton continued, when Markfield had finished his work. " The late Mr. Whalley did not care about hanging round the front of the bungalow. If he stood in front of the lighted window, anyone passing on the road would be able to see him outlined against the glare ; and that might have led to difficulties. So he passed round to the second window of the same room, which looked out on the side of the bungalow and was therefore not so conspicuous from the road. Just as he turned the corner of the building, he heard a second car stop at the gate."

Sir Clinton paused here, as though undecided about the next part of his narrative. He glanced at Markfield, apparently to see whether he was paying attention ; then he proceeded.

" The late Mr. Whalley tip-toed along to this side-window of the lighted room, and, much to his delight, I've no doubt, he found that the curtains had been carelessly drawn, so that a chink was left between them through which he could peep into the room. He stepped on to the flower-bed, bent down, and peered through the aperture. I hope I make myself clear, Dr. Markfield ? "

" Quite," said Markfield curtly.

Sir Clinton nodded in acknowledgment, glanced once more at his papers as though to refresh his memory, and continued :

" What he saw was this. The girl was lying in an arm-chair near the fireplace. The late Mr. Whalley, again misled by his limited experience, thought she'd fallen asleep—the effects of alcohol, he supposed, I believe. The young man who was with her—we may save the trouble by calling him Hassendean, I think—seemed rather agitated, but not quite in the way that the late Mr. Whalley had anticipated. Hassendean spoke to the girl and got no reply, evidently. He shook her gently, and so on ; but he got no response. I think we may cut out the details. The net result was that to Mr. Whalley's inexperienced eye, the girl looked very far gone. Hassendean seemed to be thunderstruck by the situation, which puzzled the late Mr. Whalley considerably at the time."

Markfield, apparently unimpressed, leaned across and ran some more of the liquid out of his funnel.

Flamborough guessed the movement might be intended to conceal his features from easy observation.

" The next stage in the proceedings took the late Mr. Whalley by surprise, it seems," Sir Clinton went on. " Leaving the girl where she was, young Hassendean left the room for a minute or two. When he came back, he had a pistol in his hand. This was not at all what the late Mr. Whalley had been expecting. Least of all did he expect to see young Hassendean go up to the girl, and shoot her in the head at close quarters. I'm sure you'll appreciate the feelings of the late Mr. Whalley at this stage, Dr. Markfield."

" Surprising," Markfield commented abruptly.

Sir Clinton nodded in agreement.

" What must have been even more surprising was the sequel. The glass of the front window broke with a blow, and from behind the curtains a man appeared, who fell upon Hassendean. There was a struggle, a couple of shots from Hassendean's pistol, and then Hassendean fell on the ground—dead, as Whalley supposed at the time."

Flamborough stared hard at Markfield, but at that moment the chemist again turned in his chair, ran the remainder of the liquid from the funnel into his flask, and then refilled the funnel from the bottle on the tray. This done, he turned once more with an impassive face to Sir Clinton.

" By this time, the late Mr. Whalley seems to have seen all that he wanted. Just as he was turning away from the window, he noticed the new-comer take some small object from his waistcoat pocket and drop it on the floor. Then Mr. Whalley felt it was time to make himself scarce. He stepped back on to the path, made his way round the bungalow, hurried down the approach to the gate. There he came across a car—evidently the one in which the assailant had arrived. The late Mr. Whalley, even at this stage, was not quite free from his second idea : 'What is there in it for me ?' He took the number of the car, and then he made himself scarce."

Sir Clinton stopped for a moment or two and gazed across at Markfield with an inscrutable face.

"By the way, Dr. Markfield," he added in a casual tone, "what was the pet name that Mrs. Silverdale used to call you when you were alone together—the one beginning with 'B'?"

This time, it was evident to the Inspector, Sir Clinton had got home under Markfield's guard. The chemist glanced up with more than a shade of apprehension on his face. He seemed to be making a mental estimate of the situation before he replied.

"H'm ! You know that, do you ?" he said finally. "Then there's no use denying it, I suppose. She used to call me 'Bear' usually. She said I had the manners of one, at times ; and perhaps there was something in that."

Sir Clinton showed no sign that he attached much importance to Markfield's explanation.

"You became intimate with her some time in 1925, I think, just after the Silverdales came here ?"

Markfield nodded his assent.

"And very shortly after that, you and she thought it best to conceal your liaison by seeing as little of each other as possible in public, so as not to draw attention to your relations ?"

"That's true."

"And finally she got hold of young Hassendean to serve as a blind ? Advertised herself with him openly, whilst you stayed in the background ?"

" You seem to know a good deal about it," Markfield admitted coldly.

" I think I know all that matters," the Chief Constable commented. " You've lost the game, Dr. Markfield."

Markfield seemed to consider the situation rapidly before he spoke again.

" You can't make it worse than manslaughter," he said at last. " It's no more than that, on the evidence you've given me just now. I saw him shoot Yvonne, and then, in the struggle afterwards, his pistol went off twice by accident and hit him. You couldn't call that a case of murder. I shall plead that it was done in self-defence ; and you haven't Whalley to put into the box against me."

Sir Clinton took no pains to conceal a sardonic smile.

" It won't do, Dr. Markfield," he pointed out. " You might get off on that plea if it were only the bungalow business that you were charged with. But there's the murder of the maid at Heatherfield as well. You can't twist that into a self-defence affair. No jury would look at it for a moment."

" You seem to know a good deal about it," Markfield repeated thoughtfully.

" I suppose what you really wanted at Heatherfield was a packet of your love-letters to Mrs. Silverdale ? " Sir Clinton asked.

Markfield confirmed this with a nod.

" That's all you have against me, I suppose ? " he demanded after a pause.

Sir Clinton shook his head.

" No," he said, " there's the affair of the late Mr. Whalley as well."

Markfield's face betrayed neither surprise nor chagrin at this fresh charge.

"That's all, then?" he questioned again, with apparent unconcern.

"All that's of importance," Sir Clinton admitted. "Of course, in the guise of our friend Mr. Justice, you did your best to throw suspicion on Silverdale. That's a minor point, so far as you're concerned now. It's curious how you murderers can't leave well alone. If you hadn't played the fool there, you'd have given us ever so much more trouble."

Markfield made no answer at the moment. He seemed to be reviewing the whole situation in his mind, thinking hard before he broke the silence.

"Good thing, a scientific training," he said at length, rather unexpectedly. "It teaches one to realise the bearing of plain facts. My game seems to be up. You've been too smart for me."

He paused, and a grim smile crossed his face, as though he found something humorous in the situation.

"You seem to have enough stuff there to pitch a tale to a jury," he continued, "and I daresay you've more in reserve. I'm not inclined to be dragged squalling to the gallows—too undignified for my taste. I'll tell you the facts."

Flamborough, eager that things should be done in proper form, interposed the usual official cautionary statement.

"That's all right," Markfield answered carelessly. "You'll find paper over yonder on my desk, beside the typewriter. You can take down what I say, and I'll sign it afterwards if you think that necessary when I've finished."

The Inspector crossed the room, picked up a number

of sheets of typewriting paper, and returned to the table. He pulled out his fountain-pen and prepared to take notes.

" Mind if I light my pipe ? " Markfield inquired.

As the chemist put his hand to his pocket, Flamborough half-rose from his seat ; but he sank back again into his chair when a tobacco-pouch appeared instead of the pistol which he had been afraid might be produced. Markfield threw him a glance which showed he had fathomed the meaning of the Inspector's start.

" Don't get nervous," he said contemptuously. " There'll be no shooting. This isn't a film, you know."

He reached up to the mantelpiece for his pipe, charged it deliberately, lighted it, and then turned to Sir Clinton.

" You've got a warrant for my arrest, I suppose ? " he asked in a tone which sounded almost indifferent.

Sir Clinton's affirmative reply did not seem to disturb him. He settled himself comfortably in his chair and appeared interested chiefly in getting his pipe to burn well.

" I'll speak slowly," he said at last, turning to the Inspector. " If I go too fast, just let me know."

Flamborough nodded and sat, pen in hand, waiting for the opening of the narrative.

CHAPTER XVIII

THE CONNECTING THREAD

"I don't see how you did it," Markfield began, " but you got to the root of things when you traced a connection between me and Yvonne Silverdale. I'd never expected that. And considering how we'd kept our affairs quiet for years, I thought I'd be safe at the end of it all.

" It was in 1925, as you said, that the thing began—just after Silverdale came to the Croft-Thornton. There was a sort of amateur dramatic show afoot then, and both Yvonne and I joined it. That brought us together first. The rest didn't take long. I suppose it was a case of the attraction of opposites. One can't explain that sort of thing on any rational basis. It just happened."

He hesitated for a moment, as though casting his mind back to these earlier times ; then he continued :

" Once it *had* happened, I did the thinking for the pair of us. Clearly enough, the thing was to avoid suspicion. That meant that people mustn't couple our names even casually. And the way to prevent that was to see as little of each other as possible in public. I dropped out of things, cut dances, left the theatrical affair, and posed as being engrossed in work. She advertised herself as dance-mad. It suited her well enough. Result : we hardly ever were seen in the same room. No one thought of linking our names in the remotest way. I gave her no presents. . . ."

" Think again," Sir Clinton interrupted. " You gave her at least one present."

Markfield reflected for some moments ; then his face showed more than a trace of discomfiture.

" You mean a signet-ring ? Good Lord ! I forgot all about it, that night at the bungalow ! So that's where you got your story about the initial ' B.' from ? I never thought of that."

Sir Clinton made no comment, and after a few seconds Markfield continued.

" In the early days, we wrote letters to each other—just a few. Later on, I urged her to burn them, for safety's sake. But she treasured them, apparently ; and she wouldn't do it. She said they were quite safe in a locked drawer in her bedroom. Silverdale never entered her room, you know. It seemed safe enough. It was these damned letters that landed me in the end.

" Yvonne and I hadn't any reason to worry about Silverdale. He'd lost all interest in her and gone off after Avice Deepcar. Oh, that was all quite respectable and above-board. She's a decent girl—nothing against her. We'd have been quite glad to see him marry her, except that it wouldn't have suited our book. My screw was good enough for a single man. It wouldn't have kept two of us—not on the basis we needed, anyhow. And a divorce case might have got me chucked out of the Croft-Thornton. Where would we have been then ? So you see that alley was barred.

" By and by, young Hassendean turned up. When I found he was getting keen on Yvonne, I encouraged her to keep him on her string. She had no use for the boy except as a dancing-partner ; but we used him as a blind to cover the real state of affairs. So long as people could talk about him and her, they weren't likely to think of her and me. So she led him on until the brat thought he was indispensable. I suppose he fell in love with her, in a way. We never imagined he might be dangerous.

" That was the state of things up to ten days before the affair at the bungalow. There seemed to be no reason why it shouldn't have lasted for years. But just then Yvonne got news of this money that had been left her—about £12,000. That put a new light on the affair. It gave her an income of her own. We could afford to let Silverdale divorce her ; then I could have chucked the Croft-Thornton, married her, and set up in private practice somewhere. Her money would have kept us going until I had scraped a business together ; and no one cares a damn about the matrimonial affairs of a chemical expert in private practice.

" We talked it over, and we practically made up our minds to take that course. It seemed a bit too good to be true. Anyhow it would have got us out of all the hole-and-corner business. After three years of that, we were getting a bit sick of it. Another week or two, and Westerhaven would have had all the scandal it needed, if it was inclined that way. We'd have got each other. And Silverdale could have married his girl with all the sympathy of the town. Ideal, eh ? "

He puffed savagely at his pipe for a moment or two before speaking again.

" Then that young skunk Hassendean. . . . He must needs get above himself and ruin the whole scheme, damn him ! I can only guess what happened. He got to know about the properties of hyoscine. There was plenty of it at the Croft-Thornton. He must have stolen some of it and used it to drug Yvonne that night.

However, that's going a bit fast. I'll tell you what happened, as it seemed to me."

Markfield paused and glanced inquiringly at the Inspector.

"It's all right," Flamborough reassured him. "If you don't speak quicker than that, I can take it down easily."

Markfield leaned over and gave the contents of his flask a gentle shake before continuing his narrative.

"That night, I'd been out late at the Research Station on a piece of work. I mean I'd gone there after dinner for a few minutes. When I finished, I came in by the Lizardbridge Road in my car. It was a bit foggy, and I was driving slowly. Just after I'd passed the bungalow, I met an open car. We were both crawling, owing to the fog; and I had a good look at the people in the other car. One was young Hassendean. The other was Yvonne; and even as I passed them, I could see there was something queer about the business. Besides, what would she be doing with that young whelp away out of town? I knew her far too well to think she was up to any hanky-panky with him.

"It looked queer. So as soon as I was past them, I turned my car, meaning to follow them and stand by. Unfortunately in the fog, I almost ditched my car in turning; and it gave me some trouble to swing round—one wheel got into the trench at the edge of the road. It was a minute or so before I got clear again. Then I went off after them.

"I saw the car at the door of the bungalow, and some lights on in the place which hadn't been there when I'd passed it on my way down. So I stopped my car at the gate and walked up to the bungalow door. It was locked.

" I didn't care about hammering on the door. That would only have put Hassendean on the alert and left me still on the wrong side of the door. So I walked round to the lighted window and managed to get a glimpse of the room through the curtains. Yvonne was lying back in an armchair, facing me. I thought she'd fainted or something like that. The whole affair puzzled me a bit, you see. That young skunk Hassendean was wandering about the room, evidently in a devil of a state of nerves about something or other.

"Just as I was making up my mind to break the window, he bolted out of the room ; and I thought he meant to clear off from the house, leaving Yvonne there—ill, perhaps. That made me pretty mad ; and I kept my eye on the front door to see that he didn't get away without my catching him. That prevented me from breaking the window and climbing into the room.

" Then, a bit to my surprise, the young swine came back again with something in his hand—I couldn't see what it was then. He walked over to where Yvonne was, in the chair, lifted his arm, and shot her in the head. Deliberately. Nothing like an accident, remember. And there, before my eyes, I saw the whole of our dreams collapsing, just when we thought they were going to come true. Pretty stiff, wasn't it ? "

He bent forward and made a pretence of knocking the ashes from his pipe. When he looked up again, his face was set once more.

" I'm no psychologist to spin you a yarn about how I felt just then," he continued. " In fact, I doubt if I felt anything except that I wanted to down that young hound. Anyhow, I broke the glass, got my hand inside, undid the catch, and was through the curtain before he knew what was happening. I don't know what he thought when he saw me. His face was almost worth it —sheer amazement and terror. He was just bringing up his pistol when I dropped on him and got his wrist. Then there was a bit of a struggle ; but he hadn't a chance against me. I shot him twice in the body and when he dropped, with blood coming from his mouth, I knew I'd got him in the lung, and I didn't bother further about him. He seemed done for. I hoped he was."

Markfield's voice in the last few sentences had expressed the bitterness of his emotions ; but when he continued, he made a successful effort to keep his tone level.

" One thinks quick enough in a tight corner. First thing I did was to look at Yvonne."

He shrugged his shoulders to express what he seemed unable to put into words.

" That dream was done for. The only thing to do was to clear myself. I had another look at Hassendean. He seemed to have had his gruel. I'd a notion of shooting him again, just to make sure, but it didn't seem worth while. Besides, there had been row enough already. A fourth shot might draw some passer-by. So I left him. I picked up the pistol and cleaned my fingermarks off it before putting it on the floor again. Then I did the same for the window-hasp. These were the only two things I'd touched, so I wasn't leaving traces.

" Then I remembered something. Silverdale was always leaving his cigarette holder lying about the lab. He'd put it down on a bench or a desk and wander off, leaving the cigarette smouldering. That happened continually. That very afternoon, he'd left the thing in my room and I'd pocketed it, meaning to give it back to him when I saw him again. There it was, in my vest-pocket.

" In this world, it's a case of every man for himself. My business was to get out of the hole I was in. If Silverdale got into a hole himself, it was his affair to get out of it. Besides, he'd probably have an alibi, whereas I hadn't. In any case, the more tangled the business was, the better chance you fellows had of getting off my scent. If the whole story came out, I didn't see how I was to persuade a jury it had been pure self-defence when I knew myself that it wasn't that really. Besides, there were these infernal love-letters waiting at Yvonne's house, all ready for the police and pointing straight to me as a factor in the affair. I'd have had awkward questions to answer about the contents of them.

" The net result was that I cleaned Silverdale's cigarette-holder with my handkerchief to take off any finger-prints ; and I dropped it on the floor to amuse you people. It had that fly in the amber—absolutely unique and easily identifiable.

" Then I switched off the lights, got out of the window again, closed it behind me in case it should attract a passer-by. I used my handkerchief to grip the hasp when I closed it, so as not to leave any finger-prints there. In fact, as I walked down to my car, I felt I'd done remarkably well on the spur of the moment.

" As I drove in toward Westerhaven, I conned things over ; and it struck me I'd be none the worse of seeing someone as soon as I could. My housekeeper was away nursing a sick relation, so no one could swear whether I'd been at home in the evening or not. If I could drop in on someone, there was always the chance of creating some sort of alibi. The bother was, I knew I wasn't quite normal. That was only natural. But if I called on someone who saw me every day, they might spot that I was a bit on edge and that might lead to anything, you know. Then it flashed into my mind that Ringwood had come here lately. I hadn't seen him for years. He wouldn't see anything funny in my manner, even if I was a bit abnormal.

" I drove to his house, and there I had a bit of luck —a perfect gift from the gods. From a telephone message he got while I was in the room with him, I learned that Silverdale was out that night, one of his maids was in bed, and the maid wanted Ringwood to call at once. One's mind works quickly, as I told you, and I saw in five seconds what a chance I'd got. I offered to pilot Ringwood over to Heatherfield. That meant I'd a perfectly sound excuse if I was seen in the neighbourhood of the house.

" I dropped him at the end of Lauderdale Avenue, as I expect he told you. During the run, I'd had time to think over things. There was only one solution that I could see. I had to get hold of these letters, cost what it might. I calculated that Ringwood's visit wouldn't be a long one ; and as soon as he'd gone, I meant to drop into Heatherfield, silence the maid, and get the packet of letters.

" I must have run a bigger risk than I intended ; for evidently I got into Heatherfield between Ringwood's visit and yours. Can you wonder I was a bit pleased with my luck, when it all came out ? I made the tourniquet while I was waiting about. Then I went up to Silverdale's house, rang the bell, and asked for Silverdale. Of course he wasn't there ; but the maid knew me and let me in to write a note for him. Once she'd seen my face and recognised me, it was all up with her. One's own skin comes first. I might have risked it if it hadn't been that the drawer was locked and I had to burst it open. That meant leaving traces. And, since she knew me, that meant losing the game. So . . ."

He made a gesture as if using the tourniquet.

"I went home after that and destroyed these letters. Then I sat down to do the hardest bit of thinking I've done in my life. Time meant a good deal to me just then, for I had to have everything cut and dried before any questions were asked.

"Then the notion of a double game came into my mind. Why not follow up the cigarette-holder move and do my best to throw discredit on Silverdale. It was up to him to clear himself. That gave me the notion of anonymous letters. And obviously if I wanted any attention paid to them, I'd have to make a good start. That suggested giving the police the earliest information about the bungalow affair. If they got that from 'Justice' then they'd pay real attention to anything else he liked to send them. So I hit on the telegram idea as being the safest and the quickest. And, as a sequel to that, the obvious thing was to make a show in public of being on Silverdale's side, so that you wouldn't suspect me of having any possible connection with the anonymous letters."

"You overdid it just a trifle," Sir Clinton commented in a dry tone.

Markfield made a non-committal gesture, but did not argue the point.

"Then," he continued, "just as I thought I'd fixed everything neatly, this creature Whalley descended on me. He'd taken the number of my car at the gate and faked up a yarn about an accident, so that he could get me identified for him. He called on me and started blackmail. I paid him, of course, to keep him quiet. But naturally I couldn't let him stand in my way after all I'd gone through safely. He wasn't a very valuable life at the best, I gather.

" Anyhow, I got him up here one night—my housekeeper was still away—and throttled him without too much trouble. Then I took the body down into the garage, put it into my car, and drove out the Lizardbridge Road a bit before tipping him into the ditch. I left the tourniquet beside his body. It was a specially-contrived one, meant to throw some more suspicion on Silverdale. I forgot to say that I borrowed Silverdale's lab. coat to wear during the operation, in case of there being any blood. And I tore off a button and left it in Whalley's hand. Then I put the torn jacket back on Silverdale's peg, ready for the police.

" Naturally I was quite pleased to hear that Silverdale had been arrested. That was his look-out, after all. And he seemed to be in trouble over an alibi, which was better news still. The next thing was to clinch the business, if possible.

" I've told you that once upon a time I played some parts in an amateur dramatic show. I was really not bad. And it struck me, after I'd seen you once or twice, Sir Clinton, that I could make myself up into a very fair copy of you. We're about the same height to start with. I wouldn't have risked it with anyone who knew both of us ; but I'd learned that Avice Deepcar was out of town, and I thought I could manage to take in her maid easily enough.

" So I raided her place, posing as Sir Clinton

Driffield—I'd had some notion of the sort in my mind for a while and had cards printed in London all ready: one of these print-'em-while-you-wait places which left no traces behind in the way of an address or an account. In my raid, I got a valuable document."

" It was a clever enough fake, Dr. Markfield," Sir Clinton said reflectively. " But you left one or two things in it that we took hold of easily enough. By the way, I suppose you simply traced Mrs. Silverdale's writing from some old letters when you put the faked address on the code advertisements you sent to the newspapers ? "

Markfield nodded.

" You don't seem to have missed much," he admitted.

He rose slowly to his feet and put down his pipe.

" I think that's the whole story," he said indifferently. " If you've got it all down now, Inspector, I'll sign it and initial it for you. Then I suppose it'll be a case of ringing up the Black Maria or something like that."

He glanced at Sir Clinton.

" You wouldn't care to tell me how you worried the thing out, I suppose ? "

" No," said the Chief Constable bluntly. " I don't feel inclined to."

Markfield made a gesture as though regretting this decision. He drew his fountain pen from his pocket, unscrewed the cap deliberately, and moved round the table towards the sheets of paper which the Inspector had spread out for signature. A thought seemed to occur to him as he did so, and he bent forward to the apparatus on the tray. His manner was so unconcerned and the gesture so natural that neither Sir Clinton nor the Inspector thought of interfering before it was too late. Markfield put his hand on the tap of the funnel, and as he did so, his face lighted up with malicious glee.

" Now ! " he exclaimed.

He turned the tap, and on the instant the whole house shook under a terrific detonation.

CHAPTER XIX

EXCERPTS FROM SIR CLINTON'S NOTEBOOK

Written after the murder at Heatherfield.

. . . The following things seem suggestive. (1) The break-up of the Silverdale ménage, with Silverdale turning to Avice Deepcar whilst Mrs. Silverdale lets Hassendean frequent her openly. (2) Hassendean's interference with the usual routine of coffee serving after dinner at Heatherfield. (3) The " dazed " appearance of Mrs. Silverdale when she left the house after coffee. (4) The fact that the two shots which wounded Hassendean at close quarters were not fired in Ivy Lodge. (This exonerates Dr. Ringwood, who might otherwise have come under suspicion). (5) The disappearance of Mrs. Silverdale, who was last seen in Hassendean's company. (6) The words : " Caught me . . . Thought it was all right. . . . Never guessed," which Hassendean uttered before he died. (7) The murder of the maid at Heatherfield, which was clearly done by someone she knew well or she would not have admitted him at that time of night. (8) The ransacking of one particular drawer in Mrs. Silverdale's bedroom, suggesting that the murderer had full knowledge of her private affairs. (9) The envelope fragment with the date-stamp 1925, which might indicate that the drawer had held letters compromising to the murderer. (10) The old dance programmes on which asterisks stood for the name of some partner, who must have been intimate with her at that period.

The affair can hardly have been the usual social-triangle tragedy : Silverdale surprising his wife with Hassendean. This hypothesis fails to account for (*a*) the dazed appearance of Mrs. Silverdale, which suggests drugging ; (*b*) the murder and burglary at Heatherfield, Silverdale's own house in which he could come and go freely without resorting to such extremes ; and (*c*) The expression " Caught *me* . . ." in Hassendean's last words, since " Caught *us* . . ." would have been the natural phrase in the case of the triangle-drama.

Curious that Dr. Markfield should pilot Ringwood right across the town and then drop him at the end of the avenue instead of going a hundred yards or so further, to the very gate of the house. Worth keeping in mind that Dr. Markfield knew Mrs. Silverdale well at one time, though he cooled off later (Ringwood's evidence). Compare the old dance-programmes ?

Written after the discovery of the bungalow tragedy.

This is clearly the second half of the Hassendean business. Obviously Hassendean prepared the bungalow beforehand for the reception of Mrs. Silverdale. Either she consented to go there willingly ; or else, as seems more likely, he drugged her after dinner and took her there without her consent. In any case, it was premeditated on his part. Evidently he overshot the dose of the drug and killed her. His subsequent shooting the body suggests that he meant to leave an obvious cause of death, which might divert attention from the poison altogether and cause it to be overlooked in a P.M. examination. In that case, it's likely that he meant to take the body elsewhere in his car and leave it—meaning to suggest that she committed suicide. Of course the shooting may have been done accidentally or by a third party who did not know she was already dead. But this seems unlikely on the face of things.

Four people at least were at the bungalow that night: Mrs. Silverdale, Hassendean, and the two watchers at the windows. One of the watchers must be this fellow "Justice," who had the first news of the affair. One of them was probably the murderer of Hassendean, since he entered the room. The second watcher may have seen the murder committed, though this is not certain.

Apart from the general state of the bungalow, the only clues of interest are the cigarette-holder and the signet-ring on Mrs. Silverdale's finger.

Silverdale denies that he gave her the ring; and as the date 1925 in it belongs to the period of dissociation in the Silverdale ménage, it seems probable that he is speaking the truth. The initial "B" engraved in the ring evidently indicates the donor, and it may stand for either a real initial or the initial of a pet name. Possibly the donor was the person indicated by an asterisk on the dance-programmes and (or) the person who burgled Heatherfield to get hold of letters which perhaps compromised him.

The cigarette-holder found at the bungalow is undoubtedly Silverdale's, but that does not necessarily prove that Silverdale was ever there. Someone else, who had a chance of laying hands on his cigarette-holder, may have left it to mislead us. All that it tells is that someone associated with Silverdale was at the bungalow. Both Hassendean and Mrs. Silverdale fit this description.

As to Silverdale, it's evident that he wanted to get

rid of his wife and marry Miss Deepcar. But that does not prove he was prepared to go the length of murder to gain his ends. He has no alibi for the period of the bungalow affair ; but few of us could produce an alibi for a given time on the spur of the moment.

Miss Hailsham had a grudge against Hassendean, but there is no evidence connecting her with the bungalow affair.

The maid at Heatherfield seems a mere pawn in the game. Silverdale might have used her to drug the coffee ; but Hassendean's unusual interference with the normal serving of the coffee (coupled with his preparations beforehand at the bungalow) point to him as the administrator of the drug.

As to the drug, Hassendean must have had easy access to it. It's a mydriatic drug, since the eye-pupils were expanded. Miss Deepcar mentioned hyoscine when she came into the room at the Croft-Thornton Institute, so that evidently they have it on the premises there. Hyoscine narcosis has one special peculiarity : it obliterates from the patient's memory all recollection of what may have happened while the drug was acting. At least that's what they say about the " Twilight Sleep " treatment. This would be the very drug Hassendean would require for his purpose. Mrs. Silverdale would wake up from the narcosis with only the very faintest recollection of what had happened.

A preliminary hypothesis seems possible. Hassendean resolved to drug Mrs. Silverdale with hyoscine and take her to the bungalow while under the influence of the narcotic. He prepared the place beforehand and got her there successfully. But he overshot the dose he gave her, and she died in his hands at the bungalow. He then shot her in the head, meaning to take her away in his car and leave the body somewhere, arranged as though it were a case of suicide. He might hope that in these circumstances the drug might not be spotted and thus he would be completely clear. But someone else saw the shooting and, being keenly interested in Mrs. Silverdale, shot Hassendean in revenge. On the face of things, this third party must be either " Justice " or the second watcher. Then, if this third party had been intimate with Mrs. Silverdale, there might be letters in her possession which would bring out their relations ; and these letters it might be essential to secure. Hence the murder of the maid and the burglary at Heatherfield. Very sketchy, of course, but it seems suggestive.

If it be the truth or near it, then the murderer must have known when to strike at Heatherfield, for usually there were two maids on the premises, which would be too big a job for a single assailant. But, from Ringwood's evidence, *Markfield learned the state of affairs at Heatherfield that night from the 'phone call which came through when he was at Ringwood's house.* And at once he offered to pilot Ringwood through the fog—which gave him a perfectly sound excuse for being in the neighbourhood of Heatherfield if anyone happened to recognise him. Further, he deliberately avoided taking Ringwood up to the Heatherfield gate, but dropped him at the end of Lauderdale Avenue. This would avoid any chance of his being directly connected with Heatherfield that night ; and after he left Ringwood, he could easily drive round to the back of Heatherfield and watch his chance to enter the house.

Written after reading Hassendean's Journal.

Three things emerge from Hassendean's M.S. (1) He seems to have excited Miss Hailsham to the extent of a loss of control when he jilted her ; but that does not in itself prove anything. (2) Mrs. Silverdale obviously led him on and continually disappointed him. This fits in with the hypothesis I made. (3) His remark : " Only I shall know of my triumph," agrees very neatly with the memory-blotting property of hyoscine. As a whole, then, the hypothesis, seems justified.

As to Markfield, I notice he makes a parade of intense reluctance if he is asked to give evidence involving Silverdale ; but when he is actually induced to talk, he says things which tell heavily against his colleague. As he's by no means a fool, this seems worth attention.

It is possible that the moneylender might wish to ensure that young Hassendean's death should be proved to be due to murder ; but I doubt if a firm doing so well (as appears from their office, which Flamborough describes as opulent) would be likely to go the length of murder itself for the sake of a mere £5,000. And if Spratton had no hand in the actual murder, it is hard to see how he could get the first news of it. On the face of things, it's unlikely that he was " Justice." And it is practically impossible to fit him into the affair at Heatherfield, which is interlocked with the bungalow tragedy. Renard's story of Mrs. Silverdale's inheritance may have some bearing on the affair—but only if Silverdale is the murderer ; and that won't fit in with the Heatherfield business on any reasonable assumptions.

One point certainly tells badly against Silverdale's credibility. He must have told a deliberate lie when he said that on the night of the bungalow murder he was working late at the Croft-Thornton Institute. This tale seems completely exploded by the evidence which Flamborough unearthed.

Silverdale, however, is not necessarily a murderer because he has been trapped in a lie. He may have used his lie to cover up something quite other than murder; and since he was obviously being suspected of murder, his motive for lying must have been a strong one or he would have made a clean breast of the affair. The only factor of sufficient importance seems to be a woman whom he hoped to shield by his lie; and the only woman in the case, so far, whom he has a clear interest in is Miss Deepcar. One can easily imagine circumstances in which he might find it politic to lie.

Written after the identification of hyoscine in the body.

As I expected, hyoscine was the poison. That fits in with Hassendean's journal entry and with the hypothesis I made before. Hassendean, like most people at the Croft-Thornton, had access to the hyoscine in the store. The over-dose which he used gave me some trouble at first, but I think that's cleared up. All the available evidence shows that Hassendean was a careless and inaccurate worker. From his notebook, I found that he used the abbreviation *gr.* for "gramme," whereas Markfield uses *gm.* It seems probable that Hassendean looked up the normal dose of hyoscine in a book of reference, found it given in apothecaries' weights as "1/100 gr.," and copied this down as it stood, without making a note to remind him that here *gr.* meant "grain" and not "gramme." When he came to weigh out the dose he meant to give to Mrs. Silverdale, he would read "1/100 gr." as *the hundredth part of a gramme*, since in laboratory work the metric system is always used and chemists never think in terms of grains. Thus Hassendean, weighing out what in his carelessness he supposed to be a normal dose, would take 0.01 *grammes* of hyoscine. (The reference books state that serious poisoning has been caused by as little as 0.0002 gramme of hyoscine). As there are fifteen grains in a gramme, his quantity would be fifteen times the normal dose, which fits fairly well with the amount found in the body. He had no reason for killing Mrs. Silverdale, provided that the hyoscine obliterated her memory of that evening's proceedings ; and it seems most improbable that he deliberately planned to cause her death.

Miss Hailsham obviously does not wish to see Hassendean's murderer caught ; and therefore her identification with "Justice" is more than problematical. She may or may not have an alibi for the time of the bungalow affair, since she admits going to a dance in her car and coming away almost immediately. One may keep her case in reserve for the present.

Markfield's car, GX. 9074, is alleged to have been in in an accident that night. The man who complained about it might provide a clue to Markfield's movements, if we can lay hands on him.

The man who appeared at Fountain Street Police Station, fishing for a reward in connection with the bungalow affair, can hardly be anyone but one of the two watchers at the windows. Unfortunately, unless he chooses to talk, we have no power to extract information from him. Flamborough states that he can lay hands on him at any moment, as he is well known to our men.

Written after the receipt of the code advertisement.

This "Justice" is an ingenious fellow. First his trail was covered by using letters clipped from telegraph forms ; now he resorts to advertisements, so that we do not get his handwriting. However, he betrays his knowledge of the internal affairs of the Croft-Thornton, which is a bad mistake since it limits the circle of inquiry.

Written after the interview with Renard.

I don't care much for Mr. Renard. He poses too much as the honest fellow rather puzzled by the course of events. His evidence, certainly supplied a fresh motive for Silverdale in the rôle of murderer. But Silverdale will not fit into the Heatherfield affair on any reasonable basis ; and the tragedies at Heatherfield and at the bungalow are obviously interconnected. It's a nuisance that Silverdale won't tell us where he spent the night of the murders. It might save trouble if he did so.

"Justice" seems to be making a fool of himself. The fact that he forged Mrs. Silverdale's writing in the advertisement addresses limits the circle still further. We now know : (*a*) that "Justice" must have learned of the bungalow shooting almost as soon as it was done ; (*b*) that he knows hyoscine was in the Croft-Thornton stores ; (*c*) that he is in possession of specimens of Mrs. Silverdale's writing.

Markfield might fill the bill.

Other possibles are : Miss Hailsham, Miss Deepcar, and Silverdale himself.

Written after the Whalley murder.

So Flamborough has let Whalley slip through our fingers !

My impression is that Whalley was murdered elsewhere and taken out in a car to be dumped into the ditch where he was found. The man behind all this is clever, and wouldn't go in for an open-road murder in which he might be interrupted by a motorist coming round the corner.

The tourniquet was obviously intended to mislead us, or it would never have been left beside the body. The Heatherfield tourniquet was a makeshift thing which indicated no one in particular ; this new one, with its pressure-tubing and banjo-string, seems constructed specially as evidence. The tubing suggests the Croft-Thornton chemical work ; the banjo-string points to Silverdale, since I learned from Ringwood that Silverdale was a banjo-player. *Both these points would be familiar to Markfield.*

The laboratory coat was apparently left on its peg every night after work was done. It was therefore accessible to anyone in the Croft-Thornton, after Silverdale had gone for the day. *Markfield could have procured it, if necessary, and returned it when his work with it was over.* If the Whalley murder was committed in some secluded spot—say inside a house—the murderer would hardly have left a clue, like this button and shred of cloth, in his victim's hand, since he would have plenty of time to search the body at leisure. As things are, it looks like a manufactured clue, especially since the shred of cloth is so characteristic.

Silverdale again has no alibi ; *but neither has Markfield,* since his housekeeper was away nursing a relative. We shall need to wait for further evidence.

Written after the raid on Avice Deepcar's house.

Flamborough has arrested Silverdale. Perhaps it's a sound move, though not from his point of view. I hope it will bring things to a crisis, and that we may be able to fish something out of the disturbed waters.

One point is already established : Silverdale had nothing to do with this raid on Miss Deepcar's house.

The raider must have been a man. Miss Deepcar herself could not have impersonated me well enough to deceive her own maid. Miss Hailsham has a girl's figure and could hardly have posed as myself. The shape of her face, and especially her mouth, would make that impossible. No other woman that we know about is sufficiently mixed up in the business to make it worth while to run a risk like that.

Markfield, according to Ringwood's evidence, used to go in for amateur theatricals. Further, Markfield knew—for he told me so at the Croft-Thornton—that Miss Deepcar was out of town on the night of the raid on her house, so if he was the raider, he could be sure that he wouldn't have to meet her and run the risk of meeting (*a*) a person who knew him when undisguised ; and (*b*) a person who knew my appearance well enough.

What was he after ? Letters, evidently. And again this limits the circle, since the raider must be someone who has knowledge of the relations between Silverdale and Miss Deepcar.

Miss Deepcar's evidence gives Silverdale a complete alibi for the time of the bungalow murder. On the other hand, they may both have been mixed up in it ; in which case her evidence carries no weight. But the Heatherfield affair seems the key to the whole business, and Silverdale had no motive for that murder, even assuming he wanted to destroy the draft of his wife's new will. On the face of it, Miss Deepcar's evidence seems sound and clears Silverdale.

Written after the receipt of the photographs.

Curious how people will never let well alone. If this fellow "Justice" had been content to stay out of the case, we'd have had a much stiffer job. Now at last he's let us see what side he's on—anti-Silverdale definitely.

The photographs are obvious fakes if one examines them carefully. Their only importance is as a guide to the identity of "Justice."

They limit the circle still further, since the production of them implies the use of a good microphotographic camera; and the Croft-Thornton Institute has more than one of these.

Points which seem to tell against Markfield:

(1) He was intimate with Mrs. Silverdale shortly after she came here.

(2) He was near Heatherfield on the night of the murder.

(3) He knew the maid was alone in Heatherfield except for her sick companion.

(4) He could easily have obtained possession of Silverdale's cigarette-holder.

(5) Owing to his housekeeper's absence, he could move about freely with no check on the times when he left his house or returned to it.

(6) He was out at the Research Station on the Lizardbridge Road early in the evening on the night of the bungalow affair.

(7) The evidence he gave us, for all his pretence of reluctance, was directed against Silverdale.

(8) He was well acquainted with all the arrangements of the Croft-Thornton Institute.

(9) Owing to his earlier association with Mrs. Silverdale, he had access to specimens of her writing.

(10) His car's number, GX. 9074, was known to Whalley, who made inquiries about it with reference to the night of the murders.

(11) He knew that Silverdale had a banjo.

(12) He had access to Silverdale's laboratory coat.

(13) He knew of the relations between Silverdale and Miss Deepcar.

(14) He knew that Miss Deepcar would be out of town on the night when the raid was made on her house.

(15) He was a good amateur actor.

(16) He had access to a microphotographic camera.

These are established facts. Make the assumption that his earlier association with Mrs. Silverdale was a guilty and not an innocent one, and see where that leads. It suggests the following :

(*a*) That they took special care to conceal their intimacy, since Silverdale would have been glad of a divorce.

(*b*) That they themselves did not wish for a divorce, possibly for financial reasons.

(*c*) That Hassendean was utilised as a shield for the real intrigue, without understanding that he was serving this purpose.

(*d*) That he took the bit in his teeth and resorted to hyoscine to gain his ends.

(*e*) That Markfield, on his way home from the Research Station that night, caught a glimpse of

Hassendean driving Mrs. Silverdale out to the bungalow, and became suspicious.

(*f*) That he followed them and the tragedy ensued.

(*g*) That after the tragedy, Markfield realised the danger of his love-letters to Mrs. Silverdale which were in her room at Heatherfield.

(*h*) That the Heatherfield murder followed as a sequel to this.

Finally, there is the inscription in the ring which Mrs. Silverdale wore. Markfield has no initial " B " in his name ; but the " B " might stand for some pet name which she used for him.

The net result of it all is that there are strong grounds for suspicion against him, but no real proof that one could put confidently before a jury.

Possibly he might be bluffed. I'll try it.

Written some time after the explosion at Markfield's house.

One might put it down as a drawn game. We failed to hang Markfield, for the explosion killed him on the spot. Luckily, the effects were extraordinarily localised, and Flamborough and I got off alive, though badly damaged temporarily.

Markfield, one has to admit, was too clever for us at the last. From what a chemist has since told me, tetranitromethane detonates with extraordinary violence in presence of triethylamine, though it is perfectly safe to handle under normal conditions. Markfield had about half a pound or more of tetranitromethane in his conical flask ; in his dropping funnel he had alcohol, or some other harmless liquid, colourless like triethylamine ; and in his stoppered bottle he had triethylamine itself. While he talked to us, he ran the alcohol into the tetranitromethane—a perfectly harmless operation. Then, when he saw the game was up, he ran the funnel empty and refilled it from the bottle. As we saw it, this was simply a preparation for continuing the experiment which we had already found to be harmless; but in practice it meant that he had only to turn his tap and mix the two liquids in order to get his explosion. He staged it so well that neither Flamborough nor I spotted what he was after.

The house was a perfect wreck, they tell me : doors and windows blown out, ceilings down, walls cracked. The room we were in was completely gutted by the explosion ; and Markfield was torn in pieces. I didn't see it, of course. The next thing I remember was waking up in a nursing home. Possibly it was cheap at the price of getting rid of Markfield. He was a good specimen of the callous murderer. The only soft spot in him seems to have been his passion for Yvonne Silverdale.

www.ingramcontent.com/pod-product-compliance
Ingram Content Group UK Ltd.
Pitfield, Milton Keynes, MK11 3LW, UK
UKHW040434280225
455666UK00003B/57